Eden Phillpotts

The Human Boy

Eden Phillpotts

The Human Boy

ISBN/EAN: 9783337362867

Printed in Europe, USA, Canada, Australia, Japan

Cover: Foto ©Andreas Hilbeck / pixelio.de

More available books at **www.hansebooks.com**

THE
HUMAN BOY

BY

EDEN PHILLPOTTS

WITH FRONTISPIECE BY ENOCH WARD

THIRD EDITION

METHUEN & CO.
36 ESSEX STREET, W.C.
LONDON
1899

CONTENTS

THE HUMAN BOY

THE ARTFULNESS OF STEGGLES

I.

I REMEMBER the very evening he
came to Merivale. "Nubby" Tomkins
had a cold on his chest, so Mathers and I
stopped in from the half-hour "kick-about"
in the playground before tea, being chums
of Nubby's. Whenever he gets a cold on
the chest he thinks he is going to die, and
this evening, sitting by the fire in the Fifth's
classroom, he roasted chestnuts for Mathers
and me, and took a very gloomy view of his
future life.

"As you know," he said, "I hate being
out of doors excepting when I can lie about

in hay. And to make me go out walking in all weathers, as they do here, is simply murder. I know what'll be the end of it. I shall get bacilluses or microbes into some important part of me, and die. It's like those books the Doctor reads to the kids on Sundays, with choirboys in them. The little brutes sing like angels, and their voices go echoing to the top of cathedrals, and make people blub about in the pews. Then they get microbes on the chest, and kick. You know the only thing I can do is to sing; and I shall die as sure as mud."

Nubby was a corker at singing. He had all the solos in the chapel to himself, and people came miles to hear him.

"You won't die," said Mathers. "You don't give your money away to the poor, or help blind people across roads, and all that. Your voice'll crack, and you'll live."

"I wish it would," said Nubby; "I should feel a lot safer."

"Mine," continued Mathers, "cracked when my moustache came."

We looked at him as he patted it. Mathers was going next term. He had more moustache than, at least, two of the under-masters, and once he let Nubby stroke it and Nubby said he could feel it distinctly under the hand.

"That's what's done it with M.," said Nubby, looking at Mathers and opening another gloomy subject.

Mathers got redder, and began peeling a chestnut.

"I wish I was as certain as you," he said.

"None of us can be certain," I said; "but if your voice did go, Nubbs, you'd be out of the hunt for one."

"I am," declared Nubby. "Last time I had a cold in the throat she sent me a little bunch of grapes by Jane, and a packet of black-currant lozenges; but this time, though the attack is on my chest, and I may die, she hasn't sent a thing."

"Perhaps she doesn't know."

"She does. I met her going into the library yesterday, and I doubled up and barked like a dog, and she never even said she was sorry. It lies between you two chaps now."

" I believe you are going strongest just at present," said Mathers, critically, to me. "You came off last Wednesday and kicked two goals on your own, and she said afterwards to Browne that she never saw you play a bigger game. Then that little beast— Browne, I mean—sniggered, and made that noise in his throat, like a sprung bat, and said he was quite glad he hadn't kept you in. That's how he shows M. what a gulf there is even between the Fifth and masters."

" The bigger the gulf the better," I said. " It would be rough on a decent worm to put it second to Browne. In my opinion even a Double-First would be nothing if he wore salmon-coloured ties and elastic-sided boots; and Browne isn't a Double-First by long chalks. He can only teach the kids, and his desk is well known to be crammed with cribs of every kind."

In the matter of M., I may say at once

that she was Milly, Doctor Dunston's
youngest daughter—twelve and a half, fair,
blue eyes, and jolly difficult to please.
Somehow the Fifth always drew her most.
The Sixth were feeble beggars at that time.
Two of the ten wore spectacles, and one
was going out to Africa as a missionary,
and used to treat the Fifth's classroom as
a sort of training-ground for preaching and
doing good. He was called Fulcher, and
the spirit was willing in him, but the flesh
was flabby. We used to assegai him with
stumps, and pretend to scalp him and boil
him and eat him. He said he should glory
in martyrdom really; and Nubbs, who
knows a good deal about eating, used to
write recipes for cooking Fulcher, and post
them to imaginary African kings. But I
should think that to be merely eaten is not
martyrdom, properly speaking. If it is,
then everything we eat, down to peri-
winkles, must be martyrs; which is absurd,
like Euclid says.

Well, it got to be a settled idea at

Merivale that M. cared, in a sort of vague way, for either Nubby, or Mathers, or me, or all of us. The situation was too uncertain for anything like real jealousy amongst us; besides, we were chums, and had no objection to going shares in M.'s regard. At football Mathers and I fought like demons for Merivale and for M.'s good word; but any impression we might make was generally swept away in chapel by Nubby when Sunday came. He could sing, mind you. It was like cold water down your spine, and all from printed music. Besides, he could be ill, which gave him a pull over Mathers and me, who couldn't. To look at, Nubby was nothing. He had big limbs, but they were soft as sausages. If you punched him he didn't bruise yellow and afterwards black, but merely turned red and then white again. Mathers, besides being captain of the First Footer eleven, had nigger hair, that girls always go dotty about, and black eyes, and pretty nearly as much moustache as eyebrow. As for me, my biceps were the biggest in the lower school, which isn't much, of course; but things like that tell with a girl.

Then it was that conversation turned on Steggles. He was a new boy, due that afternoon. Hardly had the name passed my lips when the door opened, and the Doctor's head appeared. The next moment a chap followed him.

"Ah! there are some of the fellows by the fire," said the Doctor. "Is that you, Tomkins? But I needn't ask."

"Yes, sir," said Nubby, rising.

"You are ill-advised, Tomkins, to spend the greater part of your leisure sitting, as you do, almost upon the hob. A constitutional weakness is thereby increased. This is Steggles. You will have time for a little conversation before tea."

The Doctor disappeared, and Steggles came slowly down the room with his hands in his pockets. There was nothing to indicate a new boy about him. He had red rims to his eyes and a spot or two on his face, chiefly near his nose and on his fore-head; his hair was sandy, and he wore a gold watch-chain.

"You're called Steggles, aren't you?" said Nubby, who was an awfully civil chap in his manners.

"I am."

"Well, I hope you'll like Merivale."

"Do you?"

"All right in summer-time when there's hay. Hate it when I'm ill, which I am now."

"What can you do?" asked Mathers in his abrupt way.

"I can draw," said Steggles.

"What?"

"Devils."

"Do one," said Mathers.

He got a piece of *Cambridge demi* and a pen and ink. Then Steggles, evidently anxious to please, sat down, and did as good a devil as ever I saw. Nubby and I were greatly pleased.

"What else can you do?" said Mathers,

as if such a power to draw devils wasn't as much as you could expect from one chap.

"I can smoke."

"Cigarettes? So can anybody."

"No; a pipe."

"Oh! where did you learn that?"

"At Harrow."

Then Steggles started like a guilty thing and put his hand over his mouth—too late. A rumour we had heard was proved true.

"It would have been sure to get out, and I don't care who knows it, for that matter," said Steggles defiantly. "I had to leave there because I didn't know enough, and couldn't get up higher in the school. I'm rather backward through not being properly taught. The teaching at Harrow's simply cruel. Not but what I've taught myself a thing or two, mind you. I'm fifteen."

He looked at us out of his red-rimmed eyes, and put me in mind of a ferret I've got at home. He might have been any age up to twenty, I thought.

"Can you play anything?" asked Mathers.

B

"The piano."

Mathers shivered and Nubby grew excited.

"So can I. We'll do duets," he said.

"If you like," said Steggles.

Then the tea-bell rang.

II.

Whole books might be written about Steggles at Merivale. I heard Thompson say, after he had been there a week, that it wasn't what he didn't know had rendered it necessary for Steggles to leave Harrow, but what he did know. Certainly he had a great deal of general information about rum things. He got newspapers by post concerning sporting matters; he knew an immense deal about dogs and horses; and Nubbs, who was a judge, said his piano-playing surpassed his devil-drawing for sheer brilliance. Yet, with all these accomplishments, he only managed to get into the Fourth. As to his smoking, it was certainly wonderful. And he ate things afterwards to hide the smell. He had a genius for wriggling out of rows and for getting them up between other fellows. He loved to look on at fighting and knew all the proper rules. On the whole he was rather a beast, and if it hadn't been for Nubby, Mathers and I should have barred him. But all I'm going to tell about now is the hideous discovery of Steggles and M., and the thing that happened on the day of the match with Buckland Grammar School.

M. had been very queer for a fortnight— queer, I mean, with all three of us—which was unusual. Then, seeing how the cat had taken to jumping, I tackled her one morning going through the hall to the Doctor's study.

" How d' you like Steggles ? " I said.

" Very well. He's clever," she said.

" He's fifteen," I said; "he ought to know something if he's ever going to. He's only in the Fourth, anyway."

" You're jealous, and so is Mathers," she said.

" Jealous of a chap with ferret-eyes ! Not likely," I said.

"You are, though."

"Not more than Nubbs and Mathers, any-way," I said.   "It's off with the old friends and on with the new, I suppose."

"Steggles knows how to treat a girl. You might learn manners from him, and so might the others," she said.

"And also the piano, perhaps?"

"He plays beautifully."

"Have you seen him play football?"

"No."

"Lucky for you."

"Football isn't everything."

"No, not since he came; I've noticed that."

This bitter speech stung M., and her eyes jolly well flashed sparks.

"Nor singing either," I went on.   "Nubbs nearly burst himself last Sunday in chapel; and all the time you were watching Steggles making a rabbit with his pocket-handker-chief."

"I'll thank you not to interest yourself in me any more," she said, "either in chapel or out of it."

"All right. I daresay I shall still live,"
I said. "Does that remark apply equally
to Mathers and Nubby, or only to me?"

"To Mathers, yes," she said. "He's as
bad as you are. Not to Nubbs."

Then she went.

Well, there it stood. When I told them
Mathers seemed to think I needn't have
dragged him in, and Nubbs got clean above
himself with hope, not seeing that he was
really just as much out of it as we were. Of
course we chucked Steggles for good and
all then, and told him what we thought
of him. That was when he said something
about only the brave deserving the fair, and
Mathers made him sit down in a puddle for
cheeking him in the playground. Steggles'
eyes looked like one of his own devils while
he sat there, but he took it jolly quietly
at the time. That got Nubby's wool off
though, because he supported Steggles, and
things were, in fact, rather difficult all
round till the day of the Buckland Grammar
School match. Buckland was two miles

from Merivale, and most of the team went by train; but Mathers and I, the day being fine, decided to walk; and at the last moment Nubbs asked if he might come with Steggles.

Out of consideration for Nubby we agreed, and the four of us started on a fine bright afternoon just after dinner. Mathers and I had our football things on, of course; Nubbs was dressed in his usual style, and Steggles, who used to get himself up tremendously on half-holidays, wore yellow spats over his boots, and a sort of white thing under his waistcoat, and gloves. We had rather more than half an hour's walk before us, and hardly were we out of sight of Merivale when Steggles pulled out his pipe and lighted it.

III.

The artfulness of Steggles properly begins here. He knew several things we didn't. He knew, for instance, that M. was coming to the football match, that she was going to ride her bicycle over on the road by which we walked, that only the day before he had quarrelled with her, and that his position with regard to her was at that hour most risky. All these things Steggles well knew, and we didn't. So he lighted his pipe with an air of long practice. The smell was fine, and he smacked his lips now and then.

"Nice pouch," he said, handing me a velveteen pouch with his initials on it in green silk.

"I'll bet a girl did that," said Mathers.

"It's a secret," said Steggles, smiling to himself.

Then he asked very civilly if we would care to join him, explaining that he generally kept a few spare pipes about him for friends.

"I would if it wasn't for the match," said Mathers.

"So would I," I said.

"Well, my baccy might turn you fellows up. Perhaps you are wise," declared Steggles, puffing away. Then he tried

Nubby with a little cherry-wood pipe, and Nubbs thought a whiff or two wouldn't hurt him, and began rather nervously, but gathered courage as he went on.

"I heard my father say once that life without tobacco would be hell," said Steggles; "and I agree with him."

"So do I; it's very soothing," said Nubby.

Then Mathers burst out. He had been sulking ever since Steggles hinted that the contents of his velveteen pouch were too strong for us.

"If you think I funk your tobacco you're wrong," Mathers said. "I've smoked three parts of a cigar before to-day."

"A chocolate one, perhaps?" said Steggles, but in such a humble, inquiring voice that Mathers couldn't hit him.

"No, a tobacco one; and if you've got another pipe I'll show you."

"So will I," I chimed in. Mathers' lead was always good enough for me.

Steggles immediately lugged out two

more pipes. He seemed to be stuffed with them.

"Get it well alight at the start," he explained, handing a fusee.

"All right, all right, I know," said Mathers. Soon we were at it like four chimneys, and Steggles praised us in such a way that we could take no offence.

"You've all smoked many a time and oft, I can see that," he said.

Mathers spat about a good deal, and fancied tobacco was probably a fine steadier for the nerves before a football match; and Nubbs said he thought so too; and he also thought that after a little smoking one didn't want to talk, but ought just to keep quiet and think of interesting things.

"It widens the mind," said Steggles.

We tramped on rather silently for ten minutes till Nubbs spoke again. To our surprise his hopeful tone had changed, and we found he had turned a sort of putty-colour, with blue lips. He said:

"I'll overtake you fellows. I think I've

got—I 've got a bit of a sunstroke or something. It 'll pass off, no doubt."

" Better not smoke any more," said
Steggles.

" It isn't that, but I won't all the same.
I 'll just dodge through that hole in the
hedge and find some wild strawberries or
hazel nuts, or something."

Seeing it was a frosty day in December
Nubby's statements looked wild.   But he
went.   There was a hole in the hedge, with
tree-roots trailing across it, and Nubbs
crawled shakily through, like a wounded
rabbit, into a place where a board was stuck
up saying that people would be prosecuted
according to law if they went there.   But
he didn't seem to care, though it wasn't a
thing he would have done in cold blood.
I saw Mathers grow uneasy in his mind.

" Wasn't the pipe—eh ? "

" No, no. This tobacco—why, a child
could smoke it," said Steggles. "You know
what Nubbs is.   It 's only an excuse to
turn.   He hates football and hates walking."

We kept on again, and I began to feel a slight perspiration on my forehead and a weird sort of feeling everywhere. I had smoked about half the pipe.

"I shan't go on with this now because of the match," I said, hastily knocking out the remaining tobacco and handing his loathsome little clay back to Steggles.

"Why!" he said, "blessed if you haven't gone the same colour as Nubbs did! Don't say you've got a sunstroke too?"

There was something in the voice of Steggles I didn't much like, but I hardly felt equal to answering him then.

"You're all right, anyway, aren't you, Mathers?" he asked.

"Of course I am. What the dickens d'you mean?"

"Nothing. Glad you like my baccy. There's plenty of time for another pipe."

"No there isn't," said Mathers. "I very much wish there was."

We walked on a few yards farther.

"D'you drink that rich, brown cod-liver

oil, the same as Nubby?" asked Steggles
of Mathers suddenly. Mathers looked at
him, and I knew how things were in a
moment. For a moment my own sufferings
were forgotten before the awful spectacle
of the ruin of Mathers. He gave his pipe
back quietly, took great gasps of air,
mopped his forehead, and rolled his eyes
about. Then he said:

"I'm not quite happy about Nubbs.
You push on, and I'll overtake you."

"Hanged if you're not queer too!" exclaimed Steggles. "Whoever would have
thought that Three Castles——?"

"Shut up," said Mathers hoarsely. "It
was the boi—boiled beef at dinner."

He spoke the words with an awful effort.

"So it was," I said feebly. "We never
could stand it—either of us."

"A steaming glass of hot grog is what
you want," said Steggles sympathetically.

"Go!" gasped Mathers, who really looked
horrid now; "go! or I'll kick you, if it kills
me to do it."

"Blessed if you haven't turned green, Mathers," said Steggles. "You look as if you'd been buried and dug up again. I don't say it unkindly, but it's jolly curious."

At the same moment ting! ting! went a bicycle bell; and there was Milly, looking fine.

"You'll all be late," she said.

We prayed she would hurry on and not observe us too narrowly. Then that beast, Steggles, made her stop.

"Look here," he said, "it's frightfully serious because of the match—these poor chaps are ill—just cast your eye at the colours they've gone. They worried me to let them try to smoke, and——"

"I'll break your neck for this!" interrupted Mathers. Then he turned to M.

"If you're a lady, if you ever cared an atom about us, please ride on round that corner. We're ill—can't you see it?"

"Yes, I can—anybody could. I'm sorry. But you won't hurt Steggles if I go?" said M.

"No; I promise. Say we're on the road and shall be there in ten—ten— Go!"

M. took the hint and rode off, with Steggles frisking beside her, like the dog he was.

"Thank the Lord!" said Mathers. Then horrid things happened both to him and me.

We crawled to the match more dead than alive and found a crowd waiting, and Browne and several of the other masters. We were fully twenty minutes late. "This is very unsportsmanlike, the days being so short too!" Browne squeaked. Then we took off our coats and tottered into the field of play.

Of course Buckland Grammar School won. Our side would have done a long way better without us. I couldn't take a pass or shoot for the life of me—it occupied all my time wrestling with nature, let alone the Bucklanders. And Mathers, who played back, was worse. The roughs "guyed" him, and asked him what he'd been drinking. If they'd asked him what he'd been smoking there might have been some sense in it. He told me afterwards that he often saw three footballs at one time when he tried to kick and sometimes four, and the ball he kicked always turned out to be an apparition. Bradwell kept goal grandly too; but it was no good with Mathers like that, and he utterly ruined Ashby Major, the other back.

Nubbs had gone to bed when we got back, and the matron, knowing Nubbs had a tricky system, sent for Doctor Barnes. Nubbs, therefore, gave himself away.

M. never looked at any of us again, and she and Steggles undoubtedly became frightful pals; but the next term, just before Easter, I had the pleasure of writing a fine letter to Mathers, who had left Merivale, and was reading for six months with a private tutor before going to Cambridge. This is part of the letter :—

"Dear Mathers," I wrote, "you will be interested to know that Browne has come down on Steggles at last. I fancy Browne knew the Doctor was fairly sick of Steggles and wanted to be rid of him. In fact, I heard the Doctor call Steggles a canker-worm myself. Anyway, Browne blew up on the smoking, and Steggles will soon probably vanish, like the dew upon the fleece. M. cried a bit, I fancy, when she heard. it, but Nubbs says she smiled at him two mornings afterwards coming out of chapel. Nubbs expects to crack (his voice) any day, but he hopes to gét a definite understanding with M. before it happens. It 'll be too late after. Of course she never looks at me. She told Steggles, and he told me, that she could not possibly care for a person she had once seen the hue of a Liberty Art Fabric —meaning me. I scragged Steggles after he told me. But it is all over now. I believe he is to go into his father's business —Steggles and Stote, Wine Merchants. M. is more beautiful than ever, though I 'm afraid she 's got a bad disposition. To reflect on a fellow's colour at such a time as that was a bit rough."

THE PROTEST OF THE WING DORMITORY

I.

THIS is the story of the most tremendous thing that ever happened at Dunston's, or any other school, I should think. Though in it, luckily I didn't do any of the big part, being merely one of those chaps who were flogged and not expelled afterwards. Trelawny and Bradwell carried the thing through, and all the other fellows in the Wing Dormitory followed their lead. And, mind you, everybody had the welfare of the school at heart. It seemed a jolly brave sort of thing to do, and jolly interesting. Trelawny arranged the military side of the business, and Bradwell, whose father is known as the "Whiteley" of some place in Yorkshire, looked to the commissariat, which means feeding. As to Trelawny, who really captained the dormitory, he was Cornish, and a relation of that very chap fifty thousand Cornishmen wanted to know the reason why about long ago. He was going to be a soldier, read history books for choice, and already knew many military words.

I was Bradwell's fag at the time, because Watson minor had failed in some secret enterprise, and I remember the first conversation which led to everything. Happening to take some tuck in to Bradwell in the Fifth classroom, I found Trelawny there and heard him say :—

"The only way. A protest, and a jolly dignified one, must be made. It's for the credit of the school, and if the Doctor will not see it we must show him. I've thought about it a lot, and I think if a section of chaps could put themselves in a strong, fortified position they might demand to be heard, and even be able to offer an—an ultimatum. Of course, doing the thing for the good of the school and not for ourselves makes us morally right."

"Of course," said Bradwell.

"But we must be physically strong. In warfare the relative positions of the sides are always taken into account when the treaties of peace are arranged."

"What are you staring at?" said Bradwell to me. "You hook it."

So I hooked. But I knew perfectly well what they were talking about. Everybody in the Wing Dormitory did, because they often discussed the same question after they thought the rest of the chaps were asleep. It was the new mathematical master, Thompson, who troubled not only Trelawny and Bradwell but a lot of the other fellows. Trelawny had called him an "unholy bounder" the third day he was there, and that seemed to be a general opinion. Yet, with all his bounderishness, he was awfully clever, and meant well. But he didn't know anything about chaps in a general way, and he left out his h's and stuck them in with awfully rum effects. Thompson tried hard to be friendly to everybody, but only the kids liked him. He couldn't understand, somehow, and insulted chaps in the most frightful way, not seeing any difference between fellows at the top of the school and mere kids at the bottom. Captains of elevens were as nothing to him. He seemed to have read up boys like he read mathematics and stuff—from rotten books. He would say sometimes, "Now, you fellows, let's 'ave a jolly game of leap-frog before the bell rings," and things like that. Boys never do play leap-frog except in books, really. Once he offered to show Trelawny how to make a kite, and he asked Chambers—*Chambers*, mind you, the Captain of the First Eleven at Cricket— whether he knew a shop where there were capital iron hoops for sale at a shilling each. I heard him say it, and he put it like this: "I say, Chambers, do you know those splendid 'oops they sell at Burford's in 'Igh

Street? It's out of bounds, but if you like
I'll get you one this evening. They've got
iron crooks and everything. I make this
offer because you understood a little of what
I said about Conic Sections this afternoon."
Thompson meant so jolly well that nobody
could get in a wax with him personally; and,
as I say, the kids, who didn't see the
"unholy bounder" side of him, and only
knew he stood gallons of ginger-beer on
half-holidays in the playing-fields, liked him
better than anybody. But Trelawny took
big views, and so ·did Bradwell, and they
decided to make a definite protest.

Nothing happened till one day Thompson
said something about Trelawny's "Celtic
thickness of skull." That stung Trelawny
like nettles, and he set to work and arranged
the great plot of the Wing Dormitory. He
decided that the fifteen chaps who slept in
the isolated Wing Dormitory of Dunston's
were to fortify the place, and hold it before
the world and the Doctor as a protest against
Thompson. Every chap in the dormitory,

from Trelawny and Bradwell to Watson
minor, signed their names in their own
blood on a paper Trelawny drew out; and
Watson minor fainted while he was doing
it, not being able to see his own gore on a
pen without going off. We swore by a
tremendous swear to obey Trelawny, to
fortify the Wing Dormitory against siege,
to devote every penny of our week's pocket-
money to provisions, and to hold out till we
starved, having first signed another paper
for Doctor Dunston explaining our united
protest against Thompson, and hoping for
the good of the school that he would be
removed. I didn't understand much about
it really. In fact I don't believe anybody
did but Trelawny and Bradwell. Only
they said we were acting for the good of
the school, and they also said that if we
held the Wing Dormitory properly nothing
short of cannon or starvation could dislodge
us. It was a tremendously tall building,
complete in itself, with iron fire-proof doors
constructed to cut it off from the rest of the

school, and with a bathroom and a lavatory adjoining, all at a great height above the ground. The windows were barred to keep chaps getting out. The bars would also keep chaps getting in, as Trelawny pointed out. He found also that it was possible when the iron doors were closed to pull down some woodwork, and stick things behind the doors so as they could not be opened again. The only entrance to the Wing Dormitory was through these iron doors, so once shut we were safe against anything but gunpowder; and Trelawny said Doctor Dunston was not the man to resort to physical means, especially if it meant knocking the place about. Bradwell came out wonderfully about the food, and knowing jolly well that they would turn the water out of the bathroom when the siege started, he made every chap fill his basin and jug the night before; because fresh water is vital to a siege.

There were fifteen chaps, and the time came at last, and one night we laid the manifesto on the mat outside the iron door, made everything fast, and waited to see what would happen. Some fellows thought that Thompson would be sent away at once, to avoid the affair becoming serious; others fancied we should be starved out or expelled to a man. Trelawny never hazarded any guess at what would be the end of it. "We are doing our duty in the interests of the school," he said, "and whatever happens we mean well; and if it gets into print the sympathy of all chaps in public schools will be on our side."

II.

When the gas was turned out at the meter on the night preceding the siege, Trelawny made a short speech. First he lighted two candles and made us sign the protest; then he explained his military system of night and day watches and guards. Each of the four windows had a guard at all hours, and two chaps were to be stationed at the iron door. This was

made doubly strong by beds piled against
it, after the manifesto had been finally
signed and left outside. The document
ran thus :—

"We, the undersigned, thinking that the
fame of Dunston's is tarnished by Mr.
Thompson, M.A., Fellow of Trinity College,
Camb., hereby protest, and formally assert
themselves to call attention to Mr.
Thompson. We, the undersigned, have
no personal grudge to Mr. Thompson, but
think him unsuited to carry on the great
reputation of Dunston's. We, the undersigned, take this important step fully alive
to the gravity of it, for we are prepared to
suffer if necessary to call attention to the
subject. We do not doubt Mr. Thompson's
goodness, and wish it to be understood that
the action is abstract and not personal. A
string will be lowered from the third window
of the Wing Dormitory to-morrow at 8.30
a.m. Any answer to the protest will receive
instant attention from us the undersigned."

Then followed the names.

Of course, it was all Greek to the kids, but they put their trust in Trelawny and signed to a kid.

Inside the dormitory we were jolly busy, too, because after Trelawny, as commander, had made his rules and regulations clear, Bradwell, as the head of the commissariat, drew up a list of the total supplies, and showed what each fellow had contributed to the store. This list I copied for Bradwell at the time, with notes about the different supplies. It comes in here, and I must give it, just to show what different ideas different chaps have about the things you ought to eat in a siege.

TRELAWNY.—Two hams, eight loaves of bread.

BRADWELL.—Three tins potted salmon, two seed cakes (big), box of biscuits.

ASHBY MAJOR.—Ten tins sardines. (Ashby has five shillings a week pocket-money, his father being rather rich. Bradwell said it was rather a pity he spent it all in sardines.)

ASHBY MINOR.—Three pats of butter,

three tins Swiss milk, one tin Guava jelly. (Bradwell was awfully pleased about the milk, because he said it was at once nourishing and pleasant to the taste.)

WILSON.—Six dried herrings, two pots veal and ham paste, one pot marmalade. (Herrings useless, unless eaten raw.)

WEST.—Four bottles raspberry vinegar. (I am West, and I thought raspberry vinegar would be a jolly good thing to break the monotony of a siege. But Bradwell said it was simply a luxury.)

MORRANT. — One hamper containing twenty-four apples, twenty-seven pears, two pots blackberry jam. (Morrant has no pocket-money, but Bradwell said the fruit was good for a change.)

GIDEON.—Nothing. (Gideon is a Jew by birth, and gets ten shillings a week pocket-money. He pretended he had forgotten. Trelawny says he will suffer for it in the course of the siege.)

MATHERS.—Eight pieces of shortbread, five slabs of toffee, seven sausage-rolls.

(The rolls were cut in half, to be eaten first thing before they went bad. But Bradwell said Mathers had made the selection of a fool, and so Mathers was rather vexed with Bradwell.)

NEWNES.—Ten loaves (five brown), one packet of beef tabloids. (Trelawny congratulated Newnes.)

McINNES.—A lot of spring onions and lettuces, costing one-and-sixpence. (McInnes had been reading a book about chaps getting scurvy on a raft, and he thought a siege would be just the place for scurvy, so he bought all green stuff; and Bradwell said it was good.)

CORKEY MINIMUS. — Three pounds of mixed sweets. (Bradwell smacked his head when he heard what Corkey minimus had got; but Trelawny pointed out that a few sweets served out from time to time might distract the mind.)

DERBYSHIRE.—A pigeon-pie and thirteen currant buns with saffron in them.

FORREST.—Four pots Bovril, one bottle

cider. (Bovril can be taken on bread like treacle, and once saved the lives of several shipwrecked sailors.)

WATSON MINOR.—One pound dog biscuits, one pound dried figs, one box of dates, one tin of shrimp paste. (Asked why he took dog biscuits, he explained it was because he had seen an advertisement about the goodness of them. It said they had dried buffalo meat in them, which was a thing you could live for an immense duration of time on. Trelawny said that was pretty fair sense for a kid.)

All this splendid food was brought out of boxes where it had been hidden and placed in the hands of Bradwell; and that night he sat up with a candle and drew out bills of fare and made calculations. We were rather surprised in the morning to hear the rations would not last more than a fortnight, but Trelawny said the siege must be over long before that. Nobody slept much, and many had dressed before the

first bell rang. When the second rang
Trelawny and Bradwell went to the door
to listen.

Presently Thompson, of all people, came
up and tried to get in and couldn't. He
shook the door, then saw the envelope
addressed to the Doctor, and said :—

"What's the meaning of this, you
fellows? Let me in at once!"

But nobody answered. Then he cleared
off. At 8.30 the string was lowered from
the window, and Trelawny went and
stood by it to pull up any letter that might
be fastened to it. But none was. Some
of the chaps were prowling about outside
looking at the Wing Dormitory, but Trelawny wouldn't let anybody go to the
windows except himself.

Then, as nothing happened, we had
breakfast. McInnes and Forrest were told
off to help Bradwell, and each chap's rations
were put on his bed after he had made it.
We all got the same except Gideon—a slice
of bread, two sardines, half one of Mathers'

sausage-rolls, and half a tumbler of water.
So we began at once to see what a jolly
serious thing a siege is. And Gideon saw
it more than we did, because he had no
sardines and no sausage-roll. He offered
Trelawny money for a little more food, but
Trelawny said he shouldn't have as much
as one mixed sweet, though he might pay
gold for it. He said, "You will have barely
enough to keep you alive." And Gideon
turned awfully white when he heard it.

Breakfast didn't take more than about
five minutes, then there was a tremendous
knocking at the iron door, and Bradwell
said the trouble had begun, but Trelawny
said it was the summons to a parley. Anyway, we heard the Doctor's voice, and it
wasn't much of a parley, strictly speaking,
because he spoke first, and merely gave us
two minutes to be in our places downstairs.

"If you don't obey, one and all of you,"
said the Doctor, "you must take the conse-
quences. As it is, they will be sufficiently
grave. Any further offence I shall know
how to treat."

" If you please, sir," said Trelawny, "the string is out of the window. We are doing this for the good of the school, and——"

Then he stopped, because he had heard the Doctor go away.

" He'll try a blacksmith first," said Forrest; "then, when they find they can't do anything with this iron door, he'll send for policemen."

But nothing was done, strangely enough, and Trelawny made the chaps lie down and sleep if they could in the afternoon, because he expected a night attack with ladders. To get in it would be necessary to remove the bars from the windows, and anybody attempting to do so would, of course, be at our mercy with the windows open.

For dinner that day we had one of Trelawny's hams cut into fifteen pieces, with two rather thin slices of bread, one spring onion, and three mixed sweets each, and as much raspberry vinegar as would go into a bullet-mould that Wilson had. Gideon ate the ham like anybody else, which shows

Jews don't refuse pork in any shape at times of siege, whatever they say. Trelawny wouldn't give him any raspberry vinegar, but Ashby minor let him have one of his mixed sweets, which was green and had arsenic in it, Ashby minor thought.

It seemed a frightfully long day, and nothing being done against us made it longer. Bradwell tried to cook Wilson's herrings with stuff out of a pillow-case, but unfortunately failed. Trelawny explained that Dunston was working out tactics, and would do something when the moon rose. He said our motto was to be " Defence, not defiance"; but Derbyshire said they were going to starve us out like rats, so as to reduce the glory as much as possible. One or two chaps had private rows that day, and Trelawny was pretty short and sharp. He said we were to regard ourselves as under martial law, and he stopped Forrest having any tea at all because he looked out of the window and waved his hand to Steggles in the playground. What made it worse

D

for Forrest was that we opened one of his pots of Bovril at that very tea, and of course he didn't have any. But Trelawny said it was good discipline, and wouldn't let Mathers divide his share with young Forrest, though he wanted to.

The day dragged out. Nothing was done, and no letter was put on the string. Then night came and moonlight, and Trelawny set watches at each window and door with directions to wake him instantly if anything happened or anybody assembled outside below. But he didn't sleep really. In fact only a few of the kids did. Bradwell got a bit down in the mouth after dark, and I heard him say to Trelawny it wasn't turning out like he thought, and Trelawny said :—

" It's always the same when a position is impregnable. I could show you a dozen similar sieges in history. Of course, it's the most uninteresting sort of siege when chaps simply sit and see the enemy get to the end of their food supplies, but they won't do

that with us.   The day boys will talk, and
old Dunston will raise heaven and earth
to keep it out of the printed papers.   I bet
he'll tie something to the string to-morrow."

Some of us tried to take a bright view
like Trelawny, but when we heard him tell
Bradwell to run no risks and serve out as
little bread as possible, we felt that he did
not really feel as hopeful of a short siege
as he seemed.   Just before dusk Corkey
minimus was caught in the act of flinging
a letter out of the window addressed to
his mother.   It was torn up, and he was
cautioned.   That ended the day, and nothing
else happened until a quarter to one o'clock.
Then Bradwell, whose watch it was, called
"Cave!" and came to Trelawny with frightful excitement to say that there was the
head of a ladder at his window, and a man
climbing up.   Trelawny was there in a
second, and asked in a loud voice what the
man wanted, and said he'd throw the ladder
down if the man came up another rung.
But the man said :—

"Hush! you silly fellow; I'm a friend with news from the enemy. The least you can do is to 'ear what I've got to say."

"Good Lord!" said Trelawny, "it's Thompson!"

And so it was, and his huge head soon got level with the window, and looked like a bull's against the moonlight. Trelawny made everybody get out of earshot except Bradwell; but he didn't happen to see me, being rolled up in bed near the window, so I heard.

First Thompson said :—

"Look 'ere, you Cornish boy, I'm sorry to find we 'aven't 'it it off by any means, and you want me to go, and you've locked yourself and friends up 'ere as a protest. Now, 'ow 'ave I 'urt your feelings, and what have I done?"

Which was a bit difficult for Trelawny; but he fell back on the manifesto to the Doctor.

"It's no personal matter, sir. We wish it to be understood that the action is abstract."

"Oh! Well, I can't say I know what the devil you mean by that; but I like you all better than ever, and I understand this much, that you don't like me. I'm not proud. I'm quite as ready to learn as to teach. Tell me what makes you do this, you queer things."

"We don't think you are the right man for Dunston's, sir," said Trelawny firmly.

"Well, but isn't Doctor Dunston the best judge? His experience reaches back rather farther than yours. Anyway, I'm not going. You'll 'ave to tolerate me. You'll 'ave to like me too. I've disobeyed all orders by climbing up 'ere now to advise you to give in to-morrow. Take my advice, and come out at the first bell, and with ropes round your necks. Measures are in 'and; and as your protest has utterly failed, the sooner you give in and take your punishment the better. I've done my best to make it as light as I can; but boys mustn't do this sort of thing in big schools, you know. It's very naughty indeed."

"We shall keep up the protest for another day at least, sir," said Trelawny, with a lot of side in his voice.

"No, my lad, you won't," answered Thompson. "The Doctor has taken my advice, and by very simple means, with the least possible waste of time, trouble, and money, we shall enter your stronghold to-morrow. I am quite good-tempered to-day. To-morrow I shall probably be quite cross and 'ot. The matter is in my 'ands. Do be good boys and yield while there is time. The sooner the better."

"I regret we cannot comply with your terms, sir," said Trelawny.

"I'm not offering any," answered Mr. Thompson. "I only want to make your foolishness fall as light as possible. Your mothers' and fathers' 'earts will ache over this headstrong business."

"The parley is ended," said Trelawny.

"All right," said Mr. Thompson. "I'm afraid you're a hawful little prig, Trelawny." Then he went down the ladder, and looking out, Bradwell reported that he saw him taking it back to the gardener's shed in the shrubbery.

III.

There is not much more to be said about the protest of the Wing Dormitory. I suppose Thompson was better up in tactics really than Trelawny. Anyway, he found a weak spot that Trelawny never thought of, and he ended the siege by half-past seven the following morning.

About six Ashby major, whose watch it was, reported that the school fire-escape was coming round the corner. With it appeared Mr. Thompson, Mr. Mannering, who is an Oxford "Blue" and not much smaller than Mr. Thompson, the Doctor, the gardener, and the military sergeant who drills our volunteer corps and teaches gymnastics. They put the escape against the wall of the Wing Dormitory, between two windows where it couldn't be reached by us. Then Thompson and Mannering went up, and the sergeant and gardener followed. The Doctor waited at the foot of the ladder.

"They'll get through the roof!" said Trelawny, "I never thought of that!"

Trelawny turned awfully rum in the face, and tried to think out a way of repelling a roof attack; but there wasn't time. In about ten minutes or so the end of an iron bar came through the ceiling; then followed a regular avalanche of plaster and dust, that fell on Watson minor and jolly nearly smothered him. Then came Thompson, Mannering followed, and the gardener and the sergeant dropped after them as quick as lightning. Of course we were done, because only half of us were fighters, the rest being kids; and Trelawny himself being just fifteen and Bradwell fourteen and Ashby major twelve and a half, and I only eleven and a half, it was no good.

"We surrender," said Trelawny.

"Surrender, you little brute, I should think you did surrender!" said Mannering, who had cut his hand getting the slates off the roof, and was in a rare bate.

"You needn't insult a defeated force, sir," said Trelawny, keeping his nerve jolly well. "We are prepared to pay the penalty of failure, and having meant well we—we don't care."

But whether we meant well or not, I know Trelawny and Bradwell both got expelled, though Thompson was said to have tried very hard for them. Dunston didn't seem to realise what frightfully good motives prompted them to protest against Thompson in an abstract way. Nothing was done to anybody else except Ashby major and me and Wilson. We were flogged by Mr. Mannering for the Doctor; and he did it as you might expect from a "Blue."

As for Thompson, he stayed on, and the protest never got into print; and there wasn't much disgrace for Trelawny or Bradwell after all, because the first afterwards got into Woolwich ten from the top, through an army crammer's, and the second joined his father, who was the Whiteley of the North I spoke of.   He wrote to me only a week ago to say that he was getting a hundred pounds a year from his governor for doing much less than he had to do at Dunston's.   Mind you, Thompson is a jolly good sort, really, and we know it now ; and, as I heard my uncle say of somebody else, I don't suppose it's a matter of life and death whether or no a chap puts his h's in the wrong places if his heart's in the right one.

"FRECKLES" AND "FRENCHY."

H E was the most peculiar chap that ever came to Merivale, not excepting even Mason, who shot the Doctor's wife's parrot with a catapult, and, after he had been flogged, offered to stuff it in the face of the whole school, and nearly got expelled. Freckles was so called owing to his skin, which was simply a complicated pattern much like what you can see in any map of the Grecian Archipelago. This arose, he thought, from his having been born in Australia. Anyway it was rum to see; and so were his hands, which had reddish down on the backs. His eyes were also reddish— a sort of mixture of red and grey specks, and they glimmered like a cat's when he was angry, which was often. His real name was Maine, and he had no side. His father had made a big fortune selling wool at Sydney, and his grandfather was one of the

last people to be transported to Botany Bay
—through no fault of his own. After he
had been on a convict ship five years, a chap
at home confessed on his death-bed that he
had done the thing Maine's grandfather
was transported for. So they naturally let
Maine's grandfather go free; and he was so
much annoyed about it that he never came
back home again, but married a farmer's
daughter near Sydney and settled out there
for good.

Maine didn't think great things of England,
and was always talking about the Australian
forests of blue gum trees and bush, and
sneering rather at the size of our forests
round Merivale, though they were good ones.
He never joined in games, but roamed away
alone for miles and miles into the country on
half-holidays, and trespassed with a cheek I
never saw equalled. He could run like a
hare—especially about half a mile or so,
which, as he explained to me, is just about
a distance to blow a keeper. Certainly,
though often chased, he was never caught

and never recognised, owing to things he
did which he had learned in Australia and
copied from famous bushrangers. His
great hope some day was to be a bushranger himself, and he practised in a quiet
way every Saturday afternoon, making it a
rule to go out of bounds always. His get-
up was fine. My name is Tomkins, called
"Nubby" because I happen to have a rather
large sort of Roman-shaped nose, and being
fond of the country and not keen on games,
Maine rather took to me, and after I had
sworn on crossed knives not to say a word
to a soul (which I never did till Freckles
left) he told me his secrets and showed me
his things. If you'd seen Freckles starting
for an excursion you wouldn't have said
there was anything remarkable about him;
but really he was armed to the teeth, and
had everything a bushranger would be likely
to want in a quiet place like Merivale.
Down his leg was the barrel of an air-gun,
strong enough to kill any small thing like a
cat at twenty-five yards; the rest of the

gun was arranged inside the lining of his coat, and the slugs it fired he carried loose in his trousers-pockets.   Round his waist he had a leather belt he got from a sailor for a pound.   Inside the leather was human skin, said to be flayed off a chap by cannibals somewhere, which was a splendid thing to have for your own, if it was true; and in the belt a place had been specially made for a knife.   Freckles, of course, had a knife in it—a "bowie" knife that made you cold to see. He never used it, but kept it ready, and said if a keeper ever caught him he possibly might have to.   In addition to these things he carried in his coat-pockets a little spirit lamp and a collapsible tin pot and a bag of tea.

He said tea was the very life of men in the bush, and that often after a hard escape, when he was out of danger, he would get away behind a woodstack or under banks of a stream, or some such secret place, and brew a cup and drink it, and feel the better for it.

Lastly, Freckles had a flat lead mask with holes for the eyes and mouth, which he always fitted on when trespassing. He said it was copied from the helmet Ned Kelly, the King of the Bushrangers, used to wear, but it was not bullet-proof, but only used for a disguise. We were in the same dormitory, and one night, when all the chaps had gone to sleep, he dressed up in these things and stood where some moonlight came in, and certainly looked jolly.

Once, as an awful favour — me being smaller than him, and not fast enough to run away from a man—he let me come and see what he did when bushranging on a half-holiday in winter. " I shan't run my usual frightful risks with you," he said, "because I might have to open fire to save you, and that would be very disagreeable to me ; but we'll trespass a bit, and I'll shoot a few things, if I can. I don't shoot much, only for food."

He made me a mask with tinfoil off chocolate smoothed out and gummed on cardboard ; but I had no weapons, and he said I had better not try and get any.

We started for the usual walk. Chaps were allowed to go through a public pine-wood to Merivale; but half through, by a place where was a board which warned us to keep to the path, Freckles branched off into some dead bracken, and squatted down and put on his mask. I also put on mine. Then he fastened his air-gun together and loaded it, and told me to walk six paces behind him and do as he did. His eyes were awfully keen, and now and then he pointed to a feather on the ground, or an old nest or a patch of rum fungus or a crab-apple still hanging on the tree, though all the leaves were off.

Once he fired at a jay and missed it, then fell down in the fern as if he was shot himself, and remained quite motionless for some time. He told me that he always did so after firing, that he might hear if anybody had been attracted by the sound. It was a well-known bushman's dodge. Once we saw a keeper through a clearing, and Freckles lay flat on his stomach, and so did I. He knew the keeper well, and told me that he had many times escaped from him. We waited half an hour, and turned to go back a different way from that of the keeper.

Then, where a glade sloped down to some water and the grass was all dewy and covered with mole-hills, Freckles went to inspect a trap he had set a week before. He was collecting skins for a mole-skin waistcoat, but he said skinning moles was one of the beastliest tasks a hunter ever had. However, there was a mole caught, and he skinned it and wrapped up the skin in leaves and put it in his hat.

Then we had some real sport, for on the other side of the glade we saw rabbits lopping about, and Freckles stalked them through the fern while I waited motionless, and finally he shot a young one. I wanted to take it back and get cook to do it for us, but he said I was a fool.

"If you want any you must have it now. It's about the time I take a meal," he said,

E

"and that's a part of my ranging and
hunting you haven't seen yet."

He knew the country well, and said we
were in one of the most carefully preserved
places anywhere about, which must have
been true, for there were an awful lot of
pheasants calling in the glades. But Freckles
got down into a drain and showed me a
hollow he had scooped out under a lot of
ivy where it fell over a bank.

" This is one of my caves," he said, "and
here we can feed and drink in safety;
but you mustn't talk, or I shan't be able
to hear if anything is stirring in the
woods."

He took off his mask, set down his gun,
and lighted his spirit stove.

" Skin the rabbit and cut off his hind legs
while I make tea," he said.

So I did, and he held them over the lamp
till they were slightly cooked outside, but
not right through. He ate and drank with
his ears straining for every sound. Then
he took the rest of the rabbit and removed

all traces of eating, and buried everything
we had left.

"If I didn't," he explained, "some
keeper's dog would find my lair, and make
a row and give it away, and the keepers
would doubtless lie in wait for me and catch
me red-handed. You can't be too careful,
because every man's hand's against you;
which, of course, is the beauty of it."

We got back without anything happening,
and I've hated the sight of rabbit pretty
well ever since, but Freckles said the juices
of animals are better for the human frame
underdone.

Well, that gives you an idea of Freckles,
and the affair with Frenchy, which I am
going to tell you about, showed that he really
was cut out for bushranging. Frenchy, as
we called him, was Monsieur Michel. He
didn't belong entirely to Dunston's, but
lived in Merivale and came to us three days
a week, and went to a girls' school the other
three. He was a rum, oldish chap, whose
great peculiarities were to make puns in

English and to appeal to our honour about
everything.

He would slang a fellow horribly one day,
and wave his arms and pretty nearly jump
out of his skin; and the next day he would
bring up a whacking pear for the fellow
he'd slanged, or a new knife or something.
He pretty nearly cried sometimes, and
he told us his nerves were frightfully
tricky, and often led him to be harsh when
he didn't mean it. He couldn't keep order
or make chaps work if they didn't choose;
and Steggles, who had an awfully cunning
dodge of always rubbing him up the wrong
way, and then looking crushed and broken-
hearted so as to get things, which he did,
said that Frenchy was like damp fireworks,
because you never knew exactly when he'd
go off or how.

One day, dashing out of class with a
frightful yell, Freckles got sent for, and
went back and found Monsieur raving mad.
It seemed that Freckles had yelled too soon
—before he was out of the classroom, in

fact, and Frenchy had got palpitation of the heart from it. He let into Freckles properly then. He said he was his *"bête noire"* and *"un sot à vingt-quatre carats"*—which means an eighteen carat ass in English; but twenty-four carats in French—and "one of the aborigines who ought to be kept on a chain," and many other such-like things. Freckles turned all colours, and then white, with a sort of bluish tint to his lips. He didn't say a word, but looked at Frenchy with such a frightful expression that I felt something would happen later. All that happened at the time was that Freckles got the eighth book of Telemachus to write out into French from English, and then correct by Fenelon, which was a pretty big job if a chap. had been fool enough to try and do it; and Monsieur Michel went off to Merivale with a big card on his coat-tail with *"Ici on parle Français"* written upon it in red pencil. This I had managed to do myself while Frenchy was jawing Freckles. I told Freckles, but it didn't comfort him

much.   He said there were some things no
mortal chap could stand ; and to be called
"an aborigine" because a man was born in
Australia seemed to him about the bitterest
insult even an old frog-eating Frenchman
could have invented. Happening to *him*,
of all chaps, it was especially a thing which
would have to be revenged, seeing what his
views were.   He said :—

"I couldn't bushrange or anything with
a clear conscience in the future if I had a
thing like this hanging over me unrevenged.
It's the frightfulest slur on my character,
and I won't sit down under it for fifty
Frenchmen."

Then he said he should take a week to
settle what to do, and went into the playground alone.

Next time Frenchy came up he was just
the same as ever—awfully easy-going and
jolly, and let Freckles off the Telemachus,
and offered him as classy a knife, with a
corkscrew   and   other   things,   including
tweezers, as ever you saw—just the knife

for Freckles, considering his ways. But it
didn't come off. Freckles got white again
when he saw the knife, and said :—

"Thank you, Monsieur, I don't want
your knife; and the imposition is half done,
and will be finished next time you come."

Then Frenchy called him a silly boy, and
tried to make a joke and pinch Freckles
by the ear. But nobody saw the joke, and
Freckles dodged away. Then Frenchy
sighed, and looked round to see who
should have the knife, and didn't seem to
see anybody in particular, and left it on
his desk. He often sighed in class, and
sometimes told us he was without friends,
unless he might call us friends; and we said
he might.

When he went, Freckles told me he
considered the knife was another insult.
Then he explained what he was going to
do. He said :—

"I shall finish the impot first, so as not
to be obliged to him for anything, and then
I shall stick him up."

"Stick him up—how?" I said.

"It's a bushranging expression," he explained. "To 'stick up' a man is to make him stand and deliver what he's got. I see my way to do this with Frenchy. He always goes and comes from Merivale through the woods, as you know, and now he's up here on Friday nights coaching Slade and Betterton for their army exam. Afterwards he has supper with Mr. Thompson or the Doctor. There you are. I wait my time in the wood, which is jolly lonely by night, though it is such a potty little place, hardly worth calling a wood; then he comes along, and I stick him up."

"It's highway robbery," I said. "You might get years and years of imprisonment."

"I might," he said, "but I shan't. You must begin your career some time, and I'm going to next Friday night. I've often got out of the dormitory and been in that wood by night, and only the chaps in the dormitory have known it."

Well, the night came, and all that we
heard about it till afterwards was that about
eleven o'clock, or possibly even later than
that, there was a fearful pealing at the front
door of Dunston's, and looking out we could
see a stretcher and something on it. That
something was actually Freckles, though the
few chaps who knew what was going to
be done felt sure it must be Frenchy;
because Freckles is five feet ten and growing, and Frenchy isn't more than five feet
six at the outside, and a poor thing at
that.

But it *was* Freckles all right, and two
labouring men had brought him back, and
Frenchy had come with them.

Not until five weeks afterwards, when
Freckles could get up and limp about, did
I hear the truth; and I'll tell it in his own
words, because they must be better than a
chap's who wasn't there. He seemed frightfully down in the mouth, and said that he
could never look fellows in the eyes again;
but it cheered him telling me, and when I

told him he was thundering well out of it he admitted he was.   He said :—

"I got off all right, and the moon was as clear as day, and everything just ripe for sticking a chap up.   Then, like a fool, having a longish time to wait, I didn't simply stop in shadow behind a tree-trunk or something in the usual way, but thought I'd do a thing I'd never heard of bushrangers doing, though Indian thugs are pretty good at it.   I went and got up a tree which has a branch over the road, and I thought I'd drop down almost on top of Frenchy to start with.   And that's just what I did do, only I dropped wrong, and came down pretty nearly on my head owing to slipping somehow at the start. What did exactly happen to me as I left the tree I never shall know.   Anyway, Frenchy came along sure enough, and I dropped, and he jumped I should think fully a yard in the air; but that was all, because in falling I hit a big root (it was a beech tree), and went and broke something in my ankle and something in my chest and couldn't stand. Consequently, of course, I couldn't stick him up. The pain was pretty fair, but feeling what a fool I was seemed to make me forget it. Anyway, finding it was useless to think of sticking him up, I tried to hobble into the fern and get out of sight; and finding I couldn't crawl, I rolled. But of course you can't roll away from a chap, and he came after me, and my mask fell off while I rolled, and he recognised me.

"'*Mon Dieu!* it is the boy Maine!' he said. 'Speak, child, what in the wide world was this?'

"I disguised my voice and said I wasn't Maine, and that he'd better leave me alone or it might be the worse for him yet. But he wouldn't go, and chancing to get queer about the head somehow I went off, I suppose, though it wasn't for long. When I came to he was gone, but he rushed back in a minute with that rotten old top-hat he wears full of water he'd got from the puddle in the stone-pit. He doused my head and made me sit up with my back against a tree. Then, feeling the frightfulness of it, I begged him to clear out and let me alone. I said:—

"'You don't know what you're doing. I'm no friend to you, but the deadliest enemy you've got in the world, and if I hadn't fallen down at a critical moment and broken myself I should have stuck you up, Monsieur Michel. So now you know.'

"He said to himself, 'The poor mad boy —the poor mad boy—I will run *à toutes jambes* for succour'; but I told him not to. I began to get a rum hot pain in my side then, but I felt I would gladly have died there rather than be obliged to him. I said:—

"'You called me an "aborigine," which is the most terrible thing you can call an Australian-born chap, and you wanted to pass it off with a knife with a corkscrew and tweezers in it. But you couldn't expect

me to take it, feeling as I did. Now the
fortunes of war have given you the victory,
and, if you please, I wish you'd go.'

"But he refused. He said he wouldn't
have hurt my feelings for anything. He
seemed to overlook altogether what I was
going to do to him, and asked me where
it hurt me. I told him, and he said it
was his fault — fancy that! and wished
he was big enough to carry me back. I
kept on asking him to go, and at last,
after begging my pardon like anything, for
about a week it seemed, he went. But
I heard him shouting and yelling French
yells in the woods, and after a bit he came
back with two men and a hurdle. They
presently took me back, and what Frenchy's
said since to the Doctor I don't know. In
fact, I didn't know anything for days. Anyway, I've had nothing but a mild rowing
and very good grub, and I'm not to be even
flogged, though that's probably because I
broke a rib or two, not including the bone
in my leg. But I'm all right now, and I

think it was about the most sporting thing
a chap ever did for Frenchy to treat me
like that—eh? I shouldn't have thought it
was in a Frenchman to do it, especially after
I told him what I was going to do."

"Yes," I said, "that's all right, but what
about bushranging?"

"It's pretty sickening," he said, "but I
feel as if all the keenness was knocked out
of me. If a chap can't so much as fall out
of a tree on a wanderer's path at the nick
of time without smashing himself, what's
the good of him?"

"Besides," I said, "if it hadn't been
Frenchy, but somebody else of a different
turn of mind, he might have taken you at
a disadvantage and jolly well killed you."

"In real bushranging that is what would
have happened," admitted Freckles. "As
it is I expect months, perhaps years, will
have to go by before I feel to hanker after
it again. And meantime I shan't rest in
peace till I've paid Frenchy."

"How?" I asked.

"Well, I believe it's to be done. He's often come to see me while I was on my back in bed, and he's told me a lot about himself. He's frightfully hard up and a Roman Catholic, and hopes to lay his bones in la belle France with luck, but he doesn't think he'll ever be able to manage it. He told me all this, little knowing my father was extremely rich. Well, you see, the mater wants somebody French for the kids at home, which are girls, and knowing Frenchy bars this climate I think Australia might do him good. He's fifty-three years old, and it seems to me if the guv'nor wrote and offered him his passage and a good screw he'd go. I have made it a personal thing to myself, and told the guv'nor what a good little chap he is, and what a beautiful accent he's got, and the thing that happened in the wood."

The affair dropped then, and about six weeks after, during the next term, when Freckles was getting fit again, he walked with me one half-holiday to see the place where he was smashed up. The bough was a frightful high one to drop from even in daylight, also it was broken. Freckles got awfully excited when he spotted it.

"There! there!" he said, "that's the best thing I 've seen for twelve weeks!"

"I don't see much to squeak about," I said, "especially as the beastly tree nearly did for you."

"But can't you see it's broken? That's what did it! I thought I slipped, and if I had I shouldn't have been made of the stuff for a bushranger; but the wretched branch broke, and that is jolly different. That wasn't my fault. The most hardened old hand must have come down then. In fact, he couldn't have stopped up. Oh, what a lot of misery I 'd have been saved through all these weeks if I 'd known it broke in a natural sort of way!"

He got an awful deal of comfort out of this, and said he should return to his old ways again as soon as he could run a mile without stopping. And we found his lead mask, like Ned Kelly's, just where it had dropped when he rolled over in the fern, and he welcomed it like a dog.

That's the end, except that his father did write to Dunston about Frenchy; and Dunston, not being very keen about Frenchy himself, seemed to think he would be just the chap for the girls of Freckles' father. Anyway, he went, and he cried when he said "Good-bye" to the school; and Freckles told me that when he said "Good-bye" to him he yelled with crying, and blessed him both in French and English, and said that the sunny atmosphere of Australia would very likely prolong his life until he had saved enough to get his bones back to France.

So he went, and Freckles went after him much sooner than he ever expected to, because the keepers finally caught him in the game preserves, sitting in his hole under the stream bank, frizzling the leg of a pheasant which he had shot out of a tree with his air-gun and buried seven days

F

before. And Dunston wrote to his father and his father wrote back that Freckles, being now fourteen and apparently having less sense than when he left Australia, had better return to his native land, and go into the wool business. Freckles told me that chaps in his father's office generally got a fortnight's holiday, but that his mother would probably work up his governor to give him three weeks. Then he would get a proper outfit and track away to the boundless scrub, and fall in with other chaps who had similar ideas, and begin to take life seriously. He said I might see his name in Australian papers in about a year. But he never wrote to me, and I don't know if he really succeeded well. I'm sure I hope he did, for he was a tidy chap, though queer.

CONCERNING CORKEY
MINIMUS

I.

IF Corkey minor had been at school that term the thing would never have come about; but Corkey minor was always one of the lucky chaps, and just when, in the ordinary course of events, he would have had to begin fagging for an exam., something happened to his right lung, and he had to go on an awful fine trip to Australia in a sailing ship. That left Corkey major, who was a mere learning machine in the Sixth, and Corkey minimus, who was ten, and in the Lower Fourth.

It began like this. After Bray had licked Derbyshire and Bethune, which he did one after the other on the same half-holiday, chaps gave him "best," as a matter of course, and he became cock of the lower school. He was solid muscle all through, and harder than stone, and he had a brother in London who was runner-up in the amateur "light-weight" championship two years following. Bray fancied himself a bit, naturally, and was always roaming about seeking fellows to punch. But once, out of bounds in a private wood, a keeper caught him and licked him, which was seen by two other fellows, and remembered against Bray afterwards when he put on too much side.

He and Corkey minimus were in the same class, because Bray, though thirteen, didn't know much. At first they were great chums, and Bray bossed Corkey and palled with him; and when Browne, the under mathematical master, told Corkey minimus that he was "the least of all the Corkeys, and not worthy to be called a Corkey," because he couldn't do rule-of-three, or some rot, Bray said a thing that Browne overheard, and got sent up. But by degrees

the friendship of Bray and Corkey minimus cooled off, and the matter of Milly
settled it.

The doctor had four daughters, and Milly
was the youngest. Mabel and Ethel held
no dealings with any fellows under the Sixth,
and Mary had something wrong with her
spine and didn't count. But I never cared
for any of them myself, because you couldn't
tell what they meant. Beatrice, for instance,
was absolutely engaged to Morris, for he
told his sister so in the holidays, and his
sister told Morris minor, and he told me the
next term. Morris was the head of the
school, and he had her photograph fixed
into a foreign nut which he wore on his
watch-chain. But when he left, and she
found out he was gone into a Bank at
£80 a year, she dropped him like a
spider. Mind you, Morris had told her
he was descended, on his mother's side,
from a race of old Irish kings, which may
have unsettled her. Anyway, when she
found he came, on his father's side, from

a race of church curates, she wrote and said
it was off.

But there were other things that upset
the chumming of Bray and Corkey minimus
before the Milly row, and they ought to
be taken in turn. First, there was the Old
Testament prize, which was the only thing
Bray had the ghost of a chance of getting.
But Corkey beat him by twenty - three
marks; and Bray said afterwards that
Corkey had cribbed a lot of stuff about
Joshua, and Corkey said he hadn't, and
even declared he knew as much about
Joshua as Bray, and a bit over. Then,
on top of that, came the match with
neckties, which was rather a rum match in
its way. Both of them used to be awfully
swagger about their neckties, and each
fancied his own. So one bet the other half
a crown he would wear a different necktie
every day for a month. The month being
June, that meant thirty different neckties
each, and the chap who wore the best neckties would win. A fellow called Fowle was

judge, being the son of an artist; and neither Bray nor Corkey was allowed to buy a single new tie or add to the stock he had in his box. At the end of a fortnight they stood about equal, though Corkey's ties were rather more artistic than Bray's, which were chiefly yellow and spotted. But then came an awful falling away, and some of the affairs they wore were simply weird. The test for these was if the tie passed in class. Then the terms of the match were altered, and they decided to go on wearing different things till one or other was stopped by a master. Any concern not noticed was considered a necktie "in the ordinary acceptation of that term," as Fowle put it. At the end of the third week Corkey minimus came out in an umbrella cover done in a sailor's knot, but nobody worth mentioning spotted it; and the next day Bray wore a bit of blue ribbon off a chocolate box, which also passed. They struggled on in this sort of way till Bray got bowled over. I think Corkey was wearing a yard-measure dipped in red ink that morning, but it looked rather swagger than not. Class was just ended, when old Briggs, of all people—a man who wore two pairs of spectacles at one time very often—said to Bray :—

"What is that round your neck, boy?" And Bray said :—

"My tie, sir."

Then Briggs said :—

"Is it, sir? Let me see it, please. I have noticed an increasing disorder about your neck arrangements for a week past. You insult me and you insult the class by appearing here in these ridiculous ties."

"It shan't happen again, sir," said Bray, trying to edge out of the classroom.

"No, Bray, it shall not," said old Briggs. "Bring me that thing at once, please."

Bray handed it up, and Briggs examined it as if it was a botanical specimen or something.

"This," he announced, "is not a necktie at all. You're wearing a piece of Brussels carpet, wretched boy—a fragment of the new carpet laid down yesterday in the Doctor's study. You will kindly take it to him immediately, say who sent you, and state the purpose to which you were putting it."

So Bray, by the terms of the match, lost, and Corkey minimus won with the yard measure.

Then the feeling between them grew, especially after Bray said that he could only pay his half-crown in instalments of a penny a week.

Now we come to Milly. You see she was Corkey minor's great pal the term before, but now that he was at sea, and thousands of miles off, she chucked him and turned to Corkey minimus. That shows what she was really. Anyway, in a bad moment for young Corkey, she told him he had eyes like an eagle's, and it simply turned his head. As an eagle's eyes are yellow, I couldn't see myself what there was to be so jolly pleased about; but he was, and, to show you what a chap may come to if a girl collars him, I know for a fact that Corkey minimus tried to paint a picture for her. Whether he actually succeeded I cannot say, but he went down four places in class, and got awfully dropped on by Browne.

Then came that attempt of Bray to cut Corkey out, and, being myself a tremendous personal chum of Corkey's, I wished he had succeeded; but he didn't, and even his fighting didn't take Milly. After a month of giving her things to eat and so on, he said it was his red hair that stood between them, and told Fowle he didn't care a straw about her; but from the way he went on to Corkey minimus, any fool could see he really cared a lot. The chap called Fowle comes in here. This "obscene Fowle," as we called him out of Virgil, being really a term in a crib applied to harpies, though he would have run if a mouse had squeaked at him, was yet responsible for more fights than any fellow in the school. He sneaked about, asking chaps if they gave one another "best," and when at last he found

two who didn't funk each other, though they
might be perfectly good friends, he never
rested until there was a fight. He got
kicked sometimes, but not enough. That
was owing to the fact that his hampers from
home were most extraordinary. They came
on Roman feast days, because he was a
Roman Catholic by religion; and some
fellows even said the more you kicked
Fowle the more you were likely to get from
the hampers. That was rot, of course, and
a jolly suspicious thing happened once.
Newnes—a chap in the lower fifth—kicked
Fowle the very morning before a hamper
came; and that same evening, after prayers,
Fowle gave Newnes about half a whacking
big melon, and the next day Newnes jolly
nearly died. Fowle swore he hadn't put
anything in the melon, but it is bosh to say
that half a melon, if it's all right, is going
to do a chap any harm. Anyway, we rather
funked Fowle's hampers afterwards.

Well, this wretched, obscene Fowle met
me one day licking his fat lips and showing

great excitement.　So I knew he'd probably worked up a fight; but it wasn't that, though something worse.　He said :—

"Where's Corkey minimus?　Bray wants him."

"What for?" I said.　I may mention that I am called McInnes.

"As a matter of fact he's heard something, and he says, though he's sorry, he's got to lick Corkey."

Fowle smacked his beastly mouth as if he'd got pine-apple drops in it.

"What's Corkey done?" I said.

"It's about Milly Dunston.　Young Corkey talks jolly big with her, and doesn't even speak civil of his friends.　By quite an accident I was passing through the shrubbery from Browne's house to the chapel yesterday, and I went by the summer-house, which is out of bounds, and couldn't help overhearing Milly and Corkey minimus, who were there.　And Corkey distinctly said that Bray was as fiery as his hair, and that he had no more control of himself than a burning mountain; and Milly laughed."

"And you sneaked off and told Bray?"

"As his chum I had to."

"Ah, then I shall tell Corkey what you heard, being his chum."

"I shouldn't," said Fowle. "It's only making mischief. Besides, Bray won't take an apology now. He says he's stood all that flesh and blood can stand. Those were his very words. In fact, I'm looking for Corkey minimus at this moment to tell him that Bray wants him up in the 'gym.'"

"To lick him?"

Fowle smacked his lips again.

"He's brought it on himself."

"Well," I said, "I'll give the message. You can go back and tell Bray you've told me."

"I'd rather have done it myself," said Fowle regretfully, as though he was being robbed of tuck.

"Well, you won't," I answered him, being pretty sick with the worm of a chap by that time. "You go back and say that Corkey will turn up in ten minutes."

Then he cleared out reluctantly, leaving this tremendous responsibility entirely on my hands.

II.

I went off there and then for Corkey. It's a bit of a jar for a chap to get a message like that unexpectedly, and I didn't know what advice to give. Corkey major was no good. If I'd told him he would have blinked through his goggles and have said some bosh—very likely in Latin. And Corkey minor, being thousands of miles away, it looked blue, because you can't ask anybody but a chap's own brothers to take up a matter like this. I couldn't lick Bray myself, or I would have.

The next minute I met Corkey himself, and, from an awful rum look about him, I thought for a moment he'd had the licking already. But he hadn't, and before I could speak, he said :—

" McInnes, I 've got to fight Bray."

" My dear chap, you couldn't," I began.

" I know," he answered, " but I 've got to. Things have happened. Listen to this. I 've just left Milly, and she 's in a frightful bate. I shouldn't have thought a girl could have got in such a rage without hurting herself. Bray told Fowle that there were as good fish in the sea as ever came out of it—meaning Milly ; and Fowle wrote it on a bit of paper and dropped it where Milly was bound to see it. He didn't put his name, but she knows his writing. Now she 's pretty well mad, and says it 's a disgrace that a thick-necked, speckly, stumpy chap like Bray should be cock of the lower school. Well, I said, very likely it was, but I didn't see how it could be helped, him being such a fighter. Then she tossed her hair about, and said, ' I won't have anything more to do with the lower school at all while he 's cock of it.' Of course, I didn't think she included me, being —well, her greatest pal alive since Corkey minor went. So I said, 'Quite right; I shouldn't look at them.' Then she turned round rather suddenly and said I *was* included. So I said, 'I should be only too glad to fight him if there was a ghost of a chance, but there isn't. It's no good pretending. He's four inches taller, and miles more round the chest and round the arms, and ages older. In fact, he could lick me with one hand tied behind him.' Then she said, 'The days of chivalry are dead,' which she'd got out of a book, of course; and she added that she was tired of all boys, and that a chap with eyes like mine ought to have more 'devil' in him. Yes, she used that word. I said, 'What do you want me to do?' And she said, 'Oh, nothing. I wouldn't have a hair of your head singed for the world; only I thought that it might interest you more than other people to know I'd been insulted. Of course, if it's nothing to you——' Then she stopped and marched away, and I went after her and asked her to explain, and she answered that the explanation ought to come from me. She said, 'D'you ever read dragon stories?' And I said, 'Yes.' Then she went on, 'Well, in all the ones I've read, if a lady asked anybody to kill a dragon, the person didn't say that the dragon could beat him with one paw tied behind it, even though he thought so; but he jolly well went and did the best he could.' Naturally, after that, I saw what she meant, and I said, 'Oh, all right, Milly; of course, if you've been insulted, I must make the beggar apologise—or try to.' 'Yes,' she said, cheering up like anything; 'you are my own precious champion, and I love you.' I tell you all this because you're my chum, and you'll have to be my second. And if I can even black his eye before he settles me, it will be something."

"Well, I call it a chouse," I said. "She might as well have asked you to fight Blanchard or Sims. Look at your arms, not to mention anything else; they're like cabbage-stalks."

G

"Yes, I know all that," said Corkey minimus, "and it'll be rather rotten for her if he kills me. But the thing's got to be done, and the sooner it's over the better."

Then I suddenly remembered Bray's message, and told Corkey. He seemed surprised.

"He can't lick me on the spot if I challenge him to fight in a regular way, can he?" he asked, but rather doubtfully.

I said it seemed to me he couldn't. Then we went up to the "gym," where Bray was talking to about four chaps, including Fowle.

"Oh, you've come, you kid, have you? You'd better not keep me waiting another time when I send for you," he began. "Now I'm going to lick you for cheek."

"What cheek?" Corkey minimus said.

"Fowle heard you say I was as fiery as my hair."

"Oh, Fowle, he hears a lot, I know."

"Did you say it or didn't you?"

"Yes, I did, and I say it again; and you're a dirty bully too,"

Bray came quite close to Corkey minimus, and put his face so near that their noses were almost touching, like cats do when they're going to have a row on a wall.

"Say that just once more if it isn't troubling you too much," said Bray.

"I'll say it as often as you like," answered young Corkey, keeping his eye on Bray's, "and I'll say another thing too, which is, that before you talk so big about me being a 'kid' and licking me, you'd better find out first if I give you 'best.'"

"Golly!" said Bray, grinning like mad, "don't you?"

"No, I don't; and I'll fight you properly with seconds the first minute we can."

Corkey minimus had certainly come out of it fine so far, and I only wished he could fight as well as he talked. Of course, from Bray's point of view it was the best thing that could have happened, because now he had a right to lick Corkey, and a right to lick him as badly as he could. The bell rang a minute afterwards, and going in it was settled the fight should come off next Wednesday, that being a half-holiday. Part of Merivale Woods skirted the cricket-field, and as the second eleven, to which Bray belonged, wasn't playing a match, everything suited very comfortably. Blanchard, the cock of the school, agreed to umpire, and he and another chap in the Fifth very kindly promised to carry young Corkey home by a secluded way if he was too much smashed to walk. Fowle seconded Bray, and I saw Bray teaching him how to fan with a towel and spurt water over a fellow's face between the rounds. Of course, it was about as good fun as killing rats with a stick for Bray.

III.

Corkey minimus saw Milly once or twice before the fight, and he said he couldn't make out whether she was going mad or what. One minute she wanted him to fight, the next she implored him not to; one minute she hoped he would mutilate Bray

to pieces, the next she blubbed and prayed
him if ever he had any liking for her to give
Bray "best." She said she kept dreaming
of him brought back stark and stiff; and
then, when he began to think she meant
it, she called him her "knight" and her
"hero" and her "King Arthur" and other
frightful rot, and actually wanted him to
wear one of her Sunday gloves under his
shirt at the time of fighting! Corkey
minimus said he very likely wouldn't wear
a shirt; and then she thought he might
hang it—I mean the glove—round his neck
by a bit of string!

"Blessed if I shall ever feel quite the
same to her after this," said Corkey.

"It seems rather rough to get broken up
for life to please a skimpy girl," I said.
Then he burst out as red in the face as an
apple, and told me he would not hear a
word against Milly, so I dried up.

There were three days before the fight,
and Corkey minimus trained for it, and gave
away his pudding at dinner in exchange for

the meat of the chaps who sat next to him. But you can't get your muscle up in a day or two like that, and it only made him awfully thirsty.

The day came at last, and I may as well go on to the fight itself. The First were having a big match on our own ground, so nobody paid any attention to us, and we arranged a game that should have Corkey, Bray, and me on the same side. Then, when our chaps were in, we three sneaked away into the plantations, behind some holly trees and a woodstack. Bray arranged the preliminaries as cheerful as a bird, and Blanchard, when he came, said they were right. We marked out a ring and ran a string round and arranged corners for the seconds; and I saw that the obscene Fowle had towels and bottles of water and a basin—all, of course, for Bray between the rounds. Corkey minimus was rather waxy with me for not bringing the same for him; but I 'd brought a sponge, which I know is a thing a second chucks up in the air when his man is done for; and I explained and showed it to Corkey, and he thanked me and said he supposed that was about the only thing he should want. Blanchard said the rounds were to be one minute and a half long each, and Bray grumbled because they ought by rights to be three. But Blanchard told him to shut up and begin. When we saw Bray take his shirt off I told Corkey he ought to, and he did. Then Blanchard laughed and said :—

"By gum! they peel rather different!"

Bray was like a barrel, with muscles a lot bigger than hen's eggs on his arms. Corkey minimus seemed to be all ribs somehow, with arms about as lean as rulers. I told him to keep moving about and try and puff Bray a bit if he had time, and he said :—

"All right, I'll try. If I can get a smack at his face, so as to black an eye or something, and show I've hit him before he does for me, I don't care."

I will say for Corkey minimus that he

had about the best pluck I ever saw in a chap. He was quite calm, and just his usual colour; and when Bray tossed him for corners Corkey won; and Blanchard said I picked the right corner for him. Then he told them to fight fair, and said " Time!"

I'd prayed Corkey to try and surprise Bray at the very start if he could, and have a hit at Bray's face the moment they began. And I'm blessed if he didn't go and do it! Bray began fiddling about jolly scientifically with his hands, and I fancy he just squinted down to see if his feet were scientific too. At the same moment Corkey buzzed round his right and let Bray have it fairly on the nose. Bray jumped and looked about as much surprised as if he'd been struck by lightning; and Blanchard said :—

" First blood for Corkey minimus!"

I yelled—I oughtn't to have, but I did, because to see blood dropping about on Bray's chest was a fine sight. He sniffed and went for Corkey smiling. The smile

was the beastliest part of it, for I hoped he
would have got his wool off a bit and been
wild. But he wasn't, and when he began
to hit, Corkey got flustered and swung about
like a windmill and caught it pretty hot.
Yet he jerked his head so jolly quick that
he didn't get more than about four smacks
on it in the first round, though his body,
which was white by nature, was pretty soon
covered with red marks. He said they didn't
hurt, and I cleaned him up and blew water
over him at the end of the round. His lip
was bleeding like mad, but luckily inside
where his tooth had cut it; and he swal-
lowed all the blood, so nobody knew;
besides which the blood wasn't lost. Bray
flung himself down in his corner, and
Fowle looked after him; and even at a
solemn time like that I laughed, and so did
Corkey minimus, because Fowle tried to
be too clever, and spurted a lot of water out
of his mouth into Bray's eye. Then Bray
told him that after the fight he'd tie him
in knots and kick him, looking forward to

which, of course, wrecked Fowle's enjoyment entirely.

Blanchard said "Time!" again awfully
soon, and I saw Bray meant settling Corkey
now, because his reputation as a fighter was
at stake, and he knew Corkey hoped to get
through three rounds with luck. So Bray
began hitting him like hammers, and though
I was about as sorry for Corkey minimus as
a chap could be, nobody would have been
able to help admiring the way Bray hit. It
was just at the end of this round, when
Corkey had been knocked down once, but
got up again, that the awful rum thing with
Milly Dunston happened.

Suddenly, without any warning, there was
a noise like fowls getting up a hedge, and
she rushed out from behind the woodstack
with her eyes blazing and her hair streaming
like a comet in a bate. She'd been running
a good way, I should think, and she tore
right into the ring straight at Bray, and, not
trusting to words at a time like that, and
not remembering her father was a clergy-

man, or anything, slapped his face both sides, and jolly hard too. Bray swore the horriblest words I ever heard used by a chap, because she'd given him more in half a second than Corkey could have in a year. Then he got into his shirt upside down and hooked it with Fowle, but not before he heard her say :—

"You little, fat, red-headed coward, to fight and try and murder a boy half your age and size! I wish I could kill you, I do. It's shameful to think you're an English boy at all!"

Then she turned on the chaps from the Fifth, and told Blanchard he was a disgrace to the school. So they cleared out too; and then she cried over Corkey, and said she would rather have been torn to pieces by unchained monsters than have let him be mangled like he was. And Corkey, who was pretty well dazed, forgave her, and told her kindly to go away. And she gasped and gurgled, and went.

I took Corkey back, and one or two

things got to be known. It came out that Fowle had told Milly the place and the hour of the fight, but only after she had sworn— on some rotten saint Fowle knew—that she would not tell a single soul about it. She kept her swear all right, but came herself. And when Bray got to hear how it was she came—of course, thinking Corkey had told her, which he would rather have died than do — then Bray tried a lot of Chinese tortures on Fowle that he'd seen at a wax-works. And chaps who saw it said that Fowle was so excited at the time that he called upon about twenty different well-known Bible characters by name to come and help him and destroy Bray. But they didn't.

As for Corkey minimus, the things he got from Milly after that fight you wouldn't believe. There were bottles of stuff to rub bruises with, and lozenges and grapes, and some muck for his eye, and little baskets of strawberries, and jolly books and rose-buds. She told the Doctor about slapping

Bray's face, and wrote a long letter of apology afterwards; and a week later she broke it to Corkey minimus that she was going to a boarding-school herself next term; which she did.

When Corkey told me about it he added :—

"And she's going to write me letters, because she's said several times that there's only one chap in the world for her now, and I'm the chap."

"I shouldn't think she could change her mind after all that's happened," I said.

And Corkey minimus said :—

"I bet she will when Corkey minor turns · up again, especially if he brings rum things with him from Australia. And you needn't repeat it, but to you, McInnes, as my chum, I say that I don't care how soon he does come back either."

Which showed that there was more sense in Corkey minimus than you might have thought.

THE PIEBALD RAT

I T was all the result of old Briggs asking the Doctor if he might "instil the lads with a wholesome fondness for natural history." That's how he put it, because I heard him; and the Doctor said it was an admirable notion, and would very probably keep some boys out of mischief on half-holidays. It also kept some boys out of bounds on half-holidays; and after a time I think the Doctor was pretty savage with old Briggs, and wished he'd stuck to his regular work, which was writing and drawing and such-like; because, when one or two of the chaps really got keen about natural history, and even chucked cricket for butterflies and beetles, others, who didn't care a straw about it, pretended they did to gain their own ends. And it was these chaps, if you understand, who finally made the Doctor so unfavourable to natural history generally and old Briggs for starting it.

My chum, West, began the rage for study of "our humble relations," as old Briggs called everything down to wood-lice. He let, it be generally known that he had two live lizards in his desk; and, this being the best thing that West had ever thought of, the idea caught on well. I had a dormouse myself, my name being Ashby minor, and Ashby major kept a spider pretty nearly as big as a young bird, which he had poked out of a hole in the playground wall. He caged it in a tin matchbox, and fed it with bluebottles and wasps. At least, he got bluebottles and wasps for it, but the fool wouldn't eat them; and after a week he found it with its legs all tucked up as neatly as anything. Only it was dead. I thought the matchbox must have been too tight a fit for it, but Ashby major did not. He believed there was something about a tin matchbox which must be rather poisonous for outdoor spiders.

Then chaps went on collecting till it got to be swagger to keep big live things in your desk; and the bigger the thing the more swagger it was.

Maine, generally known as 'Freckles,' had a couple of guinea-pigs in his desk for a week. Then Mannering, the classical master in the Fifth, who must have had a nose like a gimlet, smelt them at prayers, happening to come in late and kneeling down by Freckles at the time. The Doctor didn't make much fuss then, because that was just at the beginning of the business; only he said a desk was not the place for guinea-pigs, and added that a chap in Maine's position in the school ought to have known it. He let the gardener look after them from that time forward. But Freckles naturally lost all interest in them after the gardener had them; because a guinea-pig merely *as* a guinea-pig is nothing. Anyhow, it was rough on him to be landed over it, because, as a matter of fact, guinea-pigs have no scent worth mentioning, and nobody but

Mannering would have spotted them. After that Gideon and Brookes caught a blind-worm one foot two inches long; and Gideon sold his half for fivepence, so Brookes got it all. Nobody knew what a blind-worm likes to eat, unfortunately, and it died, but not for a fortnight. Then there was another scene with my dormouse, which led to tremendous things. There's a hole in a desk where the ink-pot goes in, and one day my mouse got out through it, having climbed up two dictionaries and a Greek Testament to do so. It happened old Briggs himself was taking the Lower Fourth, which is my class, and I hoped it would be all right. But he didn't seem friendly over it, and I noticed, when he told us to find the mouse, he put his feet upon the rungs of his chair. It's a rum thing about old Briggs that he doesn't care much for natural history objects while they're alive; he likes them dead and dried, or stuffed and pinned on cards, or in glass cases all labelled and neat. My dormouse gave us a jolly good hunt round,

H

then it finally tripped over a lead-pencil and got its tail and hind legs into West's ink. So we caught it, and I was drying it with a piece of blotting-paper, and old Briggs was just telling us that dormice belong to a genus of rodents called Myoxus, and are allied to mice, though they have a squirrel's habits, which he seemed to think was a pity, when Dunston came in. The Doctor asked particulars, looked as if he could have jolly well killed my mouse, which was shivering rather badly owing to the ink on its hinder parts, and said once for all that he would allow no animals of any kind inside any of the desks or in school.

Then, unluckily, as an afterthought, he demanded a clearance on the spot; and he was pretty well staggered to find the result.

" I will ask you, Ferrars, as head boy of the class, and one, I am happy to think, above any of this childish folly, to inspect the desks, one by one, and report to me where you find indications of life," said the Doctor.

Ferrars is always right with the Doctor,
chiefly because he has a face like a stone
angel in church, and a very smooth voice,
and a remarkably swagger knowledge of the
Scriptures. He is also a tremendous worker,
and will go into the Upper Fourth next term
as sure as eggs. It was jolly awkward for.
Ferrars then, because he happened to be one
of the keenest natural history chaps of all,
and had a piebald rat, which even fellows in
the Sixth had offered him half-a-crown and
three shillings for, yet he would not part with
it. So, though we didn't like him much, we
felt almost sorry for the fix he was in now.
Of course, we thought that such a demon on
Religious Knowledge as Ferrars was would
drag out his piebald rat right away, and perhaps even give it to the Doctor, or offer to
sell it for the alms-box ; but he didn't. He
got up, rather white about the gills, and
opened the desks one by one ; and a jolly
happy family it was. Only the Doctor
scattered the things to the four winds, till
there wasn't an atom of natural history left

in the whole classroom except Ferrars' piebald rat, snug in his desk.

First Fowle, who goes in for water things,
had to empty his jam-jar of tadpoles out
into the playground, which was a beastly
cruel thing to make him do, because they
all died, still being in the gill stage; then
Freckles was sent off with a young rabbit
to the hayfield, and he got caned too,
because, strangely enough, the Doctor
hadn't forgotten his guinea-pigs; and Morrant's two sparrows were let go, which was
no kindness to them, because Morrant had
cut their wings so jolly short it would
have taken them months to grow enough
feathers to fly with, and meantime a cat
got them both; and Playfair's mole, which,
by the way, had been queer for some time,
owing to having no earth to burrow in,
was ordered to be sent to the cricket-field.
There were a lot of other things, but
Corkey minimus scored rather, because his
privet hawk-moth laid a hundred and fourteen eggs on Todhunter's algebra a few
hours before it was let free. Corkey mini-

mus says a privet hawk-moth's nothing worth mentioning after it's laid eggs, but the eggs turn into fine caterpillars.

The few things the Doctor didn't know what to do with, and didn't like to have killed, he said must be given to the gardener. He thought it would be better to put my mouse out of its misery, and turned it over on my hand with a gold pencil-case, and said it had probably got a chill to its vital organs and would die; but old Briggs explained that it might live if put in cotton-wool; so the gardener looked to it, and it did live, and I took it home at the end of that term and have it still, though it is getting oldish now, and has lost half its tail. But it's a good mouse yet.

Of course the extraordinary thing was Ferrars. After the Doctor had gone, old Briggs, to whom he had whispered something before he went, gave out that his natural history half-hours would be suspended for the rest of the term; then I got a word with Ferrars. I said:—

"However did you have the cheek—you supposed to be such a saint?"

He said :—

"I don't know. Something came over me to do it. I've got a jolly peculiar feeling to that rat. It's not an ordinary rat. I'm wrapped up in it. Even my respect for the Doctor couldn't stand against it. I know what you chaps think. I daresay you reckon I'm a hound, but I couldn't help doing what I did. Somehow that rat's a sort of 'mascotte' to me. A mascotte's a thing that brings luck. All my best luck's happened since I had it."

Of course, when a chap goes on like that, what can you do? I didn't understand Ferrars. He seemed to me to be simply talking rot. So I said :—

"Well, it's pretty measly, considering the opinion the Doctor's got of you. I shan't try to score off your rat, because I know it's a jolly fine one, and I like it; but Freckles or somebody will very likely kill it after this."

He looked in a fair funk when the dreadful thought of having his rat killed came to him. Before the end of that day he spoke to every chap in the class separately, and all but three promised and swore not to lay a finger on the rat. But Freckles, Murdoch, and Morrant wouldn't swear. Finally he paid Morrant sixpence and so got him over, and Murdoch he let crib off him in "prep." three times; and Freckles, who was an awfully sportsmanlike chap really, said he was only rotting all the time, and would be the last to do a classy rat like Ferrars' any harm. In fact, he said he'd much sooner kill Ferrars himself.

Mind you, though, of course, it was simply barbarous for Ferrars to think that his piebald rat could have any effect on his work, yet he proved to me that his success in school and his great popularity with the Doctor dated from the coming of the thing. When he first got it, it was a mere cub-rat, so to say; now, though not a year old, it had turned into as fine a rat as you could wish to meet anywhere. In appearance it had pink eyes and a white head, and a fairish amount of white fur about the body, which got thinner on its stomach, so that you could see the pink skin through to some extent. But the piebaldness of the rat was the great feature. It had two big round patches of fur like the common or garden rat, and one small patch at the nape of its neck; and in addition to this it had one large patch of beautiful yellowish fur, such as you chiefly see on guinea-pigs. Its tail was pink and long, and quite hairless.

Ferrars often kept back good things at meals for it, and the bond between them seemed to grow rummer and rummer, till he let the rat get on his mind, and Wilson said he was getting dotty about it. Which I think was true, for one day, going into the classroom to get a knife from my desk, I saw Ferrars with his rat out, talking to it. He was swatting like anything in play-hours for a special Old Testament history prize, and he had the rat and the Bible and various books of reference all before him. Then, not knowing I was there, he spoke :—

"I must win it, 'Mayne Reid.' Stick to me this time, old chap, and see me through."

He called his rat "Mayne Reid" because that was his favourite author.

And "Mayne Reid" seemed to understand, and he turned his pink eyes on to the open Bible and walked over it. Finding he'd walked over the ninth chapter of the Second Book of Kings, Ferrars got excited, and, seeing me, said, "By Jove! then I'll learn that chapter by heart, though it is so long. It's good exciting stuff anyway, and I bet my rat walking over it means that there'll be a question about Jehu and Jezebel."

"You'll go cracked about that rat," I said.

"It's part of my life," he answered. "I know it seems very peculiar, and so it is, and I don't suppose such a thing ever happened before, but something tells me my prosperity and success are bound up in that rat. He's a familiar spirit, in fact, like Saul had. If he died I should never do much more good, and very likely stick in this class for the rest of my days."

"You'd better not think like that," I said, "because rats are short-lived things, owing to the nasty food they eat. Not that 'Mayne Reid' has nasty food; but all pink-eyed animals are delicate, and you'll have to lose him sooner or later."

Ferrars didn't take warning by me, but after he really did win the Old Testament prize, and there really was a question about Jezebel, he made a sort of idol out of the rat, and some chaps declared he said his prayers to it. I know he constantly bought it cocoa-nut chips, which it was very fond of. He trained it, too, to live in his breast-pocket, and I often saw him glancing down in class just to get a glimpse of its little eyes looking up at him. That taking the piebald rat into class shows the lengths Ferrars ran.

The whole thing was very peculiar. Some chaps said there was a strong likeness growing up between Ferrars and the rat; and certainly his thin, white face had a rattish look sometimes. Other fellows told him his rat was an evil spirit, and would end by doing him a bad turn, but Ferrars turned upon them and jawed them with such frightful language that they never said it again. Meanwhile the Doctor went on taking to Ferrars more and more, and there seemed every chance of his getting the whole Bible by heart before he left Merivale.

Then came the end of the affair like this. Ferrars was so dependent on his rat now that he wouldn't do a lesson without it, and he lugged it fearlessly into the Doctor's study at those times, fortunately rare, when the Doctor took our class himself in Scripture. But Ferrars was such a flyer that we all got tarred with the same brush; and the Doctor, after questioning Ferrars for half an hour about Bible people we'd never even heard of, and getting a string of dead right answers out of him, would dismiss us all in great good temper, forgetting that he'd only been having a go at one chap.

A day came when the Doctor left us for five minutes in the middle of this class, and while most of us had a hurried dip into the plagues of Egypt, which was the business in hand, Ferrars, who knew as much about the plagues as ever Moses did, just got out his rat and gave it a bit of almond and a short breather of a yard or so along the floor. But, the Doctor coming back suddenly, he had only just time to pop it into his pocket, and even then he put the rat into an unusual pocket which it was not accustomed to, and didn't like, namely, a trouser - pocket. Ferrars also shoved a handkerchief down in the pocket to steady the rat.

Then I saw an awful rum expression come over him, and he grabbed at the pocket and his mouth fell open, and his face got the colour of new putty. At the same time I saw his eyes turn to a big bookshelf with glass doors against the side of the room.

"What's the matter, Ferrars?" said the Doctor. "You appear unwell."

"Nothing, sir; merely a little passing sickness, I think."

"Then withdraw, my boy, and ask the matron to give you a few drops of brandy and water. You need not dine to-day," said the Doctor very kindly.

But Ferrars wouldn't withdraw. He knew "Mayne Reid" had got through his pocket and down his trouser-leg; he also knew it was now behind the bookshelf, and might reappear at any moment. So he said he was better, and, actually! that it would be a grief to him to miss one of the Doctor's own lessons.

But afterwards, when the rat didn't come out and the class was dismissed, Ferrars was frightful to see. His hair all got on end somehow, and his eyes swelled and stuck out of his head like glass beads, and his cheeks got hollow. He ran awful risks

going into the Doctor's study that day, but
the rat wouldn't come out, and Ferrars
looked old enough to be a master when he
went to bed, though only eleven and a half
really.

"One of two things has happened," he
said to me, for we were in the same
dormitory; "either it's got wedged in
behind the bookshelf and will die if not
let out, or else there was a rat-hole there,
and it went down and has joined common
rats, and become a sort of king rat among
them."

"Or been killed," I said.

"No, they would not kill it," he answered.
"Anyway, to-morrow after the Doctor's class
is over, and everybody has gone, I shall stop
and make a clean breast of it, and ask him
for the sake of humanity to have the bookshelf moved.   But it's all up with me if
the rat has lost its feeling towards me and
won't come back; only if it was stuck and
couldn't come back, that's different."

He didn't sleep much that night, but he

said some prayers, which was a thing he didn't often do; and of course he was praying that the piebald rat might be allowed to return.

But next day, after the Scripture class, in which Ferrars was not nearly so much to the front as usual, and got regularly muddled over a potty question about Jacob, the Doctor saved him the trouble of asking about his rat. He—the Doctor, I mean— had been jolly glum all through class, and when it was ended he did a rum thing, which was awful to see, knowing all we did. He told us to keep our places, then went to the fireplace and picked up the shovel. From the face of it he removed a bit of newspaper, and under the newspaper was "Mayne Reid." His pink eyes had gone foggy, and there was a little streak of blood on his mouth. Otherwise his body looked all right.

"Now here," said the Doctor in an awfully solemn way, "we have a dead, piebald rat. There can be no outlet for error concerning such a rat as this. To have seen such a rat is to remember it. Already three classes have been before me to-day, but nobody knew anything about this animal. That it was a tame rat its fatness and sleekness testify. Moreover, the piebald rat is an outcome of artificiality. A wild rat in a state of nature is brown or black, as the case may be. This rat, then, had an owner, and that owner brought it into my study—*my study !* —and suffered it to escape here. That I do well to be angry you will the more easily understand when I tell you that the unsavoury creature was upon my desk last night, and has scratched and even gnawed some papers whereon were notes for my next sermon. It was discovered this morning by one of the domestics. She, seeing some object moving upon my desk, struck with the broom-handle, and destroyed this rat. Now, let there be no prevarication or evasion of the questions I am going to put to you. First, I wish to know if this rat belongs, or rather belonged, to any among you ; and secondly, I desire to learn whether, supposing the rat be not the property of any present, you happen to know whose property it is, or rather was ? "

I stole a look at Ferrars, and he appeared so frightful to see, that for some reason I thought I 'd try and help him. So, like a fool, I was just going to speak when young Corkey minimus did. He said :—

" Please, sir, it might be a foreign sort of rat that came over in that box of pine-apples and things that Ashby major had sent him from the West Indies."

" When I desire your aid in the elucida-tion of this problem I will apply for it, Corkey minimus," answered the Doctor ; so Corkey dried up.

Then, in a sort of voice that was strange to us, and seemed to come from his stomach or somewhere new, Ferrars spoke, and I never saw a chap look so ghastly. His eyes were fixed on the rat, and he came forward slowly.

" Please, sir, it was my rat," he said.

I

"Yours, Ferrars! *You* to disobey! You, of all boys, to set my orders at defiance!"

"It wasn't an ordinary rat, sir."

"I can see what sort of rat it was, sir, for myself," thundered the Doctor. "This it is to consider a boy, to devote thought to him, to particularly commend him for his theological knowledge."

"I don't take any credit for knowing anything now, sir. It was the rat as much as me."

"Robert Ferrars!" said the Doctor, in his caning voice, "you are now adding wicked buffoonery to an act in itself sufficiently disreputable!"

"I can't explain, sir; I don't mean any buffoonery. That rat was more to me than you'd think. It—it *did* help me somehow, and now it's dead it wouldn't be sportsmanlike to it to say not. And if you'll let me b-bury it properly, I'll be very thankful to you."

The Doctor looked at Ferrars awfully close during this speech.

"Either you are lying," he said, "or you suffer from some hysterical and neurotic condition, Robert Ferrars, which I have neither suspected nor discovered until this moment."

Then he told us to go; but Ferrars he kept for half an hour; and when Ferrars came in to dinner I saw he'd been blubbing.

He explained to me after we'd gone to bed. He said :—

"No, he didn't cane me or anything. He just talked, and told me a lot about several things I didn't know, and said that familiar spirits were specially barred in the Bible. I never thought he'd have even tried to understand me; but he did, and he quite saw my side about the rat. He said kind words over it, too, and was sorry it was dead. And I've got to see Doctor Barnes to-morrow too, though, of course, it's only having my rat on my mind that's upset me. And he let me have it to b-bury gladly."

"Where shall you arrange the rat?" I said.

" I 'm sending it home in a stays-box that Jane gave me. I 've written to my sister where to bury it. Jane it was who killed it. She cried like anything when I told her what ' Mayne Reid' was to me. But he 's in the book-post by now, beautifully done up in shavings and fresh geranium leaves. It 's no good talking any more. Only I will say that if he was a familiar spirit, he was a jolly good one, very different to the sort barred in the Scriptures. I don't know how I 'll get on in the exams. now. I wish I was dead, too."

Then he sniffed a bit, and went to sleep.

BROWNE, BRADWELL,
AND ME

THERE'S more stuff torked about fagging at school than anything else in the world, as far as I can see; and being the smalest boy but two at Dunston's and a fag myself I ought to know. Of corse, fags do get it pretty hot sometimes if they happen to fag for a beast, but big fellows aren't beasts to small ones as a general thing. I'm sure Bradwell was the best chap that ever came to Dunston's, and when he was expelled over the seege in the Wing Dormatery — him and Trelawny — I felt frightful. I'm Watson minor myself, my brother being Watson major, one of the reserves for the second eleven and captain of the third.

The thing I'm going to write out happened just before the seege, and was all

over before that; and it shows what a fag
can do.   It also shows what a jolly good
thing it is for big fellows to treat fags well,
and give them odds and ends so as to get
their affecksun.   If I hadn't felt what I did
to Bradwell, I shouldn't have run the awful
risks I did for him.   What I did certinnly
ruined a great project of Bradwell's, and
upsett him a good bit at the time.   But he
said afterwards, when the blow had fallen,
and when he could look back and think of
it without smacking my head, that I had
ment well.   I remember his very words, for
that matter.   He said, "Your intenshuns
were all right—I will say that—but you've
ruined my life."   No chap could say farer
than that; and, mind you, I did ruin his life
in a way.   I've heard many fellows say
Bradwell was a bounder by birth; but he
never was to me.

Well, Bradwell had a great admeration
for Mabel Dunston, the Doctor's youngest
daughter but one, and she had an equal
great admeration for him, for two terms.

Bradwell, although a great sportsman in other ways, was fond of girls. If he passed a school of them he would look awfully rum and reddish in the face an' watery in the eyes. Once, going with him to the playing-field for a football match, he made the distance half a mile longer by going up a side street to avoid the high-school girls; and I asked him why, and he said it was cheek, but told me all the same. He said, " You can't meet women got up like this." Bradwell has frightfully thin calves to his legs when seen in "knickers," though he is the best goal-keeper that was ever known at Dunston's. Of corse, his affair with Mabel Dunston would never have got to be known by me but for my great use to Bradwell in carrying notes. Being in the Doctor's house that term I was eesily able to do this, and there was a jar of green stuff in the hall where she told me to leave the notes, which I did. She was fifteen, I believe, or else sixteen, but well on in years anyway, and a few months older than Bradwell. It was his general brillance won her, for he could do anything, and his father had plenty of money, being a man like Whitely's in London, only in the North of England. Bradwell drew almost as well as pictures in books, and he used to illustrate the Latin grammar for his speshall chums. There's a part of the Latin grammar called Syntax, which I haven't come to yet myself, but it has rather rummy things in it with both the Latin and English of them. And Bradwell used to draw these things; and he drew two in my grammar out of puer kindness to me. One was, "Balbus is crowning the boy's head with a garland"; and the other was, "A snake appeared to Sulla while sacrifising"; and you never saw anything better. They were done on the marjin in ink, and the snake appearing to Sulla was about the queerest and best thing ever seen in a Latin grammar.

I have to tell you this because such a lot happened owing to it.

Now Browne took my class, which is the

lowest in the school, and I am seventh in it. And I gradually got to hate Browne, because Bradwell did, and for other reesons of my own to. Browne was said to be only twenty-two, and he looked younger than many of the chaps, his moustashe being whitish and invisibel to the eye. He wore necktyes which I remember hearing Mathers say were an insult to nature, and would have made a rainbow curl up and faint. We always noticed, at arithmetic times, that Browne, if he got a stumper, would put up the lid of his private desk and hide behind it—of course, looking the thing up in his crib. Then he would wander round, as if by accident, to the chap and do the sum off quick while he remembered it. Bradwell always hated him; and when he found that Browne was very friendly with Mabel and Mabel was very friendly with Browne, he hated him far, far wurse.

Bradwell and this girl had a row in the shrubbery at the back of the chapel, and I, being in the gardener's potting-shed at the time, feeding a cattipiller of mine, heard it. Bradwell said :—

"I 'm not blind, Mabel, I 've seen it going on ever since last term. You read his beastly books, and leave rosebuds with sented verbena leaves round them in that stone urn at the gate when he comes down from his house to class."

And she said :—

"And why shouldn't I? You must re-member, pleese, that I am my own mistress. Besides, the intelligents of a grown-up man is very refreshing."

For some reason Bradwell didn't like this. His voice squeaked up into his head in a rather rum way when he answered :—

"D' you call *him* a man? He hasn't got a muscle on him ; and he doesn't know more than enough to teach the kids."

"That 's merely mean jellousy," said Mabel. "Of course he doesn't talk to *you*, or show you what is in him. But he tells me all about his secret life, and very butiful it is. He is a jenius, in fact."

"If it comes to that, what can he do?"
said Bradwell awfully clevverly. "Can he
draw?"

"No, he doesn't draw."

"Oh! can he sing?"

"No."

"Can he play the piano?"

"No."

Now all of these things Bradwell could
do to perfecksun, so he got cheerfuller and
cheerfuller.

"What *can* he do then, besides jaw the
kids and always sneak to the Doctor?"

"I never saw such jellousy as this," said
Mabel; "but if you must know I'll tell you
what he can do: he can write poetry out
of his own head, and he has got a solid
book of it reddy to print some day—there!"

I suppose Bradwell couldn't write poetry.
Anyway, he got very glum in the face at
this. He didn't say anything—appeering to
be frightfully shocked at what he'd heard.
Then Mabel said :—

"When you can quote Browning and

Biron and Shelley, and write poems yourself, it will be soon enough to sneer at Mr.
Browne."

"You love him," said Bradwell in a very
tragik voice.

"I don't love anybody but my own
family," said Mabel; "but I admire him,
and I admire his poetry, which is very much
out of the common indeed."

"It's all over then, I suppose," said
Bradwell.

"I don't know what you mean," she re-
plied to him.   "A thing that has never
begun can't be all over"; which words of
Mabel's seemed to knock the heart out of
Bradwell.

Then the gardener came along, and I
didn't hear anything else.   Of corse, I
couldn't *help* hearing what I had done,
though I tried hard not to, and kept feeding my catterpeller like anything all the
time.

Two days after I had to carry another
note to Mabel, and found one waiting for

Bradwell in the usual place; so they must have made it up. Then came the beginning of my misforchunes with Browne. He found the snake appeering to Sulla in my Latin grammar, and called me up and said he knew very well I hadn't drawn it myself, but wanted to know who had. He said it was wrong to the Doctor to ruin our books, and that he had seen in several different books the same snake, evidently done by the same boy, owing to them being so much similar.

But the very identical thing had happened in another class — to Steggles, Bradwell having drawn him the same picture; and knowing what Steggles said, being a chap who is frightfully cunning, I said the same now to Browne. I said I left the book on my desk, and somebody came along and done it while I was out of the room. Browne seemed inclined not to believe this. Anyway, he took the Latin grammar away with him. But I heard no more about it till the next evening, when I wanted the book in prep. Remembering Browne had it, I went off to his study and knocked and walked in.

Browne wasn't there for the moment, and the room was empty. I took the oppertunity to look at a rather butiful tobacco-jar of Browne's which I have seen at a distance on his mantlepiece many times. Passing his table to get to it, I chanced to glance there, and juge of my surprise when the first words I saw at the top of a big sheet of paper were, "To Mabel"! Underneeth was a lot of writing, and the whole table seemed to be littered with paper covered with small bits of sepparate writing, much of it scratched out and done over again. But the peece with "To Mabel" at the top was all butiful and clean, without anything scratched, being, I suppose, the result of all the other bits put together and neetly copied out.

Well, there I was with my duty towards Bradwell as his fag. Browne had evidently done a verse out of his own head for Mabel

Dunston, and had written it in this butiful style, on thick white paper, to send to her. I felt if she got it, knowing what she'd said to Bradwell about Browne, that it was certin she would abbandon Bradwell, him not being any good at poems. I wouldn't have done it for anybody else in the world *but* Bradwell; I wouldn't have done it at all if I had known what the end of it was going to be; but, anyway, at the time it seemed to me, as Bradwell's fag, I ought to do it; so I did.

I took the poem and rolled it up so as not to hurt it, and hooked off to Bradwell. He was in his study, and Trelawny, who shares it with him, being out of the room, I was able to explain. I said:—

"If you please, Bradwell, I've come from Mr. Browne's study, and he was not there, and happening by a curious axcident to glance on the table I saw this. Knowing about you and Mabel, and being your fag, I took it."

"Took what?" said Bradwell.

I put the thing in front of him, and he got red and excited.

"It's a poem to Mabel by that beast Browne," he said.

Then he read it out, half to himself, but I heard. The thing ran like this:—

"TO MABEL.

"Oh let my Muse sing to the name of Mabel,
Whose azure eyes are fastened to my soul,
Like to forget-me-nots in button-hole.
To tell of my heart's torment I'm unable.
My thoughts they spin; my brain it grows unstable
When fixed on Thee.   Perchance it is my rôle
Never to reach my mad ambition's Goal,
But to live ever 'midst scholastic babel.
Thy glances brighten all my lonely lot.
Prometheus-like a vulture gnaws my heart,
In biting blasts and under sunshine hot.
My dreams are shattered by a barbed dart,
And, waking wild, I scream that I may not
Whisper the oaths I yearn to Thee impart."

I told Bradwell I didn't quite understand it, and he sat on me.

"You wouldn't," he said, "a kid like you. But I do.   It's a sonnit, and an extreamly fine one. I *hate* the chap, but it's no good pretending he's not a poet, because this jolly well proves he is. Look at the rimes and the smoothness!"

It seemed a fine thing of Bradwell to say that, feeling as he did to Browne. He thought for a bit, but told me not to go.

"Of corse," he said, "this must be returned. All's fair in—in a case of this kind, but——"

Then he thought very deeply and read the sonnit again. Suddenly he took a bit of paper and copied down Browne's poem word for word. Then he told me to cut back like lightning to Browne's study, and to put the poem back on his desk if I could —if not, to most carefully keep it till the first chance of getting it back to Browne's room without being spotted.

"You're a splendid fag," he said, "and I shan't forget this. It's the sort of thing that squires did for their knights in olden times; and they got good rewards too. Now hook it."

K

It's worth a lot, mind you, to get praise like that from such a chap as Bradwell.

When I got back, Browne was rumaging over his table and sweering a good deal in a loud wisper. He told me to wait a minute, and went off to look in his bedroom. Then I seezed my opportunity, and slipped the sonnit on his table under some papers. When he came back he was worried, and went on hunting till he found it. Then he said "Ah!" to himself, and got pleasanter and asked me what I wanted. I told him my Latin grammar, and being in a very happy state now, owing to finding the poem, he gave my book back and told me to clear out; which I did.

"After prep. I met Bradwell going in to prayers, and he handed me a note for Mabel to put in the usual place. He looked awfully rum when he gave it to me, and he saw that I saw he looked rum. So he said :—

" I don't mind letting you know, owing to your being such a good fag and my

trusting you as I do. You may read the
letter in prayers, then seal it down and put
it behind the pot of ferns in the hall in the
usual place."

Of corse, it wasn't really a letter, or
Bradwell wouldn't have let me read it. It
was just Browne's sonnit coppied out by
Bradwell word for word; and at the
bottom where the words, "What about
poetry now?—A. T. B." A. T. B. are Bradwell's initials, his full name being Arthur
Thomas Bradwell. You see, he didn't
exsaxtly say he'd *written* the sonnit. He
only said, "What about poetry now?"

The excitement of it all kept me awake
for hours and hours through the night. I
don't suppose any fag ever did more for a
big fellow than I had done for Bradwell that
day. Then I began to wonder when Browne
would send off his poem, and wether Mabel
would get them both together or one at
a time. You see, of corse, Browne would
send her the thing as origenal, and there
was nothing in Bradwell's letter to exsaxtly

· say he hadn't written it; and puzzling the thing out for hours and hours, I at last came to the conklusion that she would find it very difficult which to believe, because how could she know which was telling the truth to her? Then, about three or four in the morning almost, I began to feel rather terrible over it, because I thought of what frightful trouble Browne must have had to write the sonnit. He might have taken terms and terms over it for all I could tell, not, of corse, knowing myself how long it took to write poetry. I felt rather sorry for Browne; but after all a chap's duty is to the fellow he fags for before masters; and feeling that, I went to sleep.

Three days later Bradwell had me in his room and told me the end of it all, which shows that a girl never does what you might exspect.

"As a lesson to you, young Watson," said Bradwell, "I may tell you that my career has been utterly blighted and my life ruined by that business of the sonnit."

I said I was sorry to hear it.

He said :—

"Yes, blighted; and so's his—I mean Browne's. She got my letter that night and his next morning. That night she felt all her old feeling for me return because of the sonnit, thinking I'd done it. Then, next morning, she got just the very same stuff to a word from Browne, with a letter saying he had burned the midnight oil to compose it. Well, there you are. What does she do? Insted of accepting my statement, being the first, she argues in a most elaborate way that I couldn't possibly have coppied from Browne, and Browne couldn't possibly have copied from me. But it would have been to much of a coinsidence if we'd both written exsaxtly the same sonnit out of our own heads, so what does she conklude?"

I said I didn't know.

"Why, fathead, that we both got it from somebody else—out of some book written by a well-known proper dead poet.

I 've no doubt now, on thinking over it, that Browne *did* do that ; because when I first read his poem I could hardly believe that he had written such real poetry, owing to the rimes and smoothness.   But it 's all over now.   She 's written a letter I can't show you.   To hope even for her friendship wouldn't be any good.   A girl hates a joke something frightful."

" How about Browne ? " I said.

"She 's written to him also, asking him where he got the verses out of, and exsplaining she doesn't believe they are original, and saying how another acquaintance of hers had sent the very same lot the day before. So now you see what a sinful mess you 've made of it."

I said I did, but I felt it was my duty to him.

" Yes, I know," he said ; " but the question is, What do I do now?   You see 'all 's fair,' and all that ; but now, being out of the hunt, ought I to throw up the sponge and tell the truth, or ought I not ? "

"I don't know, Bradwell," I said; "but anyway you won't mention me, I hope, because I only acted for you, and did a jolly dangerous thing."

"No, you're safe enough, and, in fact, I'm going to reward you for what you *did* do," said Bradwell. "But seeing I'm out of it, I think it will be a manly act to Browne if I tell Mabel frankly that I resorted to strateji."

"But me?" I said.

"I shall merely inform her," answered Bradwell, "that one of my emissaceries found the poem, and, of course, brought it to me; that I despatched it—as a joke, taking care not to say I was the auther. I shall end with these words: 'Browne is innosent.'"

All of which he did, and I left the letter in the usual spot. But Mabel cut him altogether from that day; and he told me girls have no humer and laughed it off, though he felt it a lot, and often smacked my head out of bitterness of mind afterwards, but not hard. He gave me an old knife for a reward, but told me at the same time never to do anything for him again without being commanded.

As for Mabel, she threw over Browne just like she threw over Bradwell, in spite of Bradwell's letter; and Bradwell said it was a nemmecis, whatever that is; and I had a nemmecis to, because a week afterwards Bradwell threw over me and made young West his fag. I felt hert, but, of corse, that didn't get known to Bradwell; and if I fag again, I wont so much as make a peece of toste unless I'm commanded to.

GIDEON'S FRONT TOOTH

I BELIEVE Gideon was the only Jew that ever came to Dunston's, and I expect, taking it all round, he might have had a better time at a school for Jews in general; though in one way he wouldn't have done as well, and wouldn't have had the adventure with old Grimbal, which turned out so splendidly for him when old Grimbal died.

Though easily the richest chap at Merivale, and getting no less than ten shillings a week pocket-money, Gideon was so awfully fond of coin that he hardly spent a penny, and the only thing he did with his money was to lend it to fellows. He didn't lend it for nothing, having a curious system by which you paid in marbles, or bats, or knives for the money, and, in spite of that, still had to pay back the money itself after

a certain time. You signed a paper, and
Gideon said that if chaps hadn't paid back
the tin on the dates named it would be very
serious for them. But it got serious for him
after a bit, because Steggles, who knew
quite as much about money as Gideon
(though he never had any), borrowed a
whole pound once, and promised to pay five
shillings for it for one term; and Gideon
was new to Steggles then, and agreed. But
when the time of payment came, Steggles
said that Gideon had better regard it as a
bad debt, because he wasn't going to pay
back even the original pound. Then Gideon
thought a bit, and asked him why, and
Steggles told him. He said: " Because you
know jolly well the Doctor doesn't allow
chaps to lend money."

And Gideon said:—

"This is the first time I've heard that."

"Anyway, it's usury, which is a crime,"
said Steggles, "and I'm not going to pay
anything; and, being less than twenty-
one, you can't make me; so it amounts to

a bad debt, as I told you just now. You've done jolly well, one way and another, and you've got two bats, and Lord knows how many indiarubber-balls, and cricket-balls, and silver pencils, and knives out of it, including Ashby minor's watch-chain, which is silver; and if you take my tip you'll keep quiet, because once all these kids get to know anybody under twenty - one can borrow money without returning it, then it's all up with your beastly financial schemes."

Gideon was remarkably surprised to know what a lot Steggles had found out about him, and accused him of looking into his play-chest; and Steggles said he had. Then Gideon went; and about three chaps who had heard the talk told others, and they told still more chaps, until, finally, a good many fellows who owed Gideon money felt there was no hurry about paying it back till it happened to be convenient. In fact, Gideon jolly soon saw he couldn't do any more good for himself like that, and at the beginning of the next term, when chaps were pretty flush of coin, he wrote up in the gym, "There will be a sale of bats, knives, and other various useful articles, between two and three o'clock, by auction, on Tuesday.— J. GIDEON."

Somebody tore it down, but not before most fellows had read it; and when Gideon and young Miller, who had a bat in the auction, and hoped to get it back if possible, were seen carrying Gideon's play-chest to the gym after dinner on the appointed day, of course we went. It passed off very well for Gideon, because the things were really good, and often almost new. He seemed to know all about auctions, and hit the chest with a stump, and explained the things, and what good points they had about them. He only took money down, and I will say nobody could have done it fairer. If a knife had a broken blade, for instance, or a bat was slightly sprung, which happened with one, he always pointed it out, so that nobody could say he had been choused over it. Young Miller got back his bat for four

shillings and eightpence; and Ashby minor
got back his silver chain for thirteen
shillings; but it wasn't much good to him,
because, in order to raise the thirteen bob,
he had to raffle the chain at once, at shilling
shares; and he took one, hoping to be lucky,
but he wasn't, Fowle unfortunately getting
it. Gideon told me afterwards that the sale
came out fairly, but not quite what he had
hoped. He rather sneered at the Dunston
chaps in general, and said they were a
poverty-stricken crew; which got me into
a bate, and I told him that I'd sooner be
the son of an officer in the Royal Navy,
which I am, than the biggest Jew diamond
dealer in the world, his father being in that
profession. He said there was no account-
ing for tastes, but he should have thought
that a man who could deliberately go and
be a sailor must be weak in the head.
Then I punched him, and he instantly
went down and apologised. I may say
here that I am Bray, the cock of the Lower
School.

Before coming to Gideon's front tooth, just to let you know exactly the chap he was, I'll mention another thing he did. An old woman was allowed to bring up fruit and tuck generally, and sell it to us after morning school. Steggles, who knows the reason for pretty nearly everything, said this was permitted by Doctor Dunston to take the edge off our appetites; but anyway, the old woman sold strawberries and raspberries in summer-time, and these were arranged with cabbage-leaves in little wicker baskets at about fourpence each. Well, one day Gideon, who never refused to eat fruit if offered it, but very seldom bought any, asked the old woman what she gave for the wicker baskets, and she said threepence a dozen. Then he asked her what she would give for those that had been used once, and she thought, and said they would be worth at least three-halfpence a dozen to her. He didn't say any more, but after that it was a rum thing how all the used baskets, which generally were seen kicking about the playground in shoals, disappeared. Nobody noticed it at the time, but afterwards we remembered clearly that they *had* disappeared. And just at the end of the term a chap, hurrying in late after the bell rang, came bang on Gideon and the old woman round a corner out of sight of the gates. And the chap saw Gideon give her a pile of baskets and get three-half-pence. Of course, it was the last three-halfpence he ever got that way, because when it became known the chaps rendered their baskets useless for commerce in many ways. And Barlow called Gideon "Shylock minor" when he heard that he'd made two shillings and fivepence-halfpenny; which name stuck to Gideon for ever. And Steggles got nine other chaps to subscribe a penny each and buy a pound of flesh from a butcher's shop, because in Shakespeare Shylock was death on his pound of flesh. The pound was put under Gideon's pillow by Steggles himself, and when Gideon shoved his watch under his pillow, which

he always did at night, he found it; and
Steggles says he turned pale, but read what
was pinned on the pound of flesh, and then
smiled and wrapped the meat up in a letter
from home, and said: "What fools you
chaps are, wasting money like that! But it
looks all right, and will mean a good feed
for nothing."

Next day he got up very early and took
his pound of flesh down to the kitchen and
got them to cook it; and he ate about half
before breakfast and had the rest cold in his
desk during Monsieur Michel's lesson, which
was a safe time. And Steggles said we
ought to have gone one better and put
poison on it.

The great affair of the tooth came on at
the beginning of next term; and first I must
tell you that next door to Dunston's lived an
old man, so frightfully ancient that his skin
was all shrivelled over his bones. He didn't
like boys much, but he would look over his
garden-wall sometimes into our playground
and scowl if anybody caught his eye.

Various things, of course, went over the wall often, and it was one of the excitements of Dunston's to go into old Grimbal's garden and get them back. Twice only he caught a chap, and both times, despite his awful age and yellowness of skin, he thrashed the chap very fairly hard with a walking-stick; but he never reported anybody to Dunston, and it was generally thought he regarded it as a sort of sport hunting for chaps in his garden. Of course, in fair, open hunting he hadn't a chance, and the two he did catch he got by stealth, hiding behind bushes on a rather dark evening.

Well, the facts would never have been known about this tooth but for Gideon's mean spirit. It happened to be necessary for him to fight me, and though not caring much about it, he couldn't help himself. Besides, though the champion of the Lower School, I was tons smaller than Gideon, and Gideon didn't know till after the fight that I was a champion, the true facts about my greatness being hid from him.

L

Just before the fight Gideon said, "Oh! my tooth, by the way. It may be hurt, and it cost my father five guineas." So, to our great interest he unscrewed one of his two top front teeth and gave it to his second. You couldn't have told it was a sham, so remarkably was it done, and it screwed on to the foundation of the original tooth much like a spike screws into the sole of a cricket-boot. Gideon had fallen downstairs when he was ten and knocked off half the tooth, so he told us; but Murray, who is well up in science, said that all Jews' front teeth are rather rocky, because in feudal times they were pulled out with pincers as a form of torture, and to make the Jews give up their secret treasures. Murray said that after many generations of pulling out Nature got sick of it, and that in modern times the front teeth of Jews aren't worth talking about. Murray is full of rum ideas like that, and he hopes to go in for engineering, having already many secret inventions waiting to be patented.

As to Gideon, I licked him rather badly in two rounds and a half. Then he was mopped up and dressed, and screwed in his front tooth again with the greatest ease.

Once it got known about this tooth, and fellows were naturally excited. Steggles said it was on the principle of a tobacco-pipe mouthpiece; and, finding the chaps were keen to see it, Gideon let it be generally known he would freely show it to anybody for threepence a time, and to friends for twopence. But this was a safe reduction to make, because, properly speaking, he hadn't any friends. Seeing there were nearly two hundred boys at Dunston's, and that certainly half, including several fellows from the Sixth, took a pleasure in seeing the tooth, and didn't mind the rather high charge, Gideon did jolly well; and in the case of Nubby Tomkins, he made actually one shilling and threepence, because the tooth had a most peculiar fascination for Nubby, and he saw it no less than five times. After that Gideon made a reduction to him, as well he might. But somehow Slade, the head of the school, was very averse to Gideon's front tooth when he heard about it, and he decided that there must be no more exhibitions of it for money. He told Gideon so himself.

However, a new boy came a week afterwards and heard about the strangeness of the tooth, and offered a shilling, in three instalments, to see it; which was too much temptation for Gideon, and he showed it, contrary to what Slade had said.

Slade, of course, heard, for the new boy happened to be his own cousin, though called Saunders; and then there was a curious scene in the playground, which I fortunately saw. Slade came up to Gideon in the very quiet way he has, and asked him in a perfectly gentlemanly voice for his front tooth. At first Gideon seemed inclined not to give it up, but he saw what an awfully serious thing that would be, and finally unscrewed it, though not willingly.

" Now," said Slade, " I 'll have no more

of this penny peep-show business at Merivale. I told you once, and you have disobeyed me. So there's an end of your beastly tooth. What's this?"

He took something out of his pocket.

"It's a catapult," said Gideon.

"It is," said Slade, "and I'm going to use your tooth instead of a bullet, and fire it into space."

"It cost five guineas," said Gideon.

"Don't care if it cost a hundred," answered Slade, still in a very gentlemanly sort of way. "We can't have this sort of thing here, you know."

Slade was just going to fire into space, as he had said, when a robin suddenly settled within thirty yards of us, on the wall between the playground and old Grimbal's. Slade being a wonderful shot with a catapult (having once shot a wood-pigeon), suddenly fired at the robin, and only missed it by about four inches. He said the shape of a front tooth was very unfavourable for shooting. But anyway, the tooth went over into

Grimbal's, and we distinctly heard it hit against the side of his house.

Then Slade went away, and we rotted Gideon rather, because not having the tooth looked rum, and made a difference in his voice. He took it very quietly, and said he rather thought his father would be able to summon Slade; and before evening school, having marked down the spot where he fancied his tooth had hit Grimbal's house, he went to look with a box of matches. What happened afterwards he told us frankly; and it was certainly true, because, with all his faults, Gideon never lied to anybody.

"I went quietly over, and began carefully looking along the bottom of the wall, using a match to every foot or so," he said, "and I had done about half when I heard a door open. I then hooked it, and ran almost on to old Grimbal. He had not opened the door at all, but was coming up the garden path at the critical moment. Of course, he caught me. He was going to rub it into me with his stick, when I said I should think it very kind if he would hear me first, as I had a perfectly good excuse for being there.

" He said :—

" 'What excuse can you have for tres-passing in my garden, you little oily wretch?'

"'Oily wretch' was what he called me; and I said that my tooth had been fired into his garden that very day, about half-past one, by a chap with a catapult; and I lighted a match, and showed him it was missing.

" He said :—

" ' How the deuce are you going to find a tooth in a garden this size ?' And I told him I had marked it down very carefully, and that it had cost five guineas, and that I rather believed my father would be able to summon the chap who had shot it away. He seemed a good deal interested, and said he thought very likely he might, if it was robbery with violence. Then he asked me if I was the boy he had seen beating down the price of a purse at Wilkinson's in

Merivale, and I said I was. Then he said, 'Come in and have a bit of cake, boy'; and I went in and had a bit of cake, and saw on a shelf in his room about fifty or sixty cricket-balls, and various things which he has collared when they went over. He asked me a lot of questions about different things, and I answered them. All he said was about money. He also asked me to be good enough to value the things he had, which came over the wall from time to time; and I did, and he thanked me. They were worth fifteen shillings and tenpence; and Wright's ball, which everybody thought was stolen by the milkman, wasn't, for old Grimbal's got it; and the milkman should be told and apologised to.

"Well, he knew a lot about money, and told me he had thousands of golden sovereigns, which he makes breed into thousands more.

"He said:—

"'You're the only boy I ever met with a grain of sense in his head. Now, if I

gave you a cheque on my bankers in Merivale for five pounds to-day, and wrote to
you to-morrow morning to say I had changed
my mind, what would you do?'

"I said, 'It would be too late, sir, because
your cheque would have been sent off to
my father that very night, to put out at
interest for me.' He said, 'That's right.
Never give back money, or anything.' Then
he asked me my name, and told me I might
come back to-morrow, and look for my tooth
by daylight."

That was Gideon's most peculiar adventure, and, though he never found the tooth
or saw old Grimbal again, yet about seven
or eight months afterwards, when old
Grimbal was discovered all curiously twisted
up and dead in bed by the man who took
him his breakfast, the result of Gideon's visit
to him came out. Old Grimbal had specially
put him into his will by some legal method,
and Doctor Dunston had Gideon into his
study three days after old Grimbal kicked.
It then was proved that old Grimbal had left

Gideon all the things that came over the wall, and also a legacy of fifty pounds in money, because, according to the bit of the will which the Doctor read to Gideon out of a lawyer's letter, he was the only boy old Grimbal had ever met with who showed any intelligence above that of the anthropoid ape.

Gideon returned all the balls and things to their owners free of charge, but not until the rightful owners proved they were so. And the money he sent to his father; and his father, he told me afterwards, was so jolly pleased about the whole affair that he added nine hundred and fifty pounds to old Grimbal's fifty. Therefore, by shooting Gideon's front tooth at a robin, Slade was actually putting the enormous sum of one thousand pounds into Gideon's pocket, which I should think was about the rummest thing that ever happened in the world.

Gideon stopped at Dunston's one term after that. Then he went away, and, I believe, began to help his father to sell

· diamonds. He was fairly good at French, and very at German ; but of other things he knew rather little, except arithmetic, and his was the most beautiful arithmetic which had ever been done at Merivale ; for I heard Stokes, who was a seventeenth wrangler in his time, tell the Doctor so.

THE CHEMISTRY CLASS

THIS story about Guy Fawkes' Night at Dunston's is worth knowing, because it shows the rumminess of Nubby Tomkins. Tomkins, I may say, was called "Nubby," owing to his nose, which was extremely huge, though he said it was Roman, and swore he wouldn't change it if he could. Anyway, Bradwell made a rhyme about it that is certainly good enough to repeat. He wrote it first on a blackboard with chalk, and a good many chaps learnt it by heart.

It ran like this :—

> "Our Nubby's nose is ponderous,
> And our Nubby's nose is long ;
> So it wouldn't disgrace
> Our Nubby's face
> If half his nose was gone."

Which was not only jolly good poetry, but also true—a thing all poetry isn't by long

chalks, as you can see in Virgil and such-
like.

Well, Nubbs sang the solos in chapel
on Sundays, and people came from far to
hear him do it; in consequence of which,
so Steggles said, the Doctor favoured him,
and regarded him as an advertisement to
Dunston's. But his singing wasn't in it
compared with the advertisement he gave
the Doctor on Guy Fawkes' Night the term
before Slade left.

To explain the whole tremendous thing
I must tell you that Nubbs belonged to the
chemistry class. This class, in fact, was
pretty well started for him, his father telling
Dunston, so Nubbs said, that he shouldn't
send him at all if he couldn't be taught
chemistry; because Nubbs had shown a
good deal of keenness for chemicals
generally from the earliest days, and bought
little boxes of "serpents' eggs" and red fire
instead of sweets ever since he was old
enough to buy anything. He had also
blown off his eyebrows and eyelashes with

a mixture he was grinding up in a mortar, and they had never grown again to this day—all of which things showed he had chemistry in him to a great extent. So the Doctor started a chemistry class, and a chap called Stoddart, from Merivale, came up once a week to take it; and Nubbs joined, and so did I, not because I had chemistry in me worth speaking of, but because I was a chum of Nubby's. Wilson also joined, and so did Hodges. I may mention my name is Mathers.

I always thought that chemists simply mix the muck doctors give you when you're queer, but it seems not. In fact, there are several sorts of chemists, and Nubbs said he hoped to belong to the best sort, who don't have bottles of red and green stuff in the windows, and so on. He said a man who sold pills and toothbrushes, and liquorice-root and soap, could not be considered a classy chemist. The real flyers made discoveries and froze air, and sneaked one another's inventions, and got knighted by the Queen if they had luck and if they were well thought of by the newspapers. I should think really Nubbs might come to being knighted if he sticks to it, for even down to the stuff in cough lozenges nothing is hid from him.

Once the matron gave me a simply vile lozenge for my throat, which got a bit foggy owing to falling into the water during "hare and hounds." Well, the lozenge was white in colour, but even a white lozenge may be very decent sometimes, so I took a shot at it going to bed. But it was so jolly frightful to the taste that I chucked it away, and next morning found it again and examined it, after drying. On it I then found the words "Chlorate of potash." So I took it to Nubbs. He said it was certainly a chemical, and added that the stuff in it was almost the same as you make "Pharaoh's serpents" with. I could hardly believe such a thing, so he lighted the lozenge and it burnt blue, and a long, wriggling, brownish ash came curling out of it like a snake, just as Nubby said, which is well worth knowing to anybody who ever has a chlorate of potash lozenge. Many such-like remarkable and useful things Nubby could tell you; among others, how to mix sulphur and gunpowder and other ingredients for fireworks. He had, in fact, an awful fine book devoted to the subject, and wooden affairs to load cases; and once when Stoddart didn't turn up and the Doctor put us on our honour to do the proper things in the laboratory alone, Nubbs finished off analysing some mess in about five minutes, and spent the complete rest of the time making a rocket. It had four blue stars and thirteen yellow ones, and the case was made out of a stiff brown paper roll in which his mother had that morning sent Nubbs a photograph of her new baby at home. And Nubbs forgot the photograph and stuffed the mixture in upon it, and made a separate compartment for the stars on top. So the photograph of Nubby's mother's new baby, curiously enough, went off with the rocket, and was never more seen by mortal eye. Not that Nubbs cared. He kept the rocket till the Doctor's birthday, and after prayers, when he knew he was in his study, with the windows open and the blinds up, being summer-time, Nubbs let it off in the front garden, and we helped. It turned out very good in a way, though not quite a perfect rocket, because instead of going up it tore along the ground. But it tore for an enormous distance, and then turned and came back all of itself. And the blue stars did not go off, but the yellow ones did—or some—in a bed of rather swagger geraniums, unfortunately.

The Doctor didn't care much about it, not understanding our motives. But Nubbs explained that he had done it out of honour to the day. Then the Doctor thanked him, and said he had doubtless meant well, and that from the earliest times of the Chinese the pyrotechnist's art had been employed upon occasions of legitimate festivity and rejoicing.

M

I mention this because it was the encouragement he had over this creeping rocket that made Nubbs get so above himself, if you understand me. He never forgot it, and next autumn term he actually asked the Doctor if he might have a regular firework display in the playground on the night of the Fifth of November. He asked rather cunningly, just after an English History lesson, during which the Doctor had been slating Guy Fawkes frightfully; and having said such a heap of hard things about the beggar, Doctor Dunston couldn't very well refuse.

He said:—

"Your request is unusual, Tomkins; but I can see no objection at the moment. However, I will let you have my answer at no distant date."

And I said to Nubbs:—

"That means he'll think and think till he's got a reason why you shouldn't, and let you know then."

But Nubbs said to me:—

"I believe he'll let me do it, feeling so jolly bitter as he does about Guy Fawkes."

And blessed if he didn't! Nubbs undertook to make the things himself. Nothing was to be bought but chemicals in a raw, unmixed condition, and Doctor Dunston actually headed the subscription list with 2s. 6d.; and Thompson gave the same, and Mannering 2s., and "Frenchy" 3s. Fifty-two chaps also contributed various sums from 1s. to 1d.; and Nubbs became rather important, and went down gradually to the bottom of the Lower Fifth owing to the strain upon his mind.

He gathered together £2 7s. 5d. in all, and made it up to £2 10s. himself; and Fowle's father, who was in some business where they used sulphur in terrific quantities, got four pounds weight of it for nothing, and Nubbs said it was a godsend for illuminating purposes. He had been to the Crystal Palace, and told us he was going to carry everything out just like they did there, as far as he could with the money. At the last moment he got a tremendous increase of funds in the shape of a pound from his father; and, strangely enough, it was that extra pound that wrecked him. Without that father's pound he couldn't have arranged the principal feature of the whole performance; and without that principal feature nothing in the way of misfortunes to Nubbs worth mentioning would have fallen out. But the pound came, and with it a letter very encouraging to Nubby.

He went on mixing away at the various proper compounds and experimenting with them till he got his rockets to go up like larks and his Roman candles to shoot out stars the length of a cricket pitch. Then his governor's pound came, and he decided on having a set piece with it. A set piece, Nubby said, is the triumph of the firework maker's art—and very likely it is in proper hands. You can have likenesses in fire, or words, or ships, or "Fame crowning Virtue," or, in fact, pretty well anything. A set piece is designed small first, then large; and it is worked out with little tiny things like squibs, only very small and without any bang at the end. These are all lighted off at once, and they burn one colour first, then change to another. Nubbs said his would start yellow, because it was cheaper, and finally turn green. The thing was what design to have, and the four chaps in the chemistry class all thought differently. I advised trying a shot at a huge portrait of the Doctor, but when it came to particulars nobody knew how to work a portrait; and Hodges thought we might do something about Guy Fawkes, but Nubbs didn't care about that. Then Hodges thought again, and suggested the words, "God bless the Doctor," and I agreed that it would be fine; but Wilson said it was profane, and might annoy the Doctor frightfully, especially when it turned green. Then Nubbs suggested the words, "Doctor Dunston is a Brick!" and Hodges said that it was good, and Wilson said it might be good, but it wasn't true, anyway. However, it was three to one, though we all admitted that, from his point of view, Wilson was right to hate the Doctor, because the Doctor hates him.

The thing was to make a licking big frame of light wood, and arrange the letters across it, and the note of exclamation at the end. This we did, and hammered it against the playground wall, and wheeled up the screens that go behind the bowler's arm in the cricket season, and hid away the set piece behind them till the time came. Likewise we arranged stakes for the Roman candles, and a board for the Catharine wheels, and a string for the flying pigeons, and so on. And also we rigged up bits of tin round the playground and by the fir trees at the top end and behind the gym. These were for Bengal lights and other illuminations. All of this Nubbs had arranged for the paltry sum of £3 10s. The chemistry class had a half-holiday as the time drew on, and we worked like niggers,

all four of us. Nubbs commanded, so to
speak, and mixed and did the grinding and
pounding and stars. Hodges and I hammered up the heavy posts and stakes in the
playground, and carried out odd jobs
generally; and Wilson manufactured cases
for everything with brown paper and paste
and string.

The set piece took two hundred and
thirteen little tubes. These Wilson made
in lengths of a yard and cut off at the
required size. And Nubbs stuffed them—
with green fire first and yellow on top. It
promised to be a jolly big thing altogether,
and four days before the night Nubbs began
to get awfully nervous, and to prepare yards
and yards of touch-paper.

And Corkey minimus heard the Doctor
say to Browne:—

"Really the lads have devoted no little
energy and method on their proceedings;
and it appears—so Mr. Stoddart tells me—
that the boy Tomkins has mixed his compounds quite correctly, thereby ensuring that

brilliance and variety which are looked for in an exhibition of this kind. I wonder whether we might ask the parents and friends of those who dwell at Merivale and the immediate neighbourhood."

And Browne, who never misses a chance of showing the brute he is at heart, said :—

"Really, I should think twice, Doctor Dunston. There is such an element of chance with amateur fireworks. . Unfortunately, we can't have a dress rehearsal, as with the scenes from Shakespeare and the recitations at the end of the term."

"Nevertheless," said the Doctor, "I am disposed to run the risk. A little harmless pleasure combined with courtesy to relatives at mid-term is rather desirable than not."

So about fifty people were asked, and they brought fifty more, and the cads from Merivale got to know too, and there was a good crowd of them along the fence by the gym. Also two policemen came, and

Nubbs, who was nervous before, grew much worse when he heard of it. Besides, we had a frightful shock two days before the firework night, owing to the loss of poor old Wilson. By simply sickening luck he got reported by Browne for cheek. It was when Browne came out in a new pair of awfully squeaking boots with sham pearl buttons at the side and drab tops; and Wilson said they were ugly "eighteens," and Browne heard him. The Doctor took an awfully grave view of this, and told Wilson that personality was the vilest form of cheek. Which wouldn't have mattered, but he gave him a thousand lines as well, and forbade him to see the fireworks or help any more with them.

"And that's the man you call a brick!" Wilson said rather bitterly. It certainly was rough, after the way he had worked; but from the Wing Dormitory, where he would be at the time, he might be able to see pretty well everything by leaning far out between the window bars. Which Nubbs pointed out to him, and he said he should. He also said he'd pay out Browne some day, and very likely Dunston too.

Well, the night came, and it was a fine one; and the cads likewise came and lined the fence. Then the Doctor clapped his hands twice, which was the signal to begin; and just as he did so, out burst yellow fire everywhere behind the bits of tin, lighted simultaneously by seven chaps. And everybody seemed to like it; and the Doctor said :—

" Capital! Bravo, Tomkins—a pleasing and fairy-like conceit!"

Then Nubbs let fly two rockets, and they went up well and burst out in stars, though not as many by any means as we had crammed into them; but one twisted for some reason, and, instead of falling in the direction of the cads, the stick twinkled down, with just a spark of red here and there in the line of it, bang behind the chapel. Both Nubbs and I distinctly heard it go smack through the top of the green-

house, and I rather think the Doctor heard
it too, for he didn't say "Bravo" or anything, but just sent a kid to tell Nubbs to
point future rockets the other way; which
disheartened Nubbs, because he's like a
girl at times of great excitement such as
this was. But he soon cheered up, especially
at the splendid success of the Catharine-
wheels, which he hadn't hoped much from,
and at the cheers even the cads gave for
the "golden rain" which showed up everything as bright as day, including Maude and
the other Dunston girls, and Mrs. Dunston,
and Nubby's father standing smiling very
amiably by the Doctor, and the policemen
blinking, and the crowd, and a white dab
hanging out of a high window afar off,
which I saw and knew to be Wilson.

Only the balloon failed, owing to the
nervousness of Nubbs, who set fire to the
whole show while he was trying to light the
spirit on the sponge underneath; but he
passed it off with crackers thrown among
the kids, and then, while they were all

yelling, he dragged away the cricket screens, and Nubbs let off the set piece. He lighted the touch-paper, and it snapped and crackled all over the design in a moment, and a thick smoke rose, and out of it came the set piece flaring in rich yellow fire. Of course we expected what Nubbs and Wilson had arranged, viz., "Doctor Dunston is a Brick!" but instead there came out these awful words :—

"DOCTOR DUNSTON

IS A BRUTE!"

That just shows what a frightful difference three letters will make in a thing; and the night was so dark and the letters so big that you could have read them a mile off. Only, if you will believe it, Dunston didn't. People applauded like anything at first, till the preliminary smoke cleared off and they read the truth. Then they shut up and made a sound like wind coming through a wood.

But the cads yelled and roared, and so did
the policemen, for I heard them; and to
make the frightful thing a shade more
frightful, if possible, the Doctor, who is as
blind as ten bats, and didn't realise the
end of the set piece, but only read his
name at the top, clapped his hands and
said :—

"Famous, famous! You excel yourself,
Tomkins!"

Then the words began gradually to turn
green; and, for that matter, so did Nubbs.
In fact, whether it was the reflected light
or the condition of his mind, or both, I
certainly never saw any chap become so
perfectly horrid to look at as Nubbs did
then. His nose seemed to stand out like
a great green rock, and his eyes bulged,
and his chin dropped, and the set piece
turned his teeth as bright as precious
emeralds. He just merely said, "Good
Lord!"—nothing more—then hooked it off
into the darkness, simply shattered.

At the same time Stoddart and Thompson,

and Mannering and Browne, and some chaps
from the Sixth, not knowing what colour
the beastly set piece might turn next, or
how soon the Doctor would spot it, dashed
at the thing and dragged it down, and
trampled on it; and Browne in the act
burnt the very boots that Wilson had
cheeked, which pleased Wilson a good deal
when he heard it.

After that it was all over, and the
Doctor, thinking the set piece had died a
natural death, so to speak, saw me under
the gaslight at the gate, as everybody
streamed out, and said :—

"Ah, young man, what was that last word
in the illumination? I know you and
Hodges also had a hand in it, as well as
Tomkins."

And I said :—

"Please, sir, we arranged the words
'Doctor Dunston is a Brick!'"

And he said :—

"Excellent! Pithy and concise, if a little
familiar. I only hope you all echo that senti-

ment—every one of you. Send Tomkins to me, and tell the other fellows there is cake and lemonade going in the dining-hall."

Just as if the other fellows didn't know it! But everybody gave three cheers for the Doctor and Mrs. Dunston, and I started to find Nubbs; and the policemen made the cads go, though they went reluctantly.

I looked long for Nubby, and at last found him all alone in the gym. One bit of candle was burning, which looked frightfully poor after all the brilliance of the fireworks, and Nubbs had got the parallel bars under the flying rings and was standing on them—I mean the bars.

"What the dickens are you doing, Nubby?" I said.

And he answered :—

"It's no jolly good attempting to stop me now, because it's too late. My life is ruined, and my father was there too to see it ruined; and I'm going to hang myself, as every convenience for hanging is here."

Mind you, he would have done it. Knowing Tomkins as I do and his great in-geniousness, I don't mind swearing that he would have been a hung chap in another minute. So I told him; but, though doubtful, he decided to put it off, anyway. I even got him to promise he wouldn't hang himself at all if his father believed his innocence about the set piece. And Crewe, the headmaster under the Doctor, and old Briggs and Thompson got us in a corner— Nubbs and Hodges and me—and we solemnly vowed we knew nothing of it; and Crewe went down to the *Merivale Trumpet* and made the reporter put in the original words when it came out; and Thompson explained to Mrs. Dunston how some evil-disposed, wicked person had tampered with the set piece, and begged her not to wound the feelings of the Doctor by telling him; and the Sixth hushed it up among the kids; and I sneaked a bit of cake for Wilson, and went up after the row was over and told him everything, down to the burning of Browne's boots.

He confessed to me then that he had done it, which didn't surprise me much, knowing how he had worked, and then at the last minute almost been deprived of seeing the show. It was certainly a terrible revenge; but, of course, a terrible revenge which doesn't come off owing to a master being too shortsighted to see it is pretty sickening for the revenger. Besides the risk.

Mr. Crewe worked like a demon to find out who had done it, and he suspected Wilson from the first, but couldn't prove it. But at last he did find out through Fowle, who got it out of Ferrars, who got it out of West, who got it out of Nubbs in a moment of rage. For I may say Wilson himself told Nubbs, and Nubbs never forgave him, and says he never shall, even if they ever both go to heaven.

So Crewe, having found out, had some talk with Wilson. But he didn't lick him; whereas Wilson did lick Fowle, and that pretty badly. Not that Fowle cares for an

N

ordinary licking, more than another chap cares for a smack on the head. The only way to hurt him is to twist his arm round, about twice, and then hit him hard just above the elbow. I may say I found this out myself; and everybody does it now.

DOCTOR DUNSTON'S HOWLER

MIND you, if it's interesting to watch
any ordinary person come a howler,
what must it be to see your own headmaster do it? A "howler," of course, is the
same as a "cropper," and you can come one
at cricket or football or in class or in every-
day life.

Dr. Dunston's howler was a most complicated sort, and I had the luck to be one
of the chaps who witnessed him come
it. Of course, to see any master make a
tremendous mistake is good; but when you
are dealing with a man almost totally bald
and sixty-two years of age the affair has
a solemn side, especially owing to his being
a Rev. and a D.D. In fact, Slade, who
was with me, said the spectacle reminded
him of the depths of woe beggars got into
in Greek tragedies, which often wanted half-

a-dozen gods to lug them out of. But no gods troubled themselves about Dunston; and it really was a bit awful looked at from his point of view, because it's beastly to give yourself away to kids at the best of times; and no doubt to him all of us are more or less as kids, even the Sixth.

He often had a way of bringing the parents of a possible new boy through one or two of the big classrooms and the chapel of Merivale, just to show what a swagger place it was. Then we all bucked up like mad, and the masters bucked up too, and gave their gowns a hitch round and their mortar-boards a cock up, and made more noise and put on more side generally, just to add to the splendour of the scene from the point of view of the parents of the possible new boy.

Sometimes the affair was rather spoilt by an aunt or mother or some woman or other asking the Doctor homely sort of questions about sanitary arrangements or prayers; then to see old Dunston making long-winded replies and getting even the drains to sound majestic was fine. His manner varied according to the people who came over the school. Sometimes, if it only happened to be a guardian or a lawyer, he was short and stern. Then he just swept along, calling attention to the ventilation and discipline, and looking at the chaps as if they were dried specimens in a museum; but with fathers or women he had a playful mood and an expression known as the "parent-smile." To mothers he never talked about "pupils," but called the whole shoot of us "his lads," and beamed and fluttered his gown, like a hen with chickens flutters its wings. The masters always copied him, and to see that little brute Browne trying to flutter over the kids like a hen when the Doctor came into his classroom was a ghastly sight, knowing him as we did. Also the Doctor would often pat a youngster on the head and beam at him. He generally singled Corkey minimus out for patting and beaming; and

Corkey minor said the irony of it was pretty frightful, considering that Corkey minimus, for different reasons, got licked oftener by the Doctor than almost any chap in the Lower School.

Well, one day in came the Doctor to the schoolroom of the Fourth. I'm in the Sixth myself, and a personal chum of Slade's, the head of the school; but I happened to have gone to the Fourth with a message, so I saw what happened. A very big man who puffed out his chest like a pigeon followed the Doctor. He had a blue tie on with a jolly bright diamond in it, and there were small purple veins in a regular network over his cheeks, and his moustache was yellowish-grey and waxed out as sharp as pins. A lady followed him with red rims to her little eyes and gold things hanging about her chest. The Doctor, being all arched up and rolled round from the small of the back like a wood-louse, seemed to show they were parents of perhaps more fellows than one.

The big chap wore an eyeglass, and spoke very loud, and was jolly pleasant.

"Ah!" he said, "and this is where the little boys work, eh? I expect, now, my youngster will be drafted in amongst these small men, Doctor Dunston?"

"It is very possible—nay, probable in the highest degree, my lord," said the Doctor. "We are now," he continued, "in the presence of the Fourth and Lower Fourth. The classroom is spacious, as you see, and new. A commanding panorama of the surrounding country and our playing-fields may be enjoyed from the French windows. If two of you lads will move that blackboard from there, Lord Golightly may be able to see something of the prospect."

Two of the kids promptly knocked down the blackboard nearly on to the purple-veined lord's head. Then suddenly the lady called out and attracted his attention. Looking round, we found she had got awfully excited, and stood pointing straight at young Tomlin. He was a mere kid, at the extreme bottom of the Lower Fourth; but he happened to be my fag, so I was interested. She pointed at him, in the most frantic way, with a hand in a browny - yellow glove, and a gold bracelet outside the glove and a little watch let into the bracelet.

"Good gracious!" she said, "do look, Ralph! What an astounding resemblance! Whoever is that boy?"

Tomlin turned rather red in the gills, which was natural.

"Do you know the lad?" asked the Doctor.

"Never saw him before in my life; but I hope he'll forgive me for being so rude as to point at him in that way," she said. "He's exactly like our dear Carlo; they might be twins."

Tomlin thought she meant a pet dog, and got rather rum to look at.

"Carlo is our son, you know," explained the lord.

"Singular coincidence," answered Doctor Dunston, not looking very keen about it.

In fact, he wasn't too fond of Tomlin at any time, and seemed sorry he should be dragged in now. But the kid was a very tidy sort, really—Captain of the Third Footer Eleven and a good runner. He happened to be the son of a big London hatter who had a shop of enormous dimensions in Bond Street; and the Doctor was said to get his own hats there; yet he didn't like Tomlin.

Tomlin went out into the open, and the purple-veined lord shook hands with him, and the lord's wife stood him in the light and turned him round to catch different expressions. Then they admitted that the likeness was really most wonderful, and they both hoped Tomlin and Carlo would be great friends. Tomlin, told by the Doctor to answer, stood on one leg, twisted his arms in a curious way he's got when nervous, and said he hoped they might be; but he said it as though he knew jolly well they wouldn't.

Then the lord and the lady cleared out, and a week later Carlo came. His real name was Westonleigh, and he was a viscount or something, being eldest son of an earl; but we called him Carlo, and he grew jolly waxy when he found his nickname had got to Merivale before him. He fancied himself to a most hideous extent for a kid of nine, and explained he'd only come for a year or so before going to Eton. He went into the Lower Fourth, so Tomlin ceased to be at the bottom of that class.

The likeness between Carlo and my fag was really most peculiar. It must have been for Carlo's own mother to see it; but when Carlo heard that Tomlin would be a hatter in the course of years he refused to have anything to do with him. And Tomlin loathed Carlo, too, from the start; so instead of being chums according to the wish of the purple-veined lord, they hated one another, and the first licking of any importance which Carlo got he had from Tomlin.

The chap was a failure all round, and it's no good saying he wasn't. Everybody saw it but Doctor Dunston, and he wouldn't.

Carlo proved to be a sneak and a liar of
the deepest sort—not to masters, but to the
chaps; and he was also jolly cruel to animals,
and very much liked to torture things that
couldn't hit him back, such as mice and
insects. He had a square face and snubby
nose, and a voice and eyes exactly similar
to Tomlin's; but there was no likeness in
their characters, Tomlin being a very decent
kid, as I have said. Fellows barred Carlo
all round, and he only had one real chum
in the miserable shape of Fowle. Fowle
sucked up to him and listened for hours
about his ancestors, and buttered him at all
times, hoping, of course, that some day he
would get asked to Carlo's father's castle in
the holidays. I may also note Carlo never
played games, excepting tossing behind the
gymnasium for halfpennies with Fowle and
Steggles, Steggles, of course, winning.

Happening one day to go down through
the playground, young Tomlin saw Westonleigh near a little fir tree which grew at
the top of the drill-ground. He was

alone, and seemed to be doing something queer, so Tomlin stopped and went
over.

"What are you up to?" he said.

"Frying ants," said Carlo, "though it's
no business of yours. You see, there's
turpentine juice come out of this tree where
I cut it yesterday, and you can stick the
ants in it, then fry them to a cinder with
a burning-glass, like this."

"That's what you're doing?"

"It is."

"Don't you think you're rather a little
beast?"

"What d' you mean, hatter?"

"I mean I'm going to kick you for being
such a cruel beast."

They stood the same height to an inch
and were the same age, so it was a perfectly
sportsmanlike thing for Tomlin to offer.

"You seem to forget who you're talking
to," said Carlo.

"No, I don't—no chance of that. Your
ancestors came over with William the Con-

queror—carried his portmanteau, I expect, then cleared out when the fighting came on. Yes, and another ancestor stabbed a friend of Wat Tyler's when he was face down on the ground, after somebody else had knocked him over. That's what you are, ant-fryer."

"I'll thank you to let me pass," said Carlo. "I'm not accustomed to talking to people like you, and if you think I'm going to fight with a future hatter you're wrong."

"Then you can put your tail between your legs and swallow this," said Tomlin, and he went on and licked Carlo pretty well. He also broke his burning-glass.

"You'll live to be sorry for this all your life!" yelled out Carlo, when Tomlin let him get up off some broken flower-pots on the drill-ground. "I'll never forget it; I'll get my father to make old Dunston expel you; and when I'm a man I'll devote all my time to wrecking your vile hat business and ruining you and making you a shivering, starving beggar in the streets!"

"Go and sneak, I should," said Tomlin.

And blessed if Carlo didn't! He tore straight off to the Doctor just as he was, in his licked condition.

That much I heard from my fag, young Tomlin, but the rest I saw for myself, as the Sixth happened to be before the Doctor in his study when Carlo arrived. He was white and muddy, and slightly bloody and panting; he looked jolly wicked, and his collar had carried away from the stud, and his trousers were torn behind.

"My good lad, whatever has happened?" began the Doctor. "Don't say you have met with an accident? And yet your appearance——?"

"Nothing of the sort," said Carlo, who soon found out the Doctor had a weak place for him, owing to his being a lord's son. "I've been frightfully and cruelly mangled through no fault of my own; and I believe some things inside me are broken too."

"Sit down, sit down, my unfortunate lad," said the Doctor. Then he rang the bell and told the butler to bring Viscount Westonleigh a glass of wine at once.

" It's Tomlin done it," said Carlo. " He came up behind me, and, before I could defend myself, he trampled on me and tried to tear me limb from limb. I'm not strong, and I may die of it. Anyway, he ought to be expelled, and I'll write to my father, the earl, about it, and he'll make the whole country-side resound if Tomlin isn't sent away and his character ruined."

" Hush, Westonleigh!" said the Doctor. " Have no fear that justice will not be done, my boy. You shall yourself accuse Tomlin and hear what he may have to say in defence."

Then Tomlin was sent for, and in about ten minutes came.

" Is this true, boy Tomlin?" said the Doctor, putting on his big manner. " One glance at your victim," he continued, " furnishes a more conclusive reply to my question than could any word of yours; nevertheless, I desire to hear from your own lips whether Viscount Westonleigh's assertions are true or not."

"Don't know what he's asserted, sir," said Tomlin, which was a smart thing for a kid to say. "If he said I've licked him, it's true, sir."

"That is what he *did* assert, sir, in words chosen with greater regard for my feelings than your own. And are you aware, George Tomlin, that you have 'licked' one who, in the ordinary course of nature, and subject to the will of an all-just, all-seeing Providence, will some day take his seat in the House of Lords?"

"I've heard him *say* he will, sir," answered Tomlin, as though no statement of Carlo's could be worth believing.

"Don't answer in that offensive tone, boy," answered the Doctor, his voice rising to the pitch that always went before a flogging. "If your stagnant sense of right cannot bring a blush to your cheek before the spectacle of your scandalous achievement, it will be necessary for me—for me, your headmaster, sir—to quicken the blood in your veins and bring a blush to the baser extremity of your person. Some learn through the head, George Tomlin; some can only be approached through the hide; and with the latter category you have long, unhappily, chosen to throw in your lot."

Tomlin said nothing, but looked at Carlo.

"Before proceeding, according to my custom, I shall hear both sides of this question — *audi alteram partem*, George Tomlin. Now say what you have to say; explain why your lamentable, your unholy, your aboriginal passions led you to fall upon Viscount Westonleigh from behind—to take him in the rear, sir, after the unmanly fashion of the North American Indian or other primitive savage."

"I didn't take him in the rear at all, sir," said Tomlin. "I stood right up to him, and he said he wouldn't fight a future hatter."

"A very proper decision too, sir—a natural and wise decision," declared the Doctor. "Why should the son of Lord

Golightly imbrue his hand in the blood of—
I will not say a future hatter, for I yield
to no man in my respect for your father,
Tomlin, and his business is alike honourable
and necessary; but why should he fight anybody?"

"If he's challenged he's got to, sir, or
else take a licking."

"No flippancy, sir!" thundered the Doctor
again. "Who are *you* to announce the laws
which govern the society of Merivale?
Shall it be possible in a Christian land, at
a Christian college for Christian lads, to find
infamous boys with tigrine instincts parading
the fold for the purpose of smiting when
and where they will? This, sir, is the very
apotheosis of savagery!"

"I didn't do it for nothing, sir," said
Tomlin. "I'm not going to sneak, of
course; but I—I licked Carlo for a jolly
good reason, and he knows what."

"Don't know anything of the sort,"
declared Carlo. "You flew at me like a
wolf from behind."

"That's a good one," answered Tomlin.

"Anybody can see you did from the state I'm in," said Carlo.

"You two boys," began the Doctor again, "though you know it not, stand here before me as types of a great social movement, I may even say upheaval. In the democratic age upon which we are now entering, we shall find the Tomlins at war with the Westonleighs; we shall find the Westonleighs disdaining to fight, and the Tomlins accordingly doing what pleases them in their own brutal way. Now, here I find myself met with statement and counter-statement. The indictment is all too clear against you, boy Tomlin, for even the glass of old brown sherry which he has just consumed fails to soothe your unfortunate victim's nerve-centres. He is still far from calm; his ganglions are yet vibrating. This work of destruction was yours. You do not deny it, but you refuse any explanation, making instead a vague and ambiguous reference to not sneaking. No man hates the tale-bearer more than your headmaster, sir, but there are occasions when the school's welfare and the protection of our little commonwealth make it absolutely necessary that offences should be reported to the ruler of that commonwealth. I have no hesitation in saying that Westonleigh saw the present incident in this light. He had no right to hush up the matter. Whatever his private instincts towards mercy, his duty to his companions and to me, together with a hereditary sense of justice and the fearless instincts of his race, compelled him to come before me and report the presence of a young garrotter in our midst. I select the word, George Tomlin, and I say that, having regard to the perverted, not to say inverted, sense of justice and honour all too common among every community of boys, Westonleigh's act was a brave act. I accept his statement in its entirety; consequently, Tomlin, you may join me this evening, at nine o'clock, after prayers."

That meant a flogging, and Tomlin

said, "Yes, sir," and hooked it; but the wretched Carlo thought he was going to hear Tomlin expelled. He burst out and said as much, and the Doctor started as if a serpent had stung him, and told Carlo to control the instinct of revenge so common to all human nature, and explained that chaps were not expelled for trifles. He reminded Carlo that Tomlin had an immortal soul like himself, and seemed to imply that being expelled from Merivale would ruin a chap's future in the next world as well as this one. Finally, he allowed Carlo, in consideration of the dressing he had got, to stop in the playground that afternoon with a book. So the little skunk crept off, shattered ganglions and all, pretending to walk lame; while the Doctor, evidently much bothered altogether, took up our work where he had left it.

*   *   *   *   *

Tomlin got flogged all right, and there the matter ended, excepting that a lot of fellows sent Carlo to Coventry and called him "ant-fryer" from that day.

Then, within three weeks, came the Doctor's howler, Steggles being responsible. Steggles is a bit of a hound, but his cunning is wonderful. As for the Doctor, he continued making much of Carlo and sitting on Tomlin, till one day, going into chapel, he unexpectedly patted Tomlin on the head. Tomlin was rather pleased, because he thought the Doctor was relenting to him; but when Steggles heard of it, he said :—

"Why, you fool, he thought he was patting Westonleigh!"

Then, on an evening when Tomlin was cooking a sausage for me in the Sixth's classroom, he said :—

"Please, I should like to speak to you, if I may."

So I chucked work, and told him to say what he liked.

"It's only to show how things go against a chap, no matter what he does," said the kid. "This term I have been flogged for licking Carlo, and caned three times since for other things, which were more bad luck than anything else; and now I'll be flogged again to-morrow for absolute certain."

"Why?"

"Well, it's a jolly muddle. You know Steggles?"

"Yes, you're a fool to go about with him," I said.

"Perhaps I was. Anyway, Steggles and me made a plot to get some of the medlars from the tree on the lawn, and we minched out after dark to do it. They're simply allowed to fall and rot on the ground, which is a waste of good tuck, Steggles says. We went out about ten o'clock last night, past Browne's study window; and we looked in from the shrubbery to see the window open, and soda-water and whisky and pipes on the table; but no Browne, strange to say. Then we sneaked on, and Steggles suddenly heard something and got funky, but I kept

him going. We reached the tree, and
Steggles lighted his bull's-eye lantern, sc
as to collect the medlars, when suddenly out
from behind the tree itself rushed a man.
We hooked it like lightning, naturally, and
I never saw Steggles go at such a pace in
my life, and he stuck to his lantern, too;
but I tripped and fell, and before I could
get up the man had collared me. If you'll
believe it, the man was Browne! He asked
me who the other chap was, and I said I
couldn't be quite sure; so he told me to
go back to bed, which I did. That was
last night; and the one medlar we had time
to get, Steggles had eaten before I got
back, which shows what Steggles is. To-
day Browne will tell the Doctor. He
always chooses the evening after prayers,
so that he can work the Doctor up with
his stories and get a chap flogged right
away; because it often happens when
Doctor Dunston says he'll flog a chap next
day he doesn't do it."

"And what is Steggles going to do?"

"He says he is watching events. He also says that Browne was certainly stealing the Doctor's medlars himself, and really wc surprised him, not he us; but, of course, Steggles says it's no good my telling the Doctor that. Steggles also says that he's got an idea which may come to something. I don't know; but he's a very cute chap. I've got to keep out of the way after prayers to-night, and Steggles is going to watch Browne. He won't tell me his plan. I thought once that perhaps he meant giving himself up for me, and I asked him, and he said I ought to know him better."

Tomlin then cleared out, and as the Doctor took Slade and me for a short Greek lesson every evening after prayers, because of special examinations, I had the good luck to see the end of the business that very night.

We'd just got to work by the Doctor's green-shaded reading-lamp when Browne came in with his grovelling way, pretending he was awfully sorry for having to round on Tomlin, but that his duty gave him no option, and so on.

"Last night," he said, "I was sitting correcting exercises in my study when I fancied I saw a form steal across the grass outside. Thinking some vagabond might be in the grounds, I dashed out and followed as quickly as possible. Presently I saw a light, and noted two figures under the medlar tree. Fearing they might be plotting against the house, I went straight at them, and, to my astonishment, saw that they were only boys. One darted away, and I failed to catch him; the other, I much regret to say, was Tomlin."

That is how Browne put the affair.

"Tomlin again!" exclaimed the Doctor. "Positively that boy's behaviour passes the bounds of endurance."

"Yes, taking the medlars of one who has always treated him as you have. I couldn't trust myself to speak to him. He's a very disappointing boy."

"He's a disgraceful, degenerate, disreputable boy! I can forgive much; but the stealing of fruit—and that *my* fruit! Greediness, immorality, ingratitude in the person of one outrageous lad! I thank you, Browne. Yours was a zealous act, and argued courage of high order. Oblige me by sending Tomlin hither at once. There shall be no delay."

Browne hurried off to find the wretched Tomlin; and Doctor Dunston, who always had to work up his feelings before flogging a chap, snorted like a horse, and took off his glasses, and went to the corner behind the bookcase where canes and things were kept. He seemed to forget Slade and me, so we sat tight in the gloom outside the radius of light thrown by the green-shaded lamp, and waited with regret to see Tomlin catch it. The Doctor talked to himself as he brought out a birch and swished it through the air once or twice.

"Upon my soul," he said, "Lord Golightly's son was right. His knowledge of character is remarkable in so young a lad. Tomlin will have to be expelled; Tomlin must go; such consistent, such inherent depravity appears ineradicable. Pruning is of no avail; the branch must be sacrificed. My medlars under cover of darkness! And I would have given them freely had he but asked!"

He evidently wasn't going to expel Tomlin this time, but he meant doing all he knew with the birch; and as Tomlin was some while coming, the Doctor's safety-valves were regularly humming before he turned up. When he did come he walked boldly in; and the Doctor, who had been striding up and down like a lion at the Zoo, didn't wait for any remarks, but just went straight for him, seized him by the nape of the neck, nipped his hand round his back —in a way he did very neatly from long practice—and began to administer about the hottest flogging he'd given to any boy in his life.

"So — you — add — the — eighth — com-

mand—ment—to—the—others—you—have
—already—shattered—deplorable—boy!"
roared the Doctor, giving Tomlin one between each smack. "You—would—purloin
—steal—rob—the medlars—of your pre-
ceptor. You would lead others—to—share
—your—sin. You would bring—tears—of
—grief—to—a—good—mother's—eyes."

Here the Doctor stopped a moment for
breath, but he still held on to Tomlin, who,
much to my surprise, wriggled about a good
deal. In fact, he shot out his legs over and
over again at intervals, like a grasshopper
does when it gets into the water; and when
he got a chance he yelled back at the
Doctor :—

"It's a lie—a filthy lie!" he shrieked out.
"Beast—devil! Let me go! Let me go!
I never touched your rotten old medlars—
oh!—oh!"

Then the Doctor went off again.

"Silence, miserable child! Cease your
blasphemies. Falsehood—will—not—save
—you—now!"

"I never touched them, I tell you, you muddle-headed old beast! You're killing me, and my father'll imprison you for life for it. I wish they could hang you. I'll make you smart for this, if you only live till I grow up—devil!"

But the Doctor had shot his bolt. He gave Tomlin a final smack, then shook him off like a spider, picked up his mortar-board, which had fallen off in the struggle, and put the birch in its place.

"Now go, and don't speak another word, or I shall expel you, wretched lad!"

Meantime Slade and I were fairly on the gasp, for from the time that Tomlin, as we thought, had called the Doctor a devil we realized the truth. Now his passion nearly choked him; he danced with pain and rage; only when the Doctor took a stride towards him he opened the door and hooked it.

The Doctor puffed and grunted like a traction-engine trying to get up a hill.

"These are the black days in a headmaster's life, Slade," he said. "That misguided lad thinks that I enjoyed administering his punishment, yet both mentally and physically the operation caused me far greater suffering than it brought to him. I am wounded—wounded to the heart, and the exertion causes and will cause me much discomfort for hours to come, owing to its unusual severity. I may say that not for ten years has it been necessary for me to flog a boy as I have just flogged George Tomlin. Now let us proceed."

I couldn't have broken it to him, but Slade did. He said :—

"Please, sir, it wasn't Tomlin."

"Not Tomlin—not Tomlin! What d'you mean, boy? Who was it, then?" said the Doctor, his eyebrows going up on to his forehead, which was all quite dewy from the hard work.

"It was young Carlo—I mean Westonleigh," said Slade.

"Viscount Westonleigh!" gasped the Doctor, his mouth dropping right open in

a very rum way by itself, if you understand me.

"Yes, sir."

"Then why in the name of heaven
didn't you say so? How *dare* you stand
there and watch me commit an offence
against law and justice? How did you dare
to watch me ignorantly torture an innocent
boy, and that boy—— Go! go both of you
—you, Slade, and you, Butler, also. Go
instantly, and send Browne and Viscount
Westonleigh to me. Good God! this is
terrible—terrible!"

So that was his howler, and to see him
in his chair looking so old and haggard and
queer was rather frightful. He seemed
suddenly struck with limpness, and his hands
shook like anything, and so did his bald
head; and he puffed as if he'd been running miles; and Slade said afterwards that
he looked jolly frightened too. He put
his face in his hands as we went out,
and we heard him say something about
Lord Golightly and ruin, and universal

opprobrium on his grey hairs, though really he had none worth mentioning; and Slade said he almost thought the Doctor was actually going to cry, if such a thing could be possible.

We sent Browne off to him, but Carlo wasn't to be found. He'd been seen yelling somewhere, but couldn't be traced. What had happened was this: Tomlin, in obedience to Steggles, had kept rather close after prayers; in fact, he had spent the half-hour to bed-time in a cupboard in the gymnasium, under the rubber shoes. So Browne, not finding him, had told the first boy he saw to do so; and that boy happened to be Steggles, who had been at his heels ever since he went to the Doctor. Steggles is a miserable, unwholesome thing, but his strategy certainly comes off. Once having the message all was easy, because Steggles merely found Carlo, and told him the Doctor wanted him. The result was much better than even Steggles hoped; because, though the Doctor generally fell on a chap

P

who came to be flogged straight away, like he did on Carlo, it wasn't often anybody got such a frightful strong dose as Carlo had. Afterwards, when taxed, Steggles swore, of course, that he thought he was talking to Tomlin. Seeing the likeness, this might have been perfectly true, though in their secret hearts everybody knew Steggles too jolly well to really believe it.

Carlo didn't turn up, and after an hour or more of frantic rushing about, somebody said perhaps he'd jumped down the garden well owing to the indignity of what he'd got. But soon afterwards, in reply to a special telegram sent for the Doctor by the people at the railway station, an answer came from Golightly Towers, twenty miles off, where the purple-veined lord, father of Carlo, hung out. The kid, it seemed, had sloped down to Merivale railway station after his licking, and taken a ticket right away for Golightly, and gone home by the last train but one that night. He never returned either, but next day his father dropped in on Doctor Dunston, and Fowle managed to hear a little of what went on through the keyhole. He said that as far as he could make out the lord didn't think much of the matter, and said one thrashing more or less wouldn't mar Carlo. But the lord's wife, who didn't come, evidently took the same view as Carlo, for he never returned to Dunston's again. The Doctor's howler ended in his losing the little bounder altogether, which, with his views about lords in general, and especially earls, must have been frightfully rough on him.

As to Tomlin, actually the Doctor never flogged him after all! I think his spirit had got a bit broken, and though Tomlin went at the end of the term, he wasn't expelled, but withdrawn by mutual consent, like you hear of things in Parliament sometimes. He wouldn't have gone at all, but he refused to say who was under the medlar tree with him, and stuck to it; and Steggles absolutely declined to give himself up, because, as he truly said, he had more than kept his promise to Tomlin about helping him out of the mess.

So Tomlin went. He was a very decent little chap indeed, and nearly all the fellows at Dunston's promised faithfully to buy their hats entirely at his place in Bond Street, London, when they left school; which will be very good business for him if they do. As for the Doctor, it's a peculiar fact that for a whole term after Carlo's affair he never flogged a single chap. He didn't seem to have any heart in him, somehow, owing to the rum way the howler told upon his spirit.

MORRANT'S HALF-SOV.

O F course, as Steggles said truly, the rummest thing about the whole story of Morrant's half-sov. was that he should have one. Morrant, in fact, never got any pocket-money in his life, owing to his father being a gentleman farmer. Not that he had nothing. On the contrary, his hampers were certainly the best, except Fowle's, that ever came to Dunston's, both for variety and size and fruit. The farming business, Morrant said, was all right from his point of view in the holidays, as the ferreting, both rats and rabbits, was good enough for anything, and three packs of hounds met within walking distance of his farm, one pack being harriers, which Morrant, by knowing the country well, could run with to a certain extent while they hunted. But Morrant's father was so worried about chemical manures and other farming things, including the price of wheat, that he didn't see his way to giving Morrant any pocket-money. He explained to Morrant once that he was putting every halfpenny he could spare into Morrant's education, so as to save him from having to become a gentleman farmer too when he grew up.

But Morrant didn't get a farthing in a general way; so when there arrived a hamper with an envelope in it, and in the envelope a bit of paper, and in the paper a half-sovereign, Morrant was naturally extremely surprised and also pleased. It came from his godfather, who had never taken any notice of Morrant for thirteen years, though he was a clergyman. But the previous term Morrant had got a prize for Scripture history, and when that came to his godfather's ears, through Morrant's mother mentioning it in a letter, he wrote and said it was good news, and very unexpected. So he sent the money; and really Morrant was quite bewildered with it, being so utterly unaccustomed to tin even in the meanest shape.

He had a friend by the name of Ferrars, who was much more religious than Morrant himself, and knew even more Scripture history; and as a first go-off he asked Ferrars what he ought to do with the money. And Ferrars said that before everything Morrant ought to give a tithe to charity. But when it was explained to Morrant that this meant chucking away a shilling on the poor he didn't take to the idea an atom. He said his father had set him against giving tithes, not believing in them very much.

So Morrant went to Gideon, who knew much more about money than Ferrars, and he said he mustn't dream of giving a penny away in charity, because Morrant wasn't up in the subject, and might do more harm than good. He also said that in the case of a chap who had never had a half-sovereign in his life before, it was a great question whether he could be expected to give away any; and

Morrant said there was no question about it at all, because he wasn't going to. And it made even a difference in his feeling towards Ferrars, for, as he very truly said, a chap who advised him like Ferrars had couldn't be much of a friend.

Having decided to keep it, the point was what to do with it. The novelty of the thing staggered him, and, knowing he would probably never have another half-sovereign till he grew up, Morrant felt the awful importance of spending it right, because an affair once bought could never be replaced if lost. And, as Bray said, " If you get used to a thing, like a watch-chain or a tie-ring, and then lose it, the feeling you get is much worse than if you had never had it at all."

I thought about it too for Morrant, as he once sent me a brace of rabbits by post, shot by himself in the holidays. I pointed out to him that half a sovereign was a most difficult sum really, being, as it were, not small and not exactly huge, and yet too

much to make light of, especially in
Morrant's case. If he had got a sovereign,
for instance, he might have bought a silver
watch-chain to take the place of one which
he had. It was made of the hair of his
grandmother when she was young, and
Morrant didn't much like it, and had often
tried to sell it and failed. But ten bob
wouldn't buy a silver chain worth having.
Morrant had an idea about braces, and of
course he might have bought such braces
for the money as would have been seldom
seen and very remarkable; but braces
are a poor thing to put good money into,
and I dissuaded him.

There came a change in Morrant after
he had had the half-sovereign for four days
and not thought of anything to buy. He
began to worry, because time was going on
and nothing being done. Fellows gave him
many ideas, some of which he took for an
hour or two, but always abandoned after a
while. Murray told him of a wonderful box
of new conjuring tricks which was to be

had, and he nearly bought it, but luckily remembered just in time that the new tricks would get old after a while, and some might be guessed and would become useless. Then Parkinson had a remarkably swagger paint-box, and knew where Morrant could get another with only three paints less for ten shillings. And Morrant as near as a toucher bought that, but happened to remember he couldn't paint, and didn't care in the least about trying to. Corkey minimus said he would run the risk and sell Corkey minor's bat to Morrant for ten bob, the bat having cost twelve. The bat was spliced and Corkey minor was in Australia, having, luckily for him, sailed to sea just before an exam., owing to a weak lung. If Morrant had played cricket he would certainly have bought the bat; but there again, even though Gideon told him he might easily get ten-and-six or eleven shillings for the bat next term, he hesitated, and finally Gideon bought the bat himself —as an investment, he said.

Well, there was Morrant stuck with his tin. He wouldn't even change it, because Gideon warned him against that, and told him his father knew men who had made large fortunes simply by not changing gold when they had it. Gideon said there was nothing like never changing gold; so Morrant didn't, only of course there was no good in keeping the money specially stitched into a private and unknown part of his trousers, as he did, for safety.

That half-sovereign acted like a regular cloud on Morrant's mind; and then came an extraordinary day when it acted more like a cloud than ever, owing to its disappearing.

Morrant had sewn it, with a needle and thread borrowed from the housekeeper, into a spot at the bottom of his left trouser pocket, and from this spot it mysteriously vanished in the space of two hours. He had changed in the dormitory for "footer," and left his trousers on his bed at three o'clock, returning to them at five o'clock.

Then, naturally feeling for his half-sovereign, he missed it altogether, and when he examined the spot he found his money had been cut out of the bottom of the pocket with a knife.

Very wisely Morrant, seeing what a tremendous thing had happened, did not make a lot of row, but just told about ten chaps and no more. I was one. My name is Newnes. I said :—

"The first question is, Who knew your secret hiding-place?" and Butler said it was a very good question and showed sense in me. Butler is, of course, high in the Sixth.

Morrant, on thinking it over, decided that three chaps, or four at the outside, knew his hiding-place. They were Ferrars, Gideon, Fowle, and, Morrant thought, Phipps. So first Butler, who very kindly undertook the affair for Morrant, had Phipps brought up. Phipps stammers even when most calm and collected, and being sent for by Butler caused him so much excitement, that Butler

made him write down the answers to his
questions, and even then Phipps lost his
nerve so that he spelled "yes" with two s's.
But he solemnly put down and signed that
Morrant had never told him where he kept
his half-sovereign; and after he had gone
Morrant said that, now he came to think
about it, he felt sure Phipps was right.
Which reduced the matter to Ferrars,
Gideon, and Fowle; and the first two were
set aside by Morrant because Ferrars was,
of course, his personal friend, despite the
passing coldness about Ferrars' advice, and
Gideon, though very keen about money and
a great judge of it, was known to be absolutely straight, and had never so much as
choused a kid out of a marble.

Butler said :—

"That leaves Fowle; and if you told
Fowle you were a little fool."

And Morrant said.:—

"We were both Roman Catholics by
religion, and that makes a great tie; and
though many chaps hate Fowle pretty

frightfully, I've never known him try to score off me, except once, when he failed and apologised."

And Butler said :—

"That's all right, I daresay; but he's a little beast and a cur, and also a sneak of the deadliest dye. I don't say he's taken the money, because that's a libel, and he might, I believe, go to law against me; but I do say that only one out of three people could have taken it, and we know two didn't, therefore Q.E.D. the other must have."

Morrant didn't follow this very clever reasoning on the part of Butler. He only thought that Fowle, being a Roman Catholic, would never rob another; and Butler said he would, because it wasn't like Freemasons, who wouldn't score off one another for the world. He explained that history was simply choked up with examples of Roman Catholics scoring off one another.

Butler said :—

"Religion's quite different. One Buddhist is often known to have done another Buddhist in the eye, so why shouldn't one Roman do another? In fact, they have thousands of times, as you'll know when you come to read a little history and hear about the Spanish Inquisition. Especially this may have happened seeing that Fowle is the chap. I tell you candidly that, in my opinion, after a good deal of experience of fellows in general, I take Fowle to be the most likely boy in Merivale to have done it; and knowing him to have had the secret of the private pocket reduces it to a certainty to my mind. Tax him with it suddenly in the night, and you'll see."

Morrant slept in the same dormitory with Fowle, and that night the whole room was woke up at some very late hour by the sound of Morrant taxing Fowle. Fowle took a long time to realise what was being said, and when he was awake enough to understand what Morrant was getting at, he showed tremendous indignation, and asked what he had ever done that such a charge should be brought against him, especially at such a time. He reminded Morrant that they were of the same way of thinking in holy affairs, and said he was extremely sick with Morrant, and thought Morrant's religion must be pretty rocky if it allowed him to wake a chap up in the night and charge him with such a crime. In fact, Fowle went on so that Morrant finally apologised rather humbly.

From that day forward began the extraordinary disappearance of coin in general at Dunston's. Shillings constantly went, and also half-crowns. Gideon got very excited about it, and said watches must be kept and traps set. There was evidently a big robbery going on, and Gideon said if the chaps weren't smart enough to catch the thief they deserved to lose their tin. Certainly he never lost a penny himself. But, despite tremendous precautions, money kept going in small sums. Ferrars was set to watch in the pavilion, I remember, during a football match, and Morrant himself, and even Butler once or twice, also watched.

Some chaps thought it was the ground-man; but as money also disappeared at school, that showed it couldn't be him. And then there was a theory that it might be a char-woman who came from Merivale twice a week. I believe she was a very good char-woman of her kind, and Ferrars, who is great about helping the poor and so on, told me she was a very deserving woman with a husband at home who drank, and children too numerous to mention. Which Gideon remembered against the charwoman when the money began to go, and it turned his suspicion towards her, because, as he said, with the state of her home affairs, money must be a great temptation. So a watch was set on her, and a curious thing happened.

Being small, I can get into a boot cupboard very easily, and I can also breathe anywhere through a hole bored with a gimlet. This was done to the door of the boot cupboard, and two other rather larger holes were also made for my eyes. Mrs.

Q

Gouger, which was the charwoman's name, had to do a lot of work in this room—a large one leading out of the gym. And there, on a certain half-holiday, I was watching her.

She worked jolly hard as far as I could say, and made a good deal of dust, and a curious noise through her teeth when she scrubbed, which I thought only men did when they washed horses; but there was nothing suspicious, if you understand me. She didn't touch a coat or anything, though many were hanging against a wall; and the few caps about she merely picked up and hung on the pegs.

Then, just before she finished, who should come in but Ferrars, and, to my great astonishment, Mrs. Gouger curtseyed to him as though he had been the housekeeper or the Doctor.

Ferrars treated her with great loftiness, and evidently knew all about her private affairs.

He said :—

"And how is the child that's got mumps?" and she said it was better. He then gave her some advice about her husband, which I didn't hear, and she blessed him for all his goodness to her, and said God had sent him to a lone, struggling woman, and that he would reap a thousand-fold what he had sown. All of which, coming from Mrs. Gouger to Ferrars, seemed very curious to me. Presently he · said :—

"Well, I cannot stop longer. I'm glad the child is better. Keep on at your husband about the pledge; and here's a shilling."

Then Mrs. Gouger put the shilling in her pocket and blessed him again. And Ferrars went.

That very day young Forrest lost a shilling out of his desk, which doesn't lock owing to Forrest having taken the lock off to sell to Meadowes last term.

I told Butler and Gideon what I had seen, and Butler thought it rum, and

Gideon said there was more in it than met the eye.

Butler said :—

"Evidently the kid" (Ferrars is a kid from Butler's point of view) "has given the charwoman tin before, or else she wouldn't have blessed him. Now the question is, How much pocket-money does Ferrars get?"

And I said :—

"A shilling a week."

"When does he get it?"

"Mondays."

Butler said, "Ah!" but nothing seemed to strike him, and Gideon thought that Mrs. Gouger ought to be spoken to. This Gideon undertook to do ; and the next week he did. What happened was that Mrs. Gouger said all that she had before said to Ferrars about her husband and children, but added that a young gentleman with a most Christian heart had lately interested himself in her misfortunes. Gideon asked if it was a Dunston chap, and Mrs. Gouger answered that she was not at liberty to say. She seemed rather defiant about it, Gideon thought, and, in fact, when he pressed her for the amount the chap gave her, she told Gideon to mind his own business. A watch was still kept, especially on Ferrars; and once Butler did an awfully cunning thing by setting Ferrars to watch and setting another chap to watch Ferrars, if you follow what I mean. The other chap was Butler himself, and the room was a dormitory. But it came out rather awkwardly for Butler, because he sneezed at the very start, and Ferrars got out from under the bed where he had arranged to watch, and found Butler watching behind a coat against the wall. Then they had a row, because Ferrars evidently thought Butler was there to watch him; which he was.

The end of the affair came out rather tame in its way, and only shows what awfully peculiar ideas some chaps have. Gideon finally spoke to Slade, the head of the school, and though Slade doesn't like

Gideon, owing to his way of making money by usury, yet it was such a serious affair that he listened all through and promised to go to the Doctor. Gideon had actually kept an account of all the money stolen, and it amounted now to the tremendous sum of four pounds five shillings and sixpence, including Morrant's half-sovereign.

Then, after Dr. Dunston knew, we heard one day from Fowle that he had sent for Mrs. Gouger to his study, and that she had been there fully half an hour and come out crying. Fowle had listened as best he could till the Doctor's butler had come by and told him to hook it; but he had heard nothing except one remark in the voice of Mrs. Gouger, and that remark was, "Four pound five and sixpence, sir, and a godsend if ever money was."

Gideon said her mentioning of the exact sum was a very ominous thing for Ferrars. And what was more ominous still happened that evening, for Ferrars wasn't at prep. or prayers.

There were a number of ideas about as to what it all meant, and Corkey minimus, who always tries to get among chaps bigger than himself and say clever things, came out with a theory that Mrs. Gouger was Ferrars' mother, and that Ferrars was therefore stealing and making the money over to her. But Butler merely smacked his head when he heard it, and told Corkey minimus not to be a little ass.

Gideon was the only chap who hadn't any idea. He knew Ferrars' great notions about helping the poor and giving tithes to parsons, and so on, but he said for a chap to steal money and hand it over to a charwoman in charity was contrary to human nature. All the same, if a thing actually happens, it can't be contrary to human nature. Anyway, after prayers next morning the Doctor stopped the school in chapel and explained everything.

He said:—

"My boys, while it is true that you come to Merivale to be instructed by me and those who labour here amongst you on my behalf, it is also true that I learn occasionally from those whom I teach. Indeed, new problems are almost as often set by you for my solution as by me for yours, and seldom has a more intricate difficulty confronted me than that which yesterday challenged my attention. There has recently happened amongst us a mysterious disappearance of coins of the realm. Now a shilling, a sixpence, a penny-piece, if deposited in one spot, will usually remain there until removed by human agency. And the human agent who removes money which belongs to another without that other's sanction is a thief. Boys, briefly there has been a thief amongst you—a thief whose moral obliquity has taken such an extraordinary turn, whose views of rectitude have become so distorted, that even my own experience of schoolboy ethics cannot parallel his performance. This lad has looked around him upon the world, and found in it, as we all must find, a vast amount of

suffering and privation, of honest toil and
of humble heroism, displayed by the lowest
amongst us. He has also observed that
Providence is pleased to make wide dis-
tinctions between the rich and the poor; he
has noted that where one labours for daily
bread another reaps golden harvests without
the trouble of putting in the sickle. This
extraordinary boy contrasted the position
of one of these humble workers with that
of those amongst whom his own lot was
thrown here, and he found that whereas that
obscure but necessary and excellent person,
Mrs. Gouger, she whose duty it is to
cleanse, scour, and otherwise purify the disorder produced by our assemblies—he found,
I say, that whereas Mrs. Gouger worked
extremely hard for sums not considerable,
albeit handsome in connection with the
nature of her labours, others of the human
family — yourselves — were in receipt of
weekly allowances of varying amounts for
which you toiled not, neither did you
spin.

"This unhappy lad allowed his mind to brood on the apparent injustice of such an arrangement, and instead of coming to his headmaster for an explanation of this and other problems which arose to puzzle his immature intelligence, permitted himself the immoral, the scandalous, the disgraceful and horribly mistaken course of righting the balance from his point of view. This could only be effected by defiance of those divine laws which govern all properly constituted bodies of human society. Ferrars—I need not conceal his name any longer—Ferrars broke one commandment in order to obey another. His fatuous argument, as it was elaborated yesterday to me, stands based on error; his crime was the result of the most complicated ignorance and vicious sophism it has ever been my lot to discover in a boy of twelve. He did evil that good might come. Ascertaining from the inspired Word that 'charity covereth a multitude of sins,' he imagined it must extend to cover that forbidden by the Eighth Commandment.

This commandment he broke no less than fourteen times. You ask with horror why. That the domestic affairs of Mrs. Gouger might be ameliorated. He took the pocket-money of his colleagues, and with it modified those straits into which poverty and conjugal difficulties have long cast Mrs. Gouger. It was Ferrars' unhappy, and I may say un-paralleled, design to go on appropriating the money of his schoolmates until a sum of five pounds had been raised and conveyed to Mrs. Gouger. Of this total, with deplorable ingenuity, he had already subtracted from various pockets the sum of four pounds five shillings and sixpence; it was his intention to continue these depredations until the entire sum had been collected. But the end has come. The facts have been placed before me, and I confess to you that perhaps never have I been confronted with a problem more peculiar. After a lengthy conversation with those who support me here, and after placing the proposition before a higher tribunal than any which earth has to offer,

I have come to a curious decision. I have determined to leave the fate of the boy Ferrars in your hands. This time to-morrow I shall expect Slade, as representing the school, to inform me of your decision, and to-day, contrary to custom, will be a half-holiday, that the school may debate the question and conclude upon it. I would point out that there is no middle course here, in my opinion. Either Ferrars must be forgiven after a public apology to the establishment he has outraged, or he must be expelled. As for the money, if those who have lost it will apply to me between one and two o'clock to-day, each shall have his share again."

Well, you may guess what a jaw there was that afternoon; and finally, after hours of talk, Slade decided the point must be arranged by putting papers into a hat. If you drew a cross on the paper it meant that you wanted Ferrars to be expelled; and if you drew a nought, that meant he was to be let off. You were not bound to say how you voted, and the excitement when the votes were counted was something frightful. Ferrars little knew what was going on.

At last the numbers were read out :—

For expulsion . . 124
Against expulsion . . 101

And Slade and Bradwell were mad when Slade read them, and said that Merivale was disgraced. But Gideon and Butler and Ashby major and Trelawny said not, and thought it wasn't a case for anything but justice. The Doctor made no remark when he heard what had happened, but I heard him tell the new master, Thompson, a day afterwards that perhaps the Lower School ought not to have been allowed to vote, as small boys would merely have understood that Ferrars had stolen money and nothing else. Their minds, the Doctor said, were not big enough to take in the peculiar nature of the case. But Thompson said he honestly believed the school was perfectly right, and that the subtleties of the case were not for that court; and the Doctor sighed and said it might be so.

Anyway, Ferrars went. We never saw him again, and the only cheerful thing about the end of it was that Steggles was badly scored off. You see he nipped off to the Doctor among the first, and said Ferrars had stolen ten shillings from him too. But it happened that Ferrars had kept the most careful account of all the money he had raised for Mrs. Gouger and the people he had raised it from. But he had never taken a farthing from Steggles. So Steggles was flogged by Mannering in his best form; which shows that things which are frightfully sad in themselves often produce fine results in a roundabout sort of manner.

OF corse even a kid can get a good idea sometimes, and Maine, who I was fagging for, said afterwards that the idea was alright. Whether young Bailey or me thort of it first I don't know, but Maine lent me a book about coarseers and buckeneers and such-like people, and he said it was a great life, though not much followed in present times. He was no good for a coarseer himself, becorse the sea always made him dredfully bad, and, besides, he was going to be a bushranger some day, being an Australian and well up in it. But he said that Drake and Raleigh and many other men in our English history were buckeneers of the dedliest sort and had made England what it was ; so me and Bailey thort a lot about it and wished a good deal we could begin that sort of life. Bailey said that in the books he'd read, if a boy began young, he was genrally a super-cargo and went on getting grater and grater slowly; but I thort boys began as cabin-boys and got grater very quickly by resquing people. But Bailey said that was only in books, and that nobody got on quickly at sea owing to the compettitishun. He did not much think there were any buckeneers left, but Maine said there were, cheefly off the coast of Africa, and that daring and dedly deeds were done in the Mediterranan to this day. He said the lawlessness there was awful, and that nobodi knew what went on along the north side of Africa in little bays and inletts there not marked on maps.

When Bailey herd that, he took more interest in it and wished he had been born the son of a pirit insted of a doctor, because he said we should have come eesily to it if our fathers had been in that corse of life; but when I told Maine, he sed that the best and most splendid pirits had had to overcome grate dificultees in their youth, and that it was the pirit who began as a meer boy at school who often made the gratest name.

Bailey sed he was a pirit at heart, and I sed I was to; but not untell we red a butiful book by Stevenson could we see any way to be one reelly. Then we saw that we must go away from Merivale in secret—in fact, we must fly; and Bailey sed it would have to be by night to avoid capture, and Maine sed "Yes." But it was a tremendous thing to do, and I asked Bailey about his mother, and Bailey sed his mother would blub a good deal at first, but she would live to be proud of him when his name was wringing through England. And I felt the same in a way, becorse, though I have got no mother to blub, I have got an uncle, who is my gardian, and he is a lawer and a Conservitive who has tried to get into Parleyment and failed.

Then me and Bailey talked it out when chaps were asleep in our dormitory, and the thing was what we should reelly and truly

R

be, becorse there were coarseers and buckeneers and pirits, and they all had their own
pekuliar ways. So we asked Maine which
was best, and he sed "buckeneers." He
didn't seem to know exacktly what a coarseer was; but he told us all about pirits, and
he sed they kill womin and childrin, and
Bailey said he'd rather be a docter, like his
father, than do that, and I said the same.
But a buckeneer is very diferent, being like
Raleigh and Drake; and a buckeneer may
have his name wringing through England,
but a pirit never has, being rather a beast
reelly. Maine sed it was like this: a pirit
always thinks of himself, and nobody else;
but the best sort of buckeneer thinks of
himself, of corse, but thinks of his country
to; and after he has replennished his coffers
he makes his soverein a present of islands,
and so on, which are gennerally called after
him, so that his name may never be for-
gottun. And Bailey sed that was the sort
he wanted to be, and I sed so to.

We thanked Maine a good deal, and he

sed it was a big idea for such kids as us to get, and hoped we were made of the right stuff, and promised not to say a word to a soul. And we finally desided to try it, and Bailey sed we must have a plan of ackshun; so we made one.

He said we must run away and work gradully by night to the coast and go to Plymouth, and get into the docks, and find a ship bound for the north coste of Africa. I asked him what next, and he sed, very truly, that that was enuff to begin with, and that by the time we had done that much manny adventures would have fallen to our lot, and we might alredy be in the way to become buckeneers. And I sed I hoped we should make freends at sea; but he sed the fewer freends we made the better buckeneers we should probbably be, because it is not a life where you can make freends safely. In fact, no reel buckeneer would trust his own brother a yard. And I sed that we must trust one annuther at any rate. And Bailey sed, as far as that

went, he supposed we must; but he sed
it relluctantly.

The thing was then to save up for the
diferent weppons. Maine sed we shouldn't
want arms, and that money was all we
should require till we got down south; but
Bailey felt sure we must at leest have
pistells, becorse in books the man armed
to the teath is never mollested if people
know, but the unarmed man often looses
his life for want of a weppon. We had
one shilling pocket money a week each,
and Bailey getting a birthday, very fortunately, made a whole pound by it after
we had been saving for three weeks. So
between us we suddinly had one pound
six shillings, and Bailey sed it was share
and share alike for the present, and always
would be unless some dedly hatred sprang
up between us. And I sed it never would;
but he sed it might, and if it did, it would
probabbly be about a girl if books were
true. And I larfed, becorse we both have
a grate contemp for all girls.

Well, things went alright, and on a
half-holiday we managed to get to Merivale
and buy pistells. They were five shillings
and sixpence each, and the man didn't seem
to much like selling them; but we got them,
and amunition—fifty rounds each. And
Bailey sed that would be enough. Maine
sed they were very good pistells for close
work, but advised us never to use them
unless in soar straights. And we sed we
wouldn't.

It was the day of the menaggeree at
Merivale that me and Bailey finally took
the grate step of going. We had collected
a lot of food, and studdièd geography so
as to get to Plymouth, and we arranged
that we should travel by night and hide
by day in the hart of impennetrable woods,
which we did. After the menaggeree, at
a certain point on the way home, we hooked
it round a corner, and Thompson didn't
see us, and in a breef time we were at the
edge of Merivale Woods, free.

"To-night," Bailey sed, "we will get

across this forest and do eight or ten miles along the high-road, and so reach Oakshott Woods at dawn. They are on the edge of the moor and quite impennetrable."

So we got well into Merivale Woods first and made a lair of braken under a fir-tree. And we cut off some of the fir-tree bark and licked the sap, which is very nourishing and feeding, because we wanted to save our food as much as possible. But we had each a cold sorsage and a drink of water. And then night came on, and I felt, for the first time, that we had done a tremendous deed.

"We're fairly started," I sed to Bailey. "It's just call over at Merivale now."

And he sed, "Yes; if the fellows in the Upper Third could only see us!"

I sed, "It's a small begenning."

And he sed, "It is; but if things go rite, and we are made of the propper stuff for buckeneers, we'll make England wring yet."

Then it began to rain rather hard, and

I found that a wood isn't really a dry place by night if it rains, and Bailey lighted a match, and sed it was nearly nine.

"That'll mean 'lights out' at Merivale," he sed; "but for us it'll mean the begenning of the night."

I sneazed just about then, becorse water from the fir-tree was dropping down my neck rather fast, and Bailey sed if I was going to get annything the matter with me I had better go back at once, becorse no buckeneer ever had a cold, being men of steel and iron. And I sed a sneaze was nothing.

Then we started very corsiously through the wood, and Bailey cocked his pistell, and I asked him kindly to walk in front, feeling a curious sensashun when he walked behind me with his pistell cocked. I told him, and he sed it was fear, but I sed it was kaution.

Sometimes he wispered, "Cave!" and we sunk down and got fritefully dripping in the wet, but nothing happened, and we were getting well on through the wood when

Bailey sed, "Cave!" again, and this time, when we had sunk down, we distinkly herd a footstep, and Bailey sed it was our first adventure, and I sed I wished it had come by daylight, becorse it wants grate practise to face adventures in the dark at first.

Anyway the noise got nearer and got louder, and Bailey and me both cocked our pistells, and he sed, "Reserve your fire to close range," and I sed, "Yes." Then he sed, "I see the thing. It's bigger than a beast you would expect in an English wood"; and I sed, "I have got a sort of fealing it is something out of the menaggerie"; and he sed, "Then it will be a real adventure, and I wish we were up trees."

But it was to late, and something went quite close. I sore a red spark, and Bailey sed, "Fire!" which we did. At leest my pistell went off with fereful effect; but Bailey's didn't, and he sed afterwards that he'd make the pistell man biterly rew the day he sold him a treecherous weppon.

But after I fired we herd a human voice, and it sed, "Hell!" Then it sed other fearful words, which Bailey sed we ought to remember because they were buckeneering words curiously enuff. And then the man dashed towards us, which showed I had not slain him, or even hit him in a vittle spot; and we fled, and soon we found that we had distanced him, though we had a squeek for it.

"He was a keeper," sed Bailey, "and he will think we were poachers, and raise a hew-and-cry. We must keep on and get into Oakshott Woods, or we shall very likely have to yield to supereer force."

After this eksitement I got a curious feeling in my stomach, and telling Bailey, he sed it was either hunger or fear. And I sed it was hunger; but Bailey sed, seeing what a hevy meal we had made with sorsage and bred and turpentine juice only two hours before, that it was fear.

I sed if he thought so he'd better go on without me, as I hadn't taken to this

corse of life to be cheeked by him. And
he sed he was leeder of the gang, and I
was the gang, and the first thing was to
lern to obey orders. And then I got
rather waxy with Bailey, and asked him
who he thort he was to give me orders,
and reminded him my pistell could go off
anyway, which was more than his could.
This worried him a good deal, becorse,
of course, the man whose pistell went off
had the best of it. Then he sed that it
was no use having a quarrel between
ourselves while we were not yet out of
danger. He also sed that he beleeved we
might venture to take one hour's sleep to
strengthen us before getting on to Oakshott, and I sed, "Yes," but thought that
one of us ought to watch while the other
slept. Bailey sed he would watch first,
and he sed also that we might get to the
woodman's hut in the middle of Merivale
Woods if we kept on past a ded fir-tree
with its stem white, becorse all the bark
was off, which we did, becorse the moon

was now shining very britely, and the rain had stopped. The cold was also friteful, and my teath chattered once or twice, but I broke sticks and things to attract Bailey, becorse if he had herd my teath he would have sed it was fear again.

Once a bough jumped back and hit Bailey a friteful smack in the face, and I was glad, and he sed he rather thort his eye was done for; and he sed it didn't much matter if it was, so long as he had one good eye to see with, becorse most buckeneers lost an eye sooner or later, though generally with a stroak from a cutlass.

We found the hut, and there was some dry fern in it, and we lighted a candle-end we had, and took off our boots, and wrung out our socks, and each had half a currant dumpling. Then Bailey looked at his watch and sed I might turn in for half an hour. Then he would wake me and turn in for half an hour himself. He went on gard with another candle-end, and advised me to draw my pistell and sleep with it cocked under my head. But I sed I never herd of such a dangerous thing as that being done, and kept my pistell reddy cocked near my hand. I didn't fall off to sleep, as I expected, owing to anxiaty as to our fate, but I shut my eyes and thort a good deal, and after my eyes had been shut some time I opened one a little and was grately surprised to see Bailey coming towards me steelthily. He had his pistell in his hand, and first I had a horrible thort he wanted to kill me, so that he mite have all our food and money; and then I felt sure he was coming to change pistells, so that he might have the one that went off. This made me get in a friteful wax with him, becorse I saw he was very unreliable and not reely as much of a chum as I had thort. So I waited untill I saw him stretch out his hand for my pistell, and then I leapt at his throat in a very ferocious way, that much surprized him. I also sed, "Hell!" like the keeper had.

It must have been a solumn site by the lite of the candle-end when we began to fight tooth-and-nail for the pistell which could go off. We were both desperet, and it was reelly a battle to deside which should be the leeder of the enterprise and which should be merely the gang. Then, while we wresled and straned every nerve, a curious thing happened, for we fell against the candle-end, stuck on the top of a stick, and the candle-end fell against the side of the hut, and the hut, being made of wood, with walls of dried heather, was very inflameable and cort fire almost immedeetely.

And then Bailey sed we must aggree to settle our dispute later on and fly at once. So we each took our own pistell, and were just going to leave the scene, when, to our grate horror, we herd voices, and among them the voices of Browne and Mainwaring, who were, of corse, house-masters at Merivale.

Exhorsted though we were, me and Bailey made a terrible effort to eskape, and I think we mite have done so even then, but, oweing to the moon and two other men who were with Mainwaring, we could not reach an impennetrable part of the wood, and finally Mainwaring cort me, and a man cort Bailey, and they dragged us into the lite of the blazing ruins of the hut, and we found out that Browne ' and Mainwaring had come after us, like beestly bloodhounds, and had met the keeper, who told them he had been fired upon, and then the unfortunate burning of the hut had directed their steps towards us. And it's a lesson in a way, showing what risks it is for buckeneers to fall out among themselves at kritikal moments.

Of corse we had to walk back merely as prisoners of Mainwaring, but Bailey told me not to answer questions and rather let them cut our tongues out than know the truth. So they didn't get anything out of us, but when we got back, at two o'clock in the morning, Dunston was up to meet us; and by that time, what with cold and bruises and the failure of the skeem, I wasn't equal to defying Dunston, and merely sed we wanted to change our corse of life for something diferent, and had started to do so. And I also sed that burning the hut was an axsident which might have happened to anybody. And Bailey sed the same.

Then Doctor Dunston sent for the matron, and we had brandy-and-water and a hot bath, which was very refreshing to me, but Bailey sed biterly when he was in it that he had thought that morning never to have had a bath again. He also sed we should be put in sepperate bedrooms that night, and that if either of us got an opportunety to eskape, it was his duty to reskue the other. But I sed I didn't want to eskape, being fritefully sleepy and exhorsted, and I sed that if he eskaped he needn't trubble to reskue me, becorse if I returned again to being a buckeneer it certinnly wouldn't be with him.

I didn't see any more of him until next day; then we were taken in like prisinners of war before the school, and Doctor Dunston lecktured upon us as if we were beests of pray, and he sed that a corse of falty literatuer was to blame for our running away, and sed that the school liberary must be reformed. But he never knew the grate truth, becorse he sed we were onley running away to sea becorse of the fascenation of the ocean to the British karacter, when reely it was to be buckeneers and the terrer of the Mediterranan.

Maine showed us all the points we had done wrong afterwards, and he sed the way we had fought for the best pistell was very interesting to him and a grate warning not to trust in your fellow-creetures. And, after he had lecktured upon us, Doctor Dunston flogged me and Bailey in publick, which showed the stuff we were made of, becorse, though Bailey gets very red when flogged, he has never been knone to shedd a tear; and I get very white, curiously enuff; but I have never been knone to shedd a tear either.

THE END

William Brendon & Son, Printers, Plymouth.

A CATALOGUE OF BOOKS AND ANNOUNCEMENTS OF METHUEN AND COMPANY PUBLISHERS : LONDON 36 ESSEX STREET W.C.

CONTENTS

NOVEMBER 1899

MESSRS. METHUEN'S
ANNOUNCEMENTS

Travel and Adventure

THE HIGHEST ANDES. By E. A. FITZGERALD. With
Two Maps, 51 Illustrations, 13 of which are Photogravures, and a
Panorama. *Royal 8vo.* 30s. *net.*

Also, a Small Edition on Handmade Paper, limited to 50 Copies,
4to. £5, 5s.

A narrative of the highest climb yet accomplished. The illustrations have been
reproduced with the greatest care, and the book, in addition to its adventurous
interest, contains appendices of great scientific value. It also contains a very
elaborate map, and a panorama.

THROUGH ASIA. By SVEN HEDIN. With 300 Illustrations
from Photographs and Sketches by the Author, and 3 Maps. Second
and cheaper Edition in 16 Fortnightly Parts at 1s. each net; or in
two volumes. *Royal 8vo.* 20s. *net.*

Extracts from reviews of this great book, which *The Times* has called 'one of the
best books of the century,' will be found on p. 15. The present form of issue places
it within the reach of buyers of moderate means.

THE CAROLINE ISLANDS By F. W. CHRISTIAN. With
many Illustrations and Maps. *Demy 8vo.* 12s. 6d. *net.*

This book contains a history and complete description of these islands—their physical
features, fauna, flora; the habits, and religious beliefs of the inhabitants. It is
the result of many years' residence among the natives, and is the only worthy work
on the subject.

THREE YEARS IN SAVAGE AFRICA. By LIONEL DECLE.
With 100 Illustrations and 5 Maps. Cheaper Edition. *Demy 8vo.*
10s. 6d. *net.*

A NEW RIDE TO KHIVA. By R. L. JEFFERSON. With
51 Illustrations. *Crown 8vo.* 6s.

The account of an adventurous ride on a bicycle through Russia and the deserts of
Asia to Khiva.

Poetry

PRESENTATION EDITIONS

BARRACK-ROOM BALLADS. By RUDYARD KIPLING.
60th Thousand. *Crown 8vo. Leather, gilt top,* 6s. *net.*

THE SEVEN SEAS. By RUDYARD KIPLING. 50th Thousand.
Crown 8vo. Leather, gilt top, 6s. *net.*

ENGLISH LYRICS. Selected and arranged by W. E. HENLEY. Second and cheaper Edition. *Crown 8vo.* 3s. 6d.

LYRA FRIVOLA. By A. D. GODLEY, M.A., Fellow of Magdalen College, Oxford. *Pott 8vo.* 2s. 6d.

A little volume of occasional verse, chiefly academic.

The Works of Shakespeare

General Editor, EDWARD DOWDEN, Litt. D.

MESSRS. METHUEN have in preparation an Edition of Shakespeare in single Plays. Each play will be edited with a full Introduction, Textual Notes, and a Commentary at the foot of the page.

The first volume will be:

HAMLET. Edited by EDWARD DOWDEN. *Demy 8vo.* 3s. 6d.

History and Biography

THE LETTERS OF ROBERT LOUIS STEVENSON. Arranged and Edited with Notes by SIDNEY COLVIN. *Demy 8vo.* 2 vols. 25s. net.

These highly important and interesting volumes contain the correspondence of Robert Louis Stevenson from his eighteenth year to almost the last day of his life, selected and edited, with notes and introductions, by Mr. Sidney Colvin, his most intimate friend. The letters are very various in subject and character, being addressed partly to his family and private friends, and partly to such well known living or lately deceased men of letters as Mr. Hamerton, Mr. J. A. Symonds, Mr Henry James, Mr. James Payn, Dr. Conan Doyle, Mr. J. M. Barrie, Mr. Edmund Gosse, Mr. F. Locker-Lampson, Mr. Cosmo Monkhouse, Mr. Andrew Lang, Mr. W. E. Henley, and the Editor himself. They present a vivid and brilliant autobiographical picture of the mind and character of the distinguished author. It was originally intended that a separate volume containing a full narrative and critical Life by the Editor should appear simultaneously with the letters, and form part of the work: but the publication of this has for various reasons been postponed.

THE LIFE AND LETTERS OF SIR JOHN EVERETT MILLAIS, President of the Royal Academy. By his Son, J. G. MILLAIS. With over 300 Illustrations, of which 9 are in photogravure. *Two volumes.* *Royal 8vo.* 32s. net.

An edition limited to 350 copies will also be printed. This will contain 22 of Millais' great paintings reproduced in photogravure, with a case containing an extra set of these Photogravures pulled on India paper. The price of this edition will be £4, 4s. net.

In these two magnificent volumes is contained the authoritative biography of the most distinguished and popular painter of the last half of the century. They contain the story of his extraordinary boyhood, of his early struggles and triumphs, of the founding of the Pre-Raphaelite Brotherhood, now first given to the world in authentic detail, of the painting of most of his famous pictures, of his friendships with many of the most distinguished men of the day in art, letters, and politics, of his home life, and of his sporting tastes. There are a large number of letters to his wife describing the circumstances under which his pictures were painted, letters from Her Majesty the Queen, Lord Beaconsfield, Mr. Gladstone, Mr. Watts, Sir William Harcourt, Lord Rosebery, Lord Leighton, etc., etc. Among them are several illustrated letters from Landseer, Leech, Du Maurier, and Mike Halliday. The last letter that Lord Beaconsfield wrote before his death is reproduced in fac-simile. Mr. Val Prinsep contributes his reminiscences of Millais in a long and most interesting chapter. Not the least attractive and remarkable feature of this book will be the magnificence of its illustrations. No more complete representation of the art of any painter has ever been produced on the same scale. The owners of Sir John Millais' most famous pictures and their copyrights have generously given their consent to their reproduction in his biography, and, in addition to those pictures with which the public is familiar, over two hundred pictures and sketches which have never been reproduced before, and which, in all probability, will never be seen again by the general public, will appear in these pages. The early chapters contain sketches made by Millais at the age of seven. There follow some exquisite drawings made by him during his Pre-Raphaelite period, a large number of sketches and studies made for his great pictures, water colour sketches, pen-and-ink sketches, and drawings, humorous and serious. There are ten portraits of Millais himself, including two by Mr. Watts and Sir Edward Burne Jones. There is a portrait of Dickens, taken after death, and a sketch of D. G. Rossetti. Thus the book will be not only a biography of high interest and an important contribution to the history of English art, but in the best sense of the word, a beautiful picture book.

THE EXPANSION OF EGYPT. A Political and Historical Survey. By A. SILVA WHITE. With four Special Maps. *Demy 8vo.* 15s. *net.*

This is an account of the political situation in Egypt, and an elaborate description of the Anglo-Egyptian Administration. It is a comprehensive treatment of the whole Egyptian problem by one who has studied every detail on the spot.

THE VICAR OF MORWENSTOW. A Biography. By S. BARING GOULD, M.A. A new and revised Edition. With Portrait. *Crown 8vo.* 3s. 6d.

This is a completely new edition of the well known biography of R. S. Hawker.

A CONSTITUTIONAL AND POLITICAL HISTORY OF ROME. By T. M. TAYLOR, M.A., Fellow of Gonville and Caius College, Cambridge, Senior Chancellor's Medallist for Classics, Porson University Scholar, etc., etc. *Crown 8vo.* 7s. 6d.

An account of the origin and growth of the Roman Institutions, and a discussion of the various political movements in Rome from the earliest times to the death of Augustus.

A HISTORY OF THE CHURCH OF CYPRUS. By JOHN HACKETT, M.A. With Maps and Illustrations. *Demy 8vo.* 12s. 6d. *net.*

A work which brings together all that is known on the subject from the introduction of Christianity to the commencement of the British occupation. A separate division deals with the local Latin Church during the period of the Western Supremacy.

BISHOP LATIMER. By A. J. CARLYLE, M.A. *Crown 8vo.* 3s. 6d.   [*Leaders of Religion Series.*

Theology

CHRISTIAN MYSTICISM. The Bampton Lectures for 1899. By W. R. INGE, M.A., Fellow and Tutor of Hertford College, Oxford. *Demy 8vo.* 12*s.* 6*d. net.*

A complete survey of the subject from St. John and St. Paul to modern times, covering the Christian Platonists, Augustine, the Devotional Mystics, the Mediæval Mystics, and the Nature Mystics and Symbolists, including Böhme and Wordsworth.

A BIBLICAL INTRODUCTION. By W. H. BENNETT, M.A., and W. F. ADENEY, M.A. *Crown 8vo.* 7*s.* 6*d.*

This volume furnishes students with the latest results in biblical criticism, arranged methodically. Each book is treated separately as to date, authorship, etc.

ST. PAUL, THE MASTER-BUILDER. By WALTER LOCK, D.D., Warden of Keble College. *Crown 8vo.* 3*s.* 6*d.*

An attempt to popularise the recent additions to our knowledge of St. Paul as a missionary, a statesman and an ethical teacher.

THE OECUMENICAL DOCUMENTS OF THE FAITH. Edited with Introductions and Notes by T. HERBERT BINDLEY, B.D., Merton College, Oxford, Principal of Codrington College and Canon of Barbados, and sometime Examining Chaplain to the Lord Bishop. *Crown 8vo.* 6*s.*

THE CREED OF NICAEA.   THE TOME OF LEO.
THREE EPISTLES OF CYRIL. THE CHALCEDONIAN DEFINITION.

The Churchman's Bible

General Editor, J. H. BURN, B.D., Examining Chaplain to the Bishop of Aberdeen.

Messrs. METHUEN propose to issue a series of expositions upon most of the books of the Bible. The volumes will be practical and devotional rather than critical in their purpose, and the text of the authorised version will be explained in sections or paragraphs, which will correspond as far as possible with the divisions of the Church Lectionary.

THE EPISTLE OF ST. PAUL TO THE GALATIANS. Explained by A. W. ROBINSON, B.D., Vicar of All Hallows, Barking. *Fcap. 8vo.* 1*s.* 6*d. net.* *Leather,* 2*s.* 6*d. net.*

ECCLESIASTES. Explained by W. A. STREANE, M.A. *Fcp. 8vo.* 1*s.* 6*d. net.* *Leather,* 2*s.* 6*d. net.*

The Churchman's Library

Edited by J. H. BURN, B.D.

THE WORKMANSHIP OF THE PRAYER BOOK: Its Literary and Liturgical Aspects. By J. DOWDEN, D.D., Lord Bishop of Edinburgh. *Crown 8vo.* 3*s.* 6*d.*

This volume, avoiding questions of controversy, exhibits the liturgical aims and literary methods of the authors of the Prayer Book.

The Library of Devotion

Pott 8vo.   Cloth 2s.; leather 2s. 6d. net.

NEW VOLUMES.

A SERIOUS CALL TO A DEVOUT AND HOLY LIFE.
By WILLIAM LAW. Edited, with an Introduction by C. BIGG, D.D.,
late Student of Christ Church.

This is a reprint, word for word and line for line, of the *Editio Princeps.*

THE TEMPLE. By GEORGE HERBERT. Edited, with an
Introduction and Notes, by E. C. S. GIBSON, D.D., Vicar of Leeds.

This edition contains Walton's Life of Herbert, and the text is that of the first
edition.

Science

THE SCIENTIFIC STUDY OF SCENERY. By J. E. MARR,
Fellow of St John's College, Cambridge. Illustrated. *Crown 8vo.*
6s.

An elementary treatise on geomorphology—the study of the earth's outward forms.
It is for the use of students of physical geography and geology, and will also be
highly interesting to the general reader.

A HANDBOOK OF NURSING. By M. N. OXFORD, of
Guy's Hospital. *Crown 8vo.* ' *3s. 6d.*

This is a complete guide to the science and art of nursing, containing copious
instruction both general and particular.

Classical

THE NICOMACHEAN ETHICS OF ARISTOTLE. Edited,
with an Introduction and Notes by JOHN BURNET, M.A., Professor
of Greek at St. Andrews. *Demy 8vo.* 15s. *net.*

This edition contains parallel passages from the Eudemian Ethics, printed under the
text, and there is a full commentary, the main object of which is to interpret
difficulties in the light of Aristotle's own rules.

THE CAPTIVI OF PLAUTUS. Edited, with an Introduction,
Textual Notes, and a Commentary, by W. M. LINDSAY, Fellow of
Jesus College, Oxford. *Demy 8vo.* 10s. 6d. *net.*

For this edition all the important MSS. have been re-collated. An appendix deals
with the accentual element in early Latin verse. The Commentary is very full.

ZACHARIAH OF MITYLENE. Translated into English by
F. J. HAMILTON, D.D., and E. W. BROOKS. *Demy 8vo.* 12s. 6d.
net. *[Byzantine Texts.*

Sport.

Tbe Library of Sport

THE ART AND PRACTICE OF HAWKING. By E. B.
MITCHELL. Illustrated by G. E. LODGE and others. *Demy 8vo.*
10s. 6d.

A complete description of the Hawks, Falcons, and Eagles used in ancient and
modern times, with directions for their training and treatment. It is not only a
historical account, but a complete practical guide.

THOUGHTS ON HUNTING. By PETER BECKFORD. Edited
by J. OTHO PAGET, and Illustrated by G. H. JALLAND. *Demy 8vo.*
10s. 6d.

This edition of one of the most famous classics of sport contains an introduction and
many footnotes by Mr. Paget, and is thus brought up to the standard of modern
knowledge.

General Literature

THE BOOK OF THE WEST. By S. BARING GOULD. With
numerous Illustrations. *Two volumes.* Vol. I. Devon. Vol. II.
Cornwall. *Crown 8vo.* 6s. each.

PONS ASINORUM; OR, A GUIDE TO BRIDGE. By
A. HULME BEAMAN. *Fcap. 8vo.* 2s.

A practical guide, with many specimen games, to the new game of Bridge.

TENNYSON AS A RELIGIOUS TEACHER. By CHARLES
F. G. MASTERMAN. *Crown 8vo.* 6s.

Tbe Little Guides

Pott 8vo, cloth 3s. ; leather, 3s. 6d. net.

NEW VOLUME.

SHAKESPEARE'S COUNTRY. By B. C. WINDLE, F.R.S.,
M.A. Illustrated by E. H. NEW.

Uniform with Mr. Wells' 'Oxford' and Mr. Thomson's 'Cambridge.'

Methuen's Standard Library

THE DECLINE AND FALL OF THE ROMAN EMPIRE.
By EDWARD GIBBON. Edited by J. B. BURY, LL.D., Fellow of
Trinity College, Dublin. *In Seven Volumes. Demy 8vo, gilt top.*
8s. 6d. each. *Crown 8vo.* 6s. each. *Vol. VII.*

The concluding Volume of this Edition.

THE DIARY OF THOMAS ELLWOOD. Edited by G. C.
CRUMP, M.A. *Crown 8vo.* 6s.

This edition is the only one which contains the complete book as originally published. It contains a long introduction and many footnotes.

LA COMMEDIA DI DANTE ALIGHIERI.   Edited by
PAGET TOYNBEE, M.A.   *Crown 8vo.   6s.*

This edition of the Italian text of the Divine Comedy, founded on Witte's minor
edition, carefully revised, is issued in commemoration of the sixth century of
Dante's journey through the three kingdoms of the other world.

Illustrated and Gift Books

THE LIVELY CITY OF LIGG.   By GELLETT BURGESS.
With many Illustrations by the Author.   *Small 4to.   3s. 6d.*

THE PHIL MAY ALBUM.   *4to.   7s. 6d. net.*

This highly interesting volume contains 100 drawings by Mr. Phil May, and is
representative of his earliest and finest work.

ULYSSES; OR, DE ROUGEMONT OF TROY.   Described
and depicted by A. H. MILNE.   *Small quarto.   3s. 6d.*

The adventures of Ulysses, told in humorous verse and pictures.

THE CROCK OF GOLD.   Fairy Stories told by S. BARING
GOULD, and Illustrated by F. D. BEDFORD.   *Crown 8vo.   6s.*

TOMMY SMITH'S ANIMALS.   By EDMUND SELOUS.
Illustrated by G. W. ORD.   *Fcp. 8vo. · 2s. 6d.*

A little book designed to teach children respect and reverence for animals.

A BIRTHDAY BOOK.   With a Photogravure Frontispiece.
Demy 8vo.   10s. 6d.

This is a birthday-book of exceptional dignity, and the extracts have been chosen
with particular care.
The three passages for each day bear a certain relation to each other, and form a
repertory of sententious wisdom from the best authors living or dead.

Educational

PRACTICAL PHYSICS.   By H. STROUD, D. Sc., M.A., Pro-
fessor of Physics in the Durham College of Science, Newcastle-on-
Tyne.   Fully illustrated.   *Crown 8vo.   3s. 6d.*
[*Textbooks of Technology.*

GENERAL ELEMENTARY SCIENCE.   By J. T. DUNN,
D.Sc., and V. A. MUNDELLA.   With many Illustrations.   *Crown 8vo.*
3s. 6d.
[*Methuen's Science Primers.*

THE METRIC SYSTEM. By LEON DELBOS. *Crown 8vo.* 2s.
A theoretical and practical guide, for use in elementary schools and by the general reader.

A SOUTH AFRICAN ARITHMETIC. By HENRY HILL, B.A., Assistant Master at Worcester School, Cape Colony. *Crown 8vo.* 3s. 6d.
This book has been specially written for use in South African schools.

A KEY TO STEDMAN'S EASY LATIN EXERCISES. By C. G. BOTTING, M.A. *Crown 8vo.* 3s. net.

NEW TESTAMENT GREEK. A Course for Beginners. By G. RODWELL, B.A. With a Preface by WALTER LOCK, D.D., Warden of Keble College. *Fcap. 8vo.* 3s. 6d.

EXAMINATION PAPERS IN ENGLISH HISTORY. By J. TAIT WARDLAW, B.A., King's College, Cambridge. *Crown 8vo.* 2s. 6d. [*School Examination Series.*

A GREEK ANTHOLOGY. Selected by E. C. MARCHANT, M.A., Fellow of Peterhouse, Cambridge, and Assistant Master at St. Paul's School. *Crown 8vo.* 3s. 6d.

CICERO DE OFFICIIS. Translated by G. B. GARDINER, M.A. *Crown 8vo.* 2s. 6d. [*Classical Translations.*

The Novels of Charles Dickens

Crown 8vo. Each Volume, cloth 3s., leather 4s.6d. net.

Messrs. METHUEN have in preparation an edition of those novels of Charles Dickens which have now passed out of copyright. Mr. George Gissing, whose critical study of Dickens is both sympathetic and acute, has written an Introduction to each of the books, and a very attractive feature of this edition will be the illustrations of the old houses, inns, and buildings, which Dickens described, and which have now in many instances disappeared under the touch of modern civilisation. Another valuable feature will be a series of topographical and general notes to each book by Mr. F. G. Kitton. The books will be produced with the greatest care as to printing, paper and binding.

The first volumes will be :

THE PICKWICK PAPERS. With Illustrations by E. H. NEW. *Two Volumes.*

NICHOLAS NICKLEBY. With Illustrations by R. J. WILLIAMS. *Two Volumes.*

BLEAK HOUSE. With Illustrations by BEATRICE ALCOCK. *Two Volumes.*

OLIVER TWIST. With Illustrations by E. H. NEW. *Two Volumes.*

The Little Library

Pott 8vo.   Each Volume, cloth 1s. 6d. net. ; leather 2s. 6d. net.

Messrs. METHUEN intend to produce a series of small books under the above title, containing some of the famous books in English and other literatures, in the domains of fiction, poetry, and belles lettres.   The series will also contain several volumes of selections in prose and verse.

The books will be edited with the most sympathetic and scholarly care. Each one will contain an Introduction which will give (1) a short biography of the author, (2) a critical estimate of the book.   Where they are necessary, short notes will be added at the foot of the page.

The Little Library will ultimately contain complete sets of the novels of W. M. Thackeray, Jane Austen, the sisters Brontë, Mrs. Gaskell and others.   It will also contain the best work of many other novelists whose names are household words.

Each book will have a portrait or frontispiece in photogravure, and the volumes will be produced with great care in a style uniform with that of 'The Library of Devotion.'

The first volumes will be :

A LITTLE BOOK OF ENGLISH LYRICS.   With Notes.

PRIDE AND PREJUDICE.   By JANE AUSTEN.   With an Introduction and Notes by E. V. LUCAS.   *Two Volumes.*

VANITY FAIR.   By W. M. THACKERAY.   With an Introduction by S. GWYNN.   *Three Volumes.*

PENDENNIS.   By W. M. THACKERAY.   With an Introduction by S. GWYNN.   *Three volumes.*

EOTHEN.   By A. W. KINGLAKE.   With an Introduction and Notes.

CRANFORD.   By Mrs. GASKELL.   With an Introduction and Notes by E. V. LUCAS.

THE INFERNO OF DANTE.   Translated by H. F. CARY. With an Introduction and Notes by PAGET TOYNBEE.

JOHN HALIFAX, GENTLEMAN.   By MRS. CRAIK.   With an Introduction by ANNIE MATHESON.   *Two volumes.*

THE EARLY POEMS OF ALFRED, LORD TENNYSON. Edited by J. C. COLLINS, M.A.

THE PRINCESS.   By ALFRED, LORD TENNYSON.   Edited by ELIZABETH WORDSWORTH.

MAUD, AND OTHER POEMS. By ALFRED, LORD TENNYSON. Edited by ELIZABETH WORDSWORTH.

IN MEMORIAM. By ALFRED, LORD TENNYSON. Edited by H. C. BEECHING, M.A.

A LITTLE BOOK OF SCOTTISH LYRICS. Arranged and Edited by T. F. HENDERSON.

Fiction

THE KING'S MIRROR. By ANTHONY HOPE. *Crown 8vo. 6s.*

THE CROWN OF LIFE. By GEORGE GISSING, Author of 'Demos,' 'The Town Traveller,' etc. *Crown 8vo. 6s.*

A NEW VOLUME OF WAR STORIES. By STEPHEN CRANE, Author of 'The Red Badge of Courage.' *Crown 8vo. 6s.*

THE STRONG ARM. By ROBERT BARR. *Crown 8vo. 6s.*

TO LONDON TOWN. By ARTHUR MORRISON, Author of 'Tales of Mean Streets,' 'A Child of the Jago,' etc. *Crown 8vo. 6s.*

ONE HOUR AND THE NEXT. By THE DUCHESS OF SUTHERLAND. *Crown 8vo. 6s.*

SIREN CITY. By BENJAMIN SWIFT, Author of 'Nancy Noon.' *Crown 8vo. 6s.*

VENGEANCE IS MINE. By ANDREW BALFOUR, Author of 'By Stroke of Sword.' Illustrated. *Crown 8vo. 6s.*

PRINCE RUPERT THE BUCCANEER. By C. J. CUTCLIFFE HYNE, Author of 'Captain Kettle,' etc. *Crown 8vo. 6s.*

PABO THE PRIEST. By S. BARING GOULD, Author of 'Mehalah,' etc. Illustrated. *Crown 8vo. 6s.*

GILES INGILBY. By W. E. NORRIS. Illustrated. *Crown 8vo. 6s.*

THE PATH OF A STAR. By SARA JEANETTE DUNCAN, Author of 'A Voyage of Consolation.' Illustrated. *Crown 8vo. 6s.*

THE HUMAN BOY. By EDEN PHILPOTTS, Author of 'Children of the Mist.' With a Frontispiece. *Crown 8vo. 6s.*
A series of English schoolboy stories, the result of keen observation, and of a most engaging wit.

THE HUMAN INTEREST. By VIOLET HUNT, Author of 'A Hard Woman,' etc. *Crown 8vo. 6s.*

AN ENGLISHMAN. By MARY L. PENDERED. *Crown 8vo.*
6s.

A GENTLEMAN PLAYER. By R. N. STEPHENS, Author of
'An Enemy to the King.' *Crown 8vo.* 6s.

DANIEL WHYTE. By A. J. DAWSON, Author of 'Bismillah.'
Crown 8vo. 6s.

A New Edition of the Novels of Marie Corelli

This New Edition is in a more convenient form than the Library Edition, and
is issued in a new and specially designed cover.

In Crown 8vo, Cloth, 6s. Leather, 6s. net.

A ROMANCE OF TWO WORLDS.
VENDETTA.
THELMA.
ARDATH : THE STORY OF A
DEAD SELF.

THE SOUL OF LILITH.
WORMWOOD.
BARABBAS : A DREAM OF THE
WORLD'S TRAGEDY.
THE SORROWS OF SATAN.

The Novelist

MESSRS. METHUEN are making an interesting experiment which con-
stitutes a fresh departure in publishing. They are issuing under the above
general title a Monthly Series of New Fiction by popular authors at
the price of Sixpence. Each Number is as long as the average
Six Shilling Novel. The first numbers of 'THE NOVELIST' are as
follows :—

I. DEAD MEN TELL NO TALES.   E. W. HORNUNG.
[*Ready.*

II. JENNIE BAXTER, JOURNALIST.   ROBERT BARR.
[*Ready.*

III. THE INCA'S TREASURE.   ERNEST GLANVILLE.
[*Ready.*

IV. A SON OF THE STATE.   W. PETT RIDGE.
[*Ready.*

V. FURZE BLOOM.   S. BARING GOULD.
[*Ready.*

VI. BUNTER'S CRUISE.   C. GLEIG.

[*Ready.*

VII. THE GAY DECEIVERS.   ARTHUR MOORE.
[*November.*

VIII. A NEW NOVEL.   MRS. MEADE.
[*December.*

MESSRS. METHUEN'S
PUBLICATIONS

◆

Poetry

Rudyard Kipling. BARRACK-ROOM BALLADS. By RUDYARD KIPLING. 60*th Thousand.* *Crown 8vo.* 6*s.*
'Mr. Kipling's verse is strong, vivid, full of character. . . . Unmistakeable genius rings in every line.'—*Times.*
'The ballads teem with imagination, they palpitate with emotion. We read them with laughter and tears ; the metres throb in our pulses, the cunningly ordered words tingle with life ; and if this be not poetry, what is?'—*Pall Mall Gazette.*

Rudyard Kipling. THE SEVEN SEAS. By RUDYARD KIPLING. 50*th Thousand.* *Cr. 8vo.* *Buckram, gilt top.* 6*s.*
'The new poems of Mr. Rudyard Kipling have all the spirit and swing of their predecessors. Patriotism is the solid concrete foundation on which Mr. Kipling has built the whole of his work.'—*Times.*
'The Empire has found a singer ; it is no depreciation of the songs to say that statesmen may have, one way or other, to take account of them.'—*Manchester Guardian.*
'Animated through and through with indubitable genius.'—*Daily Telegraph.*

"**Q.**" POEMS AND BALLADS. By "Q." *Crown 8vo.* 3*s.* 6*d.*
'This work has just the faint, ineffable touch and glow that make poetry.'—*Speaker.*

"**Q.**" GREEN BAYS: Verses and Parodies. By "Q." *Second Edition.* *Crown 8vo.* 3*s.* 6*d.*

E. Mackay. A SONG OF THE SEA. By ERIC MACKAY. *Second Edition.* *Fcap. 8vo.* 5*s.*
'Everywhere Mr. Mackay displays himself the master of a style marked by all the characteristics of the best rhetoric.'—*Globe.*

H. Ibsen. BRAND. A Drama by HENRIK IBSEN. Translated by WILLIAM WILSON. *Third Edition.* *Crown 8vo.* 3*s.* 6*d.*
'The greatest world-poem of the nineteenth century next to "Faust." It is in the same set with "Agamemnon," with "Lear," with the literature that we now instinctively regard as high and holy.'—*Daily Chronicle.*

"**A. G.**" VERSES TO ORDER. By "A. G." *Crown 8vo.* 2*s.* 6*d. net.*
'A capital specimen of light academic poetry.'—*St. James's Gazette.*

James Williams. VENTURES IN VERSE. By JAMES WILLIAMS, Fellow of Lincoln College, Oxford. *Crown 8vo.* 3*s.* 6*d.*
'In matter and manner the book is admirable.'—*Glasgow Herald.*

J. G. Cordery. THE ODYSSEY OF HOMER. A Translation by J. G. CORDERY. *Crown 8vo.* 7*s.* 6*d.*
'A spirited, accurate, and scholarly piece of work.'—*Glasgow Herald.*

Belles Lettres, Anthologies, etc.

R. L. Stevenson. VAILIMA LETTERS. By ROBERT LOUIS STEVENSON. With an Etched Portrait by WILLIAM STRANG. *Second Edition. Crown 8vo. Buckram. 6s.*

'A fascinating book.'—*Standard.*
'Full of charm and brightness.'—*Spectator.*
'A gift almost priceless.'—*Speaker.*
'Unique in Literature.'—*Daily Chronicle.*

G. Wyndham. THE POEMS OF WILLIAM SHAKESPEARE. Edited with an Introduction and Notes by GEORGE WYNDHAM, M.P. *Demy 8vo. Buckram, gilt top.* 10s. 6d.

This edition contains the 'Venus,' 'Lucrece,' and Sonnets, and is prefaced with an elaborate introduction of over 140 pp.
'One of the most serious contributions to Shakespearian criticism that have been published for some time.'—*Times.*
'We have no hesitation in describing Mr. George Wyndham's introduction as a masterly piece of criticism, and all who love our Elizabethan literature will find a very garden of delight in it.'—*Spectator.*
'Mr. Wyndham's notes are admirable, even indispensable.'—*Westminster Gazette.*

W. E. Henley. ENGLISH LYRICS. Selected and Edited by W. E. HENLEY. *Crown 8vo. Buckram, gilt top.* 6s.

'It is a body of choice and lovely poetry. — *Birmingham Gazette.*

Henley and Whibley. A BOOK OF ENGLISH PROSE. Collected by W. E. HENLEY and CHARLES WHIBLEY. *Crown 8vo. Buckram, gilt top.* 6s.

'Quite delightful. A greater treat for those not well acquainted with pre-Restoration prose could not be imagined.'—*Athenæum.*

H. C. Beeching. LYRA SACRA: An Anthology of Sacred Verse. Edited by H. C. BEECHING, M.A. *Crown 8vo. Buckram.* 6s.

'A charming selection, which maintains a lofty standard of excellence.'—*Times.*

"Q." THE GOLDEN POMP. A Procession of English Lyrics. Arranged by A. T. QUILLER COUCH. *Crown 8vo. Buckram.* 6s.

'A delightful volume: a really golden "Pomp."'—*Spectator.*

W. B. Yeats. AN ANTHOLOGY OF IRISH VERSE. Edited by W. B. YEATS. *Crown 8vo.* 3s. 6d.

'An attractive and catholic selection. — *Times.*

G. W. Steevens. MONOLOGUES OF THE DEAD. By G. W. STEEVENS. *Foolscap 8vo.* 3s. 6d.

'The effect is sometimes splendid, sometimes bizarre, but always amazingly clever.'—*Pall Mall Gazette.*

W. M. Dixon. A PRIMER OF TENNYSON. By W. M. DIXON, M.A. *Cr. 8vo.* 2s. 6d.

'Much sound and well-expressed criticism. The bibliography is a boon.'—*Speaker.*

W. A. Craigie. A PRIMER OF BURNS. By W. A. CRAIGIE. *Crown 8vo.* 2s. 6d.

'A valuable addition to the literature of the poet.'—*Times.*

L. Magnus. A PRIMER OF WORDSWORTH. By LAURIE MAGNUS. *Crown 8vo.* 2s. 6d.

'A valuable contribution to Wordsworthian literature.'—*Literature.*

Sterne. THE LIFE AND OPINIONS OF TRISTRAM SHANDY. By LAWRENCE STERNE. With an Introduction by CHARLES WHIBLEY, and a Portrait. *2 vols.* 7s.

'Very dainty volumes are these: the paper, type, and light-green binding are all very agreeable to the eye.'—*Globe.*

Congreve. THE COMEDIES OF WILLIAM CONGREVE. With an Introduction by G. S. STREET, and a Portrait. *2 vols.* 7s.

Morier. THE ADVENTURES OF HAJJI BABA OF ISPAHAN. By JAMES MORIER. With an Introduction by E. G. BROWNE, M.A., and a Portrait. *2 vols.* 7s.

Walton. THE LIVES OF DONNE, WOTTON, HOOKER, HERBERT AND SANDERSON. By IZAAK WALTON. With an Introduction by VERNON BLACKBURN, and a Portrait. 3s. 6d.

Johnson. THE LIVES OF THE ENGLISH POETS. By SAMUEL JOHNSON, LL.D. With an Introduction by J. H. MILLAR, and a Portrait. 3 vols. 10s. 6d.

Burns. THE POEMS OF ROBERT BURNS. Edited by ANDREW LANG and W. A. CRAIGIE. With Portrait. Second Edition. Demy 8vo, gilt top. 6s.
This edition contains a carefully collated Text, numerous Notes, critical and textual, a critical and biographical Introduction, and a Glossary.
'Among editions in one volume, this will take the place of authority.'—Times.

F. Langbridge. BALLADS OF THE BRAVE; Poems of Chivalry, Enterprise, Courage, and Constancy. Edited by Rev. F. LANGBRIDGE. Second Edition. Cr. 8vo. 3s. 6d. School Edition. 2s. 6d.
'A very happy conception happily carried out. These "Ballads of the Brave" are intended to suit the real tastes of boys, and will suit the taste of the great majority.' —Spectator.
'The book is full of splendid things.'— World.

Illustrated Books

John Bunyan. THE PILGRIM'S PROGRESS. By JOHN BUNYAN. Edited, with an Introduction, by C. H. FIRTH, M.A. With 39 Illustrations by R. ANNING BELL. Crown 8vo. 6s.
This book contains a long Introduction by Mr. Firth, whose knowledge of the period is unrivalled; and it is lavishly illustrated.
'The best "Pilgrim's Progress."'— Educational Times.

F. D. Bedford. NURSERY RHYMES. With many Coloured Pictures by F. D. BEDFORD. Super Royal 8vo. 5s.
'An excellent selection of the best known rhymes, with beautifully coloured pictures exquisitely printed.'—Pall Mall Gazette.

S. Baring Gould. A BOOK OF FAIRY TALES retold by S. BARING GOULD. With numerous Illustrations and Initial Letters by ARTHUR J. GASKIN. Second Edition. Cr. 8vo. Buckram. 6s.
'Mr. Baring Gould is deserving of gratitude, in re-writing in simple style the old stories that delighted our fathers and grandfathers.'—Saturday Review.

S. Baring Gould. OLD ENGLISH FAIRY TALES. Collected and edited by S. BARING GOULD. With Numerous Illustrations by F. D. BEDFORD. Second Edition. Cr. 8vo. Buckram. 6s.
'A charming volume.'—Guardian.

S. Baring Gould. A BOOK OF NURSERY SONGS AND RHYMES. Edited by S. BARING GOULD, and Illustrated by the Birmingham Art School. Buckram, gilt top. Crown 8vo. 6s.

H. C. Beeching. A BOOK OF CHRISTMAS VERSE. Edited by H. C. BEECHING, M.A., and Illustrated by WALTER CRANE. Cr. 8vo, gilt top. 3s. 6d.
An anthology which, from its unity of aim and high poetic excellence, has a better right to exist than most of its fellows.'— Guardian.

History

Gibbon. THE DECLINE AND FALL OF THE ROMAN EMPIRE. By EDWARD GIBBON. A New Edition, Edited with Notes, Appendices, and Maps, by J. B. BURY, LL.D., Fellow of Trinity College, Dublin. In Seven Volumes. Demy 8vo. Gilt top. 8s. 6d. each. Also Cr. 8vo. 6s.

each. Vols. I., II., III., IV., V., and VI.

'The time has certainly arrived for a new edition of Gibbon's great work. . . . Professor Bury is the right man to undertake this task. His learning is amazing, both in extent and accuracy. The book is issued in a handy form, and at a moderate price, and it is admirably printed.'—*Times.*

'The standard edition of our great historical classic.'—*Glasgow Herald.*

'At last there is an adequate modern edition of Gibbon. . . . The best edition the nineteenth century could produce.'—*Manchester Guardian.*

Flinders Petrie. A HISTORY OF EGYPT, FROM THE EARLIEST TIMES TO THE PRESENT DAY. Edited by W. M. FLINDERS PETRIE, D.C.L., LL.D., Professor of Egyptology at University College. *Fully Illustrated. In Six Volumes. Cr. 8vo. 6s. each.*

VOL. I. PREHISTORIC TIMES TO XVITH DYNASTY. W. M. F. Petrie. *Fourth Edition.*

VOL. II. THE XVIITH AND XVIIITH DYNASTIES. W. M. F. Petrie. *Third Edition.*

VOL. IV. THE EGYPT OF THE PTOLEMIES. J. P. Mahaffy.

VOL. V. ROMAN EGYPT. J. G. Milne.

'A history written in the spirit of scientific precision so worthily represented by Dr. Petrie and his school cannot but promote sound and accurate study, and supply a vacant place in the English literature of Egyptology.'—*Times.*

Flinders Petrie. RELIGION AND CONSCIENCE IN ANCIENT EGYPT. By W. M. FLINDERS PETRIE, D.C.L., LL.D. Fully Illustrated. *Crown 8vo. 2s. 6d.*

'The lectures will afford a fund of valuable information for students of ancient ethics.'—*Manchester Guardian.*

Flinders Petrie. SYRIA AND EGYPT, FROM THE TELL EL AMARNA TABLETS. By W. M. FLINDERS PETRIE, D.C.L., LL.D. *Crown 8vo. 2s. 6d.*

'A marvellous record. The addition made to our knowledge is nothing short of amazing.'—*Times.*

Flinders Petrie. EGYPTIAN TALES. Edited by W. M. FLINDERS PETRIE. Illustrated by TRISTRAM ELLIS. *In Two Volumes. Cr. 8vo. 3s. 6d. each.*

'Invaluable as a picture of life in Palestine and Egypt.'—*Daily News.*

Flinders Petrie. EGYPTIAN DECORATIVE ART. By W. M. FLINDERS PETRIE. With 120 Illustrations. *Cr. 8vo. 3s. 6d.*

'In these lectures he displays rare skill in elucidating the development of decorative art in Egypt.'—*Times.*

C. W. Oman. A HISTORY OF THE ART OF WAR. Vol. II.: The Middle Ages, from the Fourth to the Fourteenth Century. By C. W. OMAN, M.A., Fellow of All Souls', Oxford. Illustrated. *Demy 8vo. 21s.*

'The book is based throughout upon a thorough study of the original sources, and will be an indispensable aid to all students of mediæval history.'—*Athenæum.*

'The whole art of war in its historic evolution has never been treated on such an ample and comprehensive scale, and we question if any recent contribution to the exact history of the world has possessed more enduring value.'—*Daily Chronicle.*

S. Baring Gould. THE TRAGEDY OF THE CÆSARS. With numerous Illustrations from Busts, Gems, Cameos, etc. By S. BARING GOULD. *Fourth Edition. Royal 8vo. 15s.*

'A most splendid and fascinating book on a subject of undying interest. The great feature of the book is the use the author has made of the existing portraits of the Caesars and the admirable critical subtlety he has exhibited in dealing with this line of research. It is brilliantly written, and the illustrations are supplied on a scale of profuse magnificence.' —*Daily Chronicle.*

F. W. Maitland. CANON LAW IN ENGLAND. By F. W. MAITLAND, LL.D., Downing Professor of the Laws of England in the University of Cambridge. *Royal 8vo. 7s. 6d.*

'Professor Maitland has put students of English law under a fresh debt. These essays are landmarks in the study of the history of Canon Law.'—*Times.*

H. de B. Gibbins. INDUSTRY IN ENGLAND : HISTORICAL OUT-LINES. By H. DE B. GIBBINS, Litt.D., M.A. With 5 Maps. *Second Edition. Demy 8vo. 10s. 6d.*

H. E. Egerton. A HISTORY OF BRITISH COLONIAL POLICY. By H. E. EGERTON, M.A. *Demy 8vo. 12s. 6d.*
' It is a good book, distinguished by accuracy in detail, clear arrangement of facts, and a broad grasp of principles.'— *Manchester Guardian.*
' Able, impartial, clear. . . . A most valuable volume.'—*Athenæum.*

Albert Sorel. THE EASTERN QUESTION IN THE EIGH-TEENTH CENTURY. By ALBERT SOREL, of the French Academy. Translated by F. C. BRAMWELL, M.A. With a Map. *Cr. 8vo. 3s. 6d.*

C. H. Grinling. A HISTORY OF THE GREAT NORTHERN RAIL-WAY, 1845-95. By CHARLES H. GRINLING. With Maps and Illustrations. *Demy 8vo. 10s. 6d.*
' Mr. Grinling has done for a Railway what Macaulay did for English History.'— *The Engineer.*

W. Sterry. ANNALS OF ETON COLLEGE. By W. STERRY, M.A. With numerous Illustrations. *Demy 8vo. 7s. 6d.*
' A treasury of quaint and interesting reading. Mr. Sterry has by his skill and vivacity given these records new life.'— *Academy.*

Fisher. ANNALS OF SHREWS-BURY SCHOOL. By G. W. FISHER, M.A., late Assistant Master. With numerous Illustrations. *Demy 8vo. 10s. 6d.*
' This careful, erudite book.'—*Daily Chronicle.*

' A book of which Old Salopians are sure to be proud.'—*Globe.*

J. Sargeaunt. ANNALS OF WEST-MINSTER SCHOOL. By J. SAR-GEAUNT, M.A., Assistant Master. With numerous Illustrations. *Demy 8vo. 7s. 6d.*

A. Clark. THE COLLEGES OF OXFORD : Their History and their Traditions. By Members of the University. Edited by A. CLARK, M.A., Fellow and Tutor of Lincoln College. *8vo. 12s. 6d.*
' A work which will be appealed to for many years as the standard book.'— *Athenæum.*

J. Wells. A SHORT HISTORY OF ROME. By J. WELLS, M.A., Fellow and Tutor of Wadham Coll., Oxford. *Second and Revised Edition.* With 3 Maps. *Crown 8vo. 3s. 6d.*
This book is intended for the Middle and Upper Forms of Public Schools and for Pass Students at the Universities. It contains copious Tables, etc.
' An original work written on an original plan, and with uncommon freshness and vigour.'—*Speaker.*

O. Browning. A SHORT HISTORY OF MEDIÆVAL ITALY, A.D. 1250-1530. By OSCAR BROWNING, Fellow and Tutor of King's College, Cambridge. *In Two Volumes. Cr. 8vo. 5s. each.*
VOL. I. 1250-1409.—Guelphs and Ghibellines.
VOL. II. 1409-1530.—The Age of the Condottieri.

O'Grady. THE STORY OF IRE-LAND. By STANDISH O'GRADY, Author of ' Finn and his Companions. *Crown 8vo. 2s. 6d.*

Byzantine Texts

Edited by J. B. BURY, M.A.

EVAGRIUS. Edited by Professor LÉON PARMENTIER of Liége and M. BIDEZ of Gand. *Demy 8vo. 10s. 6d.*

THE HISTORY OF PSELLUS. By C. SATHAS. *Demy 8vo. 15s. net.*

A 3

Biography

S. Baring Gould. THE LIFE OF NAPOLEON BONAPARTE. By S. BARING GOULD. With over 450 Illustrations in the Text and 12 Photogravure Plates. *Large quarto. Gilt top.* 36s.
'The best biography of Napoleon in our tongue, nor have the French as good a biographer of their hero. A book very nearly as good as Southey's "Life of Nelson."'—*Manchester Guardian.*
'The main feature of this gorgeous volume is its great wealth of beautiful photogravures and finely-executed wood engravings, constituting a complete pictorial chronicle of Napoleon I.'s personal history from the days of his early childhood at Ajaccio to the date of his second interment.'—*Daily Telegraph.*

P. H. Colomb. MEMOIRS OF ADMIRAL SIR A. COOPER KEY. By Admiral P. H. COLOMB. With a Portrait. *Demy 8vo.* 16s.
'An interesting and adequate biography. The whole book is one of the greatest interest.'—*Times.*

Morris Fuller. THE LIFE AND WRITINGS OF JOHN DAVENANT, D.D. (1571-1641), Bishop of Salisbury. By MORRIS FULLER, B.D. *Demy 8vo.* 10s. 6d.

J. M. Rigg. ST. ANSELM OF CANTERBURY: A CHAPTER IN THE HISTORY OF RELIGION. By J. M. RIGG. *Demy 8vo.* 7s. 6d.

F. W. Joyce. THE LIFE OF SIR FREDERICK GORE OUSELEY. By F. W. JOYCE, M.A. 7s. 6d.
'This book has been undertaken in quite the right spirit, and written with sympathy, insight, and considerable literary skill.'—*Times.*

W. G. Collingwood. THE LIFE OF JOHN RUSKIN. By W. G. COLLINGWOOD, M.A. With Portraits, and 13 Drawings by Mr. Ruskin. *Second Edition.* 2 vols. 8vo. 32s.
'No more magnificent volumes have been published for a long time.'—*Times.*
'It is long since we had a biography with such delights of substance and of form. Such a book is a pleasure for the day, and a joy for ever.'—*Daily Chronicle.*

C. Waldstein. JOHN RUSKIN. By CHARLES WALDSTEIN, M.A. With a Photogravure Portrait. *Post 8vo.* 5s.
'A thoughtful and well-written criticism of Ruskin's teaching.'—*Daily Chronicle.*

A. M. F. Darmesteter, THE LIFE OF ERNEST RENAN. By MADAME DARMESTETER. With Portrait. *Second Edition. Cr. 8vo.* 6s.
'A polished gem of biography, superior in its kind to any attempt that has been made of recent years in England, Madame Darmesteter has indeed written for English readers "*The* Life of Ernest Renan."'—*Athenæum.*

W. H. Hutton. THE LIFE OF SIR THOMAS MORE. By W. H. HUTTON, M.A. With Portraits. *Cr. 8vo.* 5s.
'The book lays good claim to high rank among our biographies. It is excellently even lovingly, written.'—*Scotsman.*

Travel, Adventure and Topography

Sven Hedin. THROUGH ASIA. By SVEN HEDIN, Gold Medallist of the Royal Geographical Society. With 300 Illustrations from Sketches and Photographs by the Author, and Maps. 2 vols. *Royal 8vo.* 20s. *net.*
'One of the greatest books of the kind issued during the century. It is impossible to give an adequate idea of the richness of the contents of this book,

nor of its abounding attractions as a story of travel unsurpassed in geographical and human interest. Much of it is a revelation. Altogether the work is one which is in solidity, novelty, and interest must take a first rank among publications of its class.'—*Times*.

'In these magnificent volumes we have the most important contribution to Central Asian geography made for many years. Intensely interesting as a tale of travel.' —*Spectator*.

F. H. Skrine and E. D. Ross. THE HEART OF ASIA. By F. H. SKRINE and E. D. ROSS. With Maps and many Illustrations by VERESTCHAGIN. *Large Crown 8vo.* 10s. 6d. net.

'This volume will form a landmark in our knowledge of Central Asia. . . . Illuminating and convincing. For the first time we are enabled clearly to understand not only how Russia has established her rule in Central Asia, but what that rule actually means to the Central Asian peoples. This book is not only *felix opportunitate*, but of enduring value.'—*Times*.

R. E. Peary. NORTHWARD OVER THE GREAT ICE. By R. E. PEARY, Gold Medallist of the Royal Geographical Society. With over 800 Illustrations. 2 *vols. Royal 8vo.* 32s. net.

'The book is full of interesting matter—a tale of brave deeds simply told; abundantly illustrated with prints and maps.' —*Standard*.

'His book will take its place among the permanent literature of Arctic exploration.' —*Times*.

G. S. Robertson. CHITRAL: The Story of a Minor Siege. By Sir G. S. ROBERTSON, K.C.S.I. With numerous Illustrations, Map and Plans. *Second Edition. Demy 8vo.* 10s. 6d.

'It is difficult to imagine the kind of person who could read this brilliant book without emotion. The story remains immortal— a testimony imperishable. We are face to face with a great book.'—*Illustrated London News*.

'A book which the Elizabethans would have thought wonderful. More thrilling, more piquant, and more human than any novel.'—*Newcastle Chronicle*.

'One of the most stirring military narratives written in our time.'—*Times*.

'As fascinating as Sir Walter Scott's best fiction.'—*Daily Telegraph*.

'A noble story, nobly told.'—*Punch*.

H. H. Johnston. BRITISH CENTRAL AFRICA. By Sir H. H. JOHNSTON, K.C.B. With nearly Two Hundred Illustrations, and Six Maps. *Second Edition. Crown 4to.* 18s. net.

'A fascinating book, written with equal skill and charm—the work at once of a literary artist and of a man of action who is singularly wise, brave, and experienced. It abounds in admirable sketches from pencil.' — *Westminster Gazette*.

L. Decle. THREE YEARS IN SAVAGE AFRICA. By LIONEL DECLE. With 100 Illustrations and 5 Maps. *Second Edition. Demy 8vo.* 10s. 6d. net.

'A fine, full book.'—*Pall Mall Gazette*.

'Its bright pages give a better general survey of Africa from the Cape to the Equator than any single volume that has yet been published.'—*Times*.

A. Hulme Beaman. TWENTY YEARS IN THE NEAR EAST. By A. HULME BEAMAN. *Demy 8vo.* With Portrait. 10s. 6d.

'One of the most entertaining books that we have had in our hands for a long time. It is unconventional in a high degree; it is written with sagacious humour; it is full of adventures and anecdotes.'—*Daily Chronicle*.

Henri of Orleans. FROM TONKIN TO INDIA. By PRINCE HENRI OF ORLEANS. Translated by HAMLEY BENT, M.A. With 100 Illustrations and a Map. *Cr. 4to, gilt top.* 25s.

R. S. S. Baden-Powell. THE DOWNFALL OF PREMPEH. A Diary of Life in Ashanti, 1895. By Colonel BADEN-POWELL. With 21 Illustrations and a Map. *Cheaper Edition. Large Crown 8vo.* 6s.

R. S. S. Baden-Powell. THE MATABELE CAMPAIGN, 1896. By Col. BADEN-POWELL. With nearly 100 Illustrations. *Cheaper Edition. Large Crown 8vo.* 6s.

S. L. Hinde. THE FALL OF THE CONGO ARABS. By S. L. HINDE. With Plans, etc. *Demy 8vo.* 12s. 6d.

A. St. H. Gibbons. EXPLORATION AND HUNTING IN CENTRAL

AFRICA. By Major A. St. H. GIBBONS. With full-page Illustrations by C. WHYMPER, and Maps. *Demy 8vo.* 15s.

'His book is a grand record of quiet, unassuming, tactful resolution. His adventures were as various as his sporting exploits were exciting.'—*Times.*

E. H. Alderson. WITH THE MASHONALAND FIELD FORCE, 1896. By Lieut.-Colonel ALDERSON. With numerous Illustrations and Plans. *Demy 8vo.* 10s. 6d.

'A clear, vigorous, and soldier-like narrative.'—*Scotsman.*

Fraser. ROUND THE WORLD ON A WHEEL. By JOHN FOSTER FRASER. With 100 Illustrations. *Crown 8vo.* 6s.

'A very entertaining book of travel.'—*Spectator.*
'The story is told with delightful gaiety, humour, and crispness. There has rarely appeared a more interesting tale of modern travel.'—*Scotsman.*
'A classic of cycling, graphic and witty.'—*Yorkshire Post.*

Seymour Vandeleur. CAMPAIGNING ON THE UPPER NILE AND NIGER. By Lieut. SEYMOUR VANDELEUR. With an Introduction by Sir G. GOLDIE, K.C.M.G. With 4 Maps, Illustrations, and Plans. *Large Crown 8vo.* 10s. 6d.

'Upon the African question there is no book procurable which contains so much of value as this one.'—*Guardian.*

Lord Fincastle. A FRONTIER CAMPAIGN. By Viscount FINCASTLE, V.C., and Lieut. P. C. ELLIOTT-LOCKHART. With a Map and 16 Illustrations. *Second Edition. Crown 8vo.* 6s.

'An admirable book, and a really valuable treatise on frontier war.'—*Athenæum.*

E. N. Bennett. THE DOWNFALL OF THE DERVISHES: A Sketch of the Sudan Campaign of 1898. By E. N. BENNETT, Fellow of Hertford College. With Four Maps and a Photogravure Portrait of the Sirdar. *Third Edition. Crown 8vo.* 3s 6d.

J. K. Trotter. THE NIGER SOURCES. By Colonel J. K. TROTTER, R.A. With a Map and Illustrations. *Crown 8vo.* 5s.

Michael Davitt. LIFE AND PROGRESS IN AUSTRALASIA. By MICHAEL DAVITT, M.P. 500 pp. With 2 Maps. *Crown 8vo.* 6s.

W. Crooke. THE NORTH-WESTERN PROVINCES OF INDIA: THEIR ETHNOLOGY AND ADMINISTRATION. By W. CROOKE. With Maps and Illustrations. *Demy 8vo.* 10s. 6d.

'A carefully and well-written account of one of the most important provinces of the Empire. Mr. Crooke deals with the land in its physical aspect, the province under Hindoo and Mussulman rule, under British rule, its ethnology and sociology, its religious and social life, the land and its settlement, and the native peasant.'—*Manchester Guardian.*

A. Boisragon. THE BENIN MASSACRE. By Captain BOISRAGON. *Second Edition. Cr. 8vo.* 3s. 6d.

'If the story had been written four hundred years ago it would be read to-day as an English classic.'—*Scotsman.*

H. S. Cowper. THE HILL OF THE GRACES: OR, THE GREAT STONE TEMPLES OF TRIPOLI. By H. S. COWPER, F.S.A. With Maps, Plans, and 75 Illustrations. *Demy 8vo.* 10s. 6d.

W. Kinnaird Rose. WITH THE GREEKS IN THESSALY. By W. KINNAIRD ROSE, Reuter's Correspondent. With Plans and 23 Illustrations. *Crown 8vo.* 6s.

W. B. Worsfold. SOUTH AFRICA. By W. B. WORSFOLD, M.A. *With a Map. Second Edition. Cr. 8vo.* 6s.

'A monumental work compressed into a very moderate compass.'—*World.*

Naval and Military

G. W. Steevens. NAVAL POLICY: By G. W. STEEVENS. *Demy 8vo.* 6s.

This book is a description of the British and other more important navies of the world, with a sketch of the lines on which our naval policy might possibly be developed. 'An extremely able and interesting work.' . —*Daily Chronicle.*

D. Hannay. A SHORT HISTORY OF THE ROYAL NAVY, FROM EARLY TIMES TO THE PRESENT DAY. By DAVID HANNAY. Illustrated. 2 *Vols. Demy 8vo.* 7s. 6d. each. Vol. I., 1200-1688.

'We read it from cover to cover at a sitting, and those who go to it for a lively and brisk picture of the past, with all its faults and its grandeur, will not be disappointed. The historian is endowed with literary skill and style.'—*Standard.*

'We can warmly recommend Mr. Hannay's volume to any intelligent student of naval history. Great as is the merit of Mr. Hannay's historical narrative, the merit of his strategic exposition is even greater.'—*Times.*

C. Cooper King. THE STORY OF THE BRITISH ARMY. By Colonel COOPER KING. Illustrated. *Demy 8vo.* 7s. 6d.

'An authoritative and accurate story of England's military progress.'—*Daily Mail.*

R. Southey. ENGLISH SEAMEN (Howard, Clifford, Hawkins, Drake, Cavendish). By ROBERT SOUTHEY. Edited, with an Introduction, by DAVID HANNAY. *Second Edition. Crown 8vo.* 6s.

'A brave, inspiriting book.'—*Black and White.*

W. Clark Russell. THE LIFE OF ADMIRAL LORD COLLING-WOOD. By W. CLARK RUSSELL. With Illustrations by F. BRANGWYN. *Third Edition. Crown 8vo.* 6s.

'A book which we should like to see in the hands of every boy in the country.'—*St. James's Gazette.*

'A really good book.'—*Saturday Review.*

E. L. S. Horsburgh. THE CAMPAIGN OF WATERLOO. By E. L. S. HORSBURGH, B.A. With Plans. *Crown 8vo.* 5s.

'A brilliant essay—simple, sound, and thorough.'—*Daily Chronicle.*

H. B. George. BATTLES OF ENGLISH HISTORY. By H. B. GEORGE, M.A., Fellow of New College, Oxford. With numerous Plans. *Third Edition. Cr. 8vo.* 6s.

'Mr. George has undertaken a very useful task—that of making military affairs intelligible and instructive to non-military readers—and has executed it with a large measure of success.'—*Times.*

General Literature

S. Baring Gould. OLD COUNTRY LIFE. By S. BARING GOULD. With Sixty-seven Illustrations. *Large Cr. 8vo. Fifth Edition.* 6s.

'"Old Country Life," as healthy wholesome reading, full of breezy life and movement, full of quaint stories vigorously told, will not be excelled by any book to be published throughout the year. Sound, hearty, and English to the core.' —*World.*

S. Baring Gould. AN OLD ENGLISH HOME. By S. BARING GOULD. With numerous Plans and Illustrations. *Crown 8vo.* 6s.

'The chapters are delightfully fresh, very informing, and lightened by many a good story. A delightful fireside companion.' —*St. James's Gazette.*

S. Baring Gould. HISTORIC ODDITIES AND STRANGE

EVENTS. By S. BARING GOULD. *Fourth Edition. Crown 8vo. 6s.*

S. Baring Gould. FREAKS OF FANATICISM. By S. BARING GOULD. *Third Edition. Cr. 8vo. 6s.*

S. Baring Gould. A GARLAND OF COUNTRY SONG: English Folk Songs with their Traditional Melodies. Collected and arranged by S. BARING GOULD and H. F. SHEPPARD. *Demy 4to. 6s.*

S. Baring Gould. SONGS OF THE WEST: Traditional Ballads and Songs of the West of England, with their Melodies. Collected by S. BARING GOULD, M.A., and H. F. SHEPPARD, M.A. In 4 Parts. *Parts I., II., III., 3s. each. Part IV., 5s. In one Vol., French morocco, 15s.*

'A rich collection of humour, pathos, grace, and poetic fancy.'—*Saturday Review.*

S. Baring Gould. YORKSHIRE ODDITIES AND STRANGE EVENTS. By S. BARING GOULD. *Fourth Edition. Crown 8vo. 6s.*

S. Baring Gould. STRANGE SURVIVALS AND SUPERSTITIONS. By S. BARING GOULD. *Cr. 8vo. Second Edition. 6s.*

S. Baring Gould. THE DESERTS OF SOUTHERN FRANCE. By S. BARING GOULD. 2 *vols. Demy 8vo. 32s.*

Cotton Minchin. OLD HARROW DAYS. By J. G. COTTON MINCHIN. *Cr. 8vo. Second Edition. 5s.*

'This book is an admirable record.'—*Daily Chronicle.*

W. E. Gladstone. THE SPEECHES OF THE RT. HON. W. E. GLADSTONE, M.P. Edited by A. W. HUTTON, M.A., and H. J. COHEN M.A. With Portraits, *Demy 8vo. Vols. IX. and X., 12s. 6d. each.*

E. V. Zenker. ANARCHISM. By E. V. ZENKER. *Demy 8vo. 7s. 6d.*

'Herr Zenker has succeeded in producing a careful and critical history of the growth of Anarchist theory.

H. G. Hutchinson. THE GOLFING PILGRIM. By HORACE G. HUTCHINSON. *Crown 8vo. 6s.*

'Full of useful information —itb plenty of good stories.'—*Truth.*

'Without this book the golfer's library will be incomplete.'—*Pall Mall Gazette.*

'It will charm all golfers.'—*Times.*

J. Wells. OXFORD AND OXFORD LIFE. By Members of the University. Edited by J. WELLS, M.A., Fellow and Tutor of Wadham College. *Third Edition. Cr. 8vo. 3s. 6d.*

'We congratulate Mr. Wells on the production of a readable and intelligent account of Oxford as it is at the present time, written by persons who are possessed of a close acquaintance with the system and life of the University.'—*Athenæum.*

J. Wells. OXFORD AND ITS COLLEGES. By J. WELLS, M.A., Fellow and Tutor of Wadham College. Illustrated by E. H. NEW. *Third Edition. Fcap. 8vo. 3s. Leather. 3s 6d. net.*

'An admirable and accurate little treatise, attractively illustrated.'—*World.*

'A luminous and tasteful little volume.'—*Daily Chronicle.*

'Exactly what the intelligent visitor wants.'—*Glasgow Herald.*

A. H. Thompson. CAMBRIDGE AND ITS COLLEGES. By A. HAMILTON THOMPSON. With Illustrations by E. H. NEW. *Pott 8vo. 3s. Leather. 3s. 6d. net.*

This book is uniform with Mr. Wells' very successful book, 'Oxford and its Colleges.'

'It is brightly written and learned, and is just such a book as a cultured visitor needs.'—*Scotsman.*

C. G. Robertson. VOCES ACADEMICÆ. By C. GRANT ROBERTSON, M.A., Fellow of All Souls', Oxford. *With a Frontispiece. Pott 8vo. 3s. 6d.*

'Decidedly clever and amusing.'—*Athenæum.*

Rosemary Cotes. DANTE'S GARDEN. By ROSEMARY COTES. With a Frontispiece. *Second Edition. Fcp. 8vo. 2s. 6d. Leather, 3s. 6d. net.*

'A charming collection of legends of the flowers mentioned by Dante.'—*Academy.*

Clifford Harrison. READING AND READERS. By CLIFFORD HARRISON. *Fcp. 8vo.* 2s. 6d.

'We recommend schoolmasters to examine its merits, for it is at school that readers are made.'—*Academy.*
'An extremely sensible little book.'—*Manchester Guardian.*

L. Whibley. GREEK OLIGARCHIES: THEIR ORGANISATION AND CHARACTER. By L. WHIBLEY, M.A., Fellow of Pembroke College, Cambridge. *Crown 8vo.* 6s.
'An exceedingly useful handbook: a careful and well-arranged study.'—*Times.*

L. L. Price. ECONOMIC SCIENCE AND PRACTICE. By L. L. PRICE, M.A., Fellow of Oriel College, Oxford. *Crown 8vo.* 6s.

J. S. Shedlock. THE PIANOFORTE SONATA : Its Origin and Development. By J. S. SHEDLOCK. *Crown 8vo.* 5s.
'This work should be in the possession of every musician and amateur. A concise and lucid history and a very valuable work for reference.'—*Athenæum.*

E. M. Bowden. THE EXAMPLE OF BUDDHA: Being Quotations from Buddhist Literature for each Day in the Year. Compiled by E. M. BOWDEN. *Third Edition. 16mo.* 2s. 6d.

Science and Technology

Freudenreich. DAIRY BACTERIOLOGY. A Short Manual for the Use of Students. By Dr. ED. VON FREUDENREICH, Translated by J. R. AINSWORTH DAVIS, M.A. *Crown 8vo.* 2s. 6d.

Chalmers Mitchell. OUTLINES OF BIOLOGY. By P. CHALMERS MITCHELL, M.A. *Illustrated. Cr. 8vo.* 6s.

A text-book designed to cover the new Schedule issued by the Royal College of Physicians and Surgeons.

G. Massee. A MONOGRAPH OF THE MYXOGASTRES. By GEORGE MASSEE. With 12 Coloured Plates. *Royal 8vo.* 18s. *net.*
'A work much in advance of any book in the language treating of this group of organisms. Indispensable to every student of the Myxogastres.'—*Nature.*

Stephenson and Suddards. ORNAMENTAL DESIGN FOR WOVEN FABRICS. By C. STEPHENSON, of The Technical College, Bradford, and F. SUDDARDS, of The Yorkshire College, Leeds. With 65 full-page plates. *Demy 8vo.* 7s. 6d.

'The book is very ably done, displaying an intimate knowledge of principles, good taste, and the faculty of clear exposition.'—*Yorkshire Post.*

TEXTBOOKS OF TECHNOLOGY. Edited by PROFESSORS GARNETT and WERTHEIMER.

HOW TO MAKE A DRESS. By J. A. E. WOOD. *Illustrated. Cr. 8vo.* 1s. 6d.
'Though primarily intended for students, Miss Wood's dainty little manual may be consulted with advantage by any girls who want to make their own frocks. The directions are simple and clear, and the diagrams very helpful.'—*Literature.*

CARPENTRY AND JOINERY. By F. C. WEBBER. With many Illustrations. *Cr. 8vo.* 3s. 6d.
'An admirable elementary text-book on the subject.'—*Builder.*

PRACTICAL MECHANICS. By SIDNEY H. WELLS. With 75 Illustrations and Diagrams. *Crown 8vo.* 3s. 6d.

Philosophy

L. T. Hobhouse. THE THEORY OF KNOWLEDGE. By L. T. HOBHOUSE, Fellow of C.C.C., Oxford. *Demy 8vo.* 21*s.*
'The most important contribution to English philosophy since the publication of Mr. Bradley's "Appearance and Reality." '—*Glasgow Herald.*
'A brilliantly written volume.'—*Times.*

W. H. Fairbrother. THE PHILOSOPHY OF T. H. GREEN. By W. H. FAIRBROTHER, M.A. *Cr. 8vo.* 3*s.* 6*d.*
'In every way an admirable book.'—*Glasgow Herald.*

F. W. Bussell. THE SCHOOL OF PLATO. By F. W. BUSSELL, D.D., Fellow of Brasenose College, Oxford. *Demy 8vo.* 10*s.* 6*d.*
'A clever and stimulating book.'—*Manchester Guardian.*

F. S. Granger. THE WORSHIP OF THE ROMANS. By F. S. GRANGER, M.A., Litt.D. *Crown 8vo.* 6*s.*
'A scholarly analysis of the religious ceremonies, beliefs, and superstitions of ancient Rome, conducted in the new light of comparative anthropology.'—*Times.*

Theology

S. R. Driver. SERMONS ON SUBJECTS CONNECTED WITH THE OLD TESTAMENT. By S. R. DRIVER, D.D., Canon of Christ Church, Regius Professor of Hebrew in the University of Oxford. *Cr. 8vo.* 6*s.*
'A welcome companion to the author's famous "Introduction." '—*Guardian.*

T. K. Cheyne. FOUNDERS OF OLD TESTAMENT CRITICISM. By T. K. CHEYNE, D.D., Oriel Professor at Oxford. *Large Crown 8vo.* 7*s.* 6*d.*
A historical sketch of O. T. Criticism.
'A very learned and instructive work.'—*Times.*

H. Rashdall. DOCTRINE AND DEVELOPMENT. By HASTINGS RASHDALL, M.A., Fellow and Tutor of New College, Oxford. *Cr. 8vo.* 6*s.*
'A very interesting attempt to restate some of the principal doctrines of Christianity, in which Mr. Rashdall appears to us to have achieved a high measure of success. He is often learned, almost always sympathetic, and always singularly lucid.'—*Manchester Guardian.*

H. H. Henson. APOSTOLIC CHRISTIANITY: As Illustrated by the Epistles of St. Paul to the Corinthians. By H. H. HENSON, M.A., Fellow of All Souls', Oxford. *Cr. 8vo.* 6*s.*
'A worthy contribution towards same solution of the great religious problems of the present day.'—*Scotsman.*

H. H. Henson. DISCIPLINE AND LAW. By H. HENSLEY HENSON, B.D., Fellow of All Souls', Oxford. *Fcap. 8vo.* 2*s.* 6*d.*

H. H. Henson. LIGHT AND LEAVEN : HISTORICAL AND SOCIAL SERMONS. By H. H. HENSON, M.A. *Crown 8vo.* 6*s.*

W. H. Bennett. A PRIMER OF THE BIBLE. By W. H. BENNETT. *Second Edition. Cr. 8vo.* 2*s.* 6*d.*
'The work of an honest, fearless, and sound critic, and an excellent guide in a small compass to the books of the Bible.'—*Manchester Guardian.*

William Harrison. CLOVELLY SERMONS. By WILLIAM HARRISON, M.A., late Rector of Clovelly. With a Preface by 'LUCAS MALET.' *Cr. 8vo.* 3*s.* 6*d.*

Cecilia Robinson. THE MINISTRY OF DEACONESSES. By Deacon-

ness CECILIA ROBINSON. With an Introduction by the Lord Bishop of Winchester. *Cr. 8vo.* 3*s.* 6*d.*
'A learned and interesting book.'—*Scotsman.*

E. B. Layard. RELIGION IN BOYHOOD. Notes on the Religious Training of Boys. By E. B. LAYARD, M.A. 18*mo.* 1*s.*

W. Yorke Fausset. THE *DE CATECHIZANDIS RUDIBUS* OF ST. AUGUSTINE. Edited, with Introduction, Notes, etc., by W. YORKE FAUSSET, M.A. *Cr. 8vo.* 3*s.* 6*d.*

F. Weston. THE HOLY SACRIFICE. By F. WESTON, M.A., Curate of St. Matthew's, Westminster. *Pott 8vo.* 6*d. net.*
A small volume of devotions at the Holy Communion, especially adapted to the needs of servers and those who do not communicate.

À Kempis. THE IMITATION OF CHRIST. By THOMAS À KEMPIS. With an Introduction by DEAN FARRAR. Illustrated by C. M. GERE. *Second Edition. Fcap. 8vo.* 3*s.* 6*d. Padded morocco,* 5*s.*

'Amongst all the innumerable English editions of the "Imitation," there can have been few which were prettier than this one, printed in strong and handsome type, with all the glory of red initials.'—*Glasgow Herald.*

J. Keble. THE CHRISTIAN YEAR. By JOHN KEBLE. With an Introduction and Notes by W. LOCK, D.D., Warden of Keble College. Illustrated by R. ANNING BELL. *Second Edition. Fcap. 8vo.* 3*s.* 6*d. Padded morocco.* 5*s.*

'The present edition is annotated with all the care and insight to be expected from Mr. Lock.'—*Guardian.*

Oxford Commentaries

General Editor, WALTER LOCK, D.D., Warden of Keble College, Dean Ireland's Professor of Exegesis in the University of Oxford.

THE BOOK OF JOB. Edited, with Introduction and Notes, by E. C. S. GIBSON, D.D., Vicar of Leeds. *Demy 8vo.* 6*s.*

Handbooks of Theology

General Editor, A. ROBERTSON, D.D., Principal of King's College, London.

THE XXXIX. ARTICLES OF THE CHURCH OF ENGLAND. Edited with an Introduction by E. C. S. GIBSON, D.D., Vicar of Leeds, late Principal of Wells Theological College. *Second and Cheaper Edition in One Volume. Demy 8vo.* 12*s.* 6*d.*
'We welcome with the utmost satisfaction a new, cheaper, and more convenient edition of Dr. Gibson's book. It was greatly wanted. Dr. Gibson has given theological students just what they want, and we should like to think that it was in the hands of every candidate for orders.'—*Guardian.*

AN INTRODUCTION TO THE HISTORY OF RELIGION. By F. B. JEVONS, M.A., Litt.D., Principal of Bishop Hatfield's Hall. *Demy 8vo.* 10*s.* 6*d.*
'The merit of this book lies in the penetration, the singular acuteness and force of the author's judgment. He is at once critical and luminous, at once just and

suggestive. A comprehensive and thorough book.'—*Birmingham Post.*

THE DOCTRINE OF THE INCARNATION. By R. L. OTTLEY, M.A., late fellow of Magdalen College, Oxon., and Principal of Pusey House. *In Two Volumes. Demy 8vo.* 15*s.*
'A clear and remarkably full account of the main currents of speculation. Scholarly precision . . . genuine tolerance . . . intense interest in his subject—are Mr. Ottley's merits.'—*Guardian.*

AN INTRODUCTION TO THE HISTORY OF THE CREEDS. By A. E. BURNS, Examining Chaplain to the Bishop of Lichfield. *Demy 8vo.* 10*s.* 6*d.*
'This book may be expected to hold its place as an authority on its subject.'—*Spectator.*
'It is an able and learned treatise, and contains a mass of information which will be most useful to scholars.'—*Glasgow Herald.*

The Churchman's Library

Edited by J. H. BURN, B.D.

THE BEGINNINGS OF ENGLISH CHRISTIANITY. By W. E. COLLINS, M.A. With Map. *Cr. 8vo.* 3s. 6d.

An investigation in detail, based upon original authorities, of the beginnings of the English Church, with a careful account of earlier Celtic Christianity. 'An excellent example of thorough and fresh historical work.'—*Guardian.*

SOME NEW TESTAMENT PRO-

BLEMS. By ARTHUR WRIGHT, Fellow of Queen's College, Cambridge. *Crown 8vo.* 6s.

THE KINGDOM OF HEAVEN HERE AND HEREAFTER. By CANON WINTERBOTHAM, M.A., B.Sc., LL.B. *Cr. 8vo.* 3s. 6d.

'A most able book, at once exceedingly thoughtful and richly suggestive.'—*Glasgow Herald.*

The Library of Devotion

Pott 8vo, cloth, 2s.; leather, 2s. 6d. net.

'This series is excellent.'—THE BISHOP OF LONDON.
'A very delightful edition.'—THE BISHOP OF BATH AND WELLS.
'Well worth the attention of the Clergy.'—THE BISHOP OF LICHFIELD.
'The new " Library of Devotion " is excellent.'—THE BISHOP OF PETERBOROUGH.
'Charming.'—*Record.*
'Delightful.'—*Church Bells.*

THE CONFESSIONS OF ST. AUGUSTINE. Newly Translated, with an Introduction and Notes, by C. BIGG, D.D., late Student of Christ Church. *Second Edition.*

'The translation is an excellent piece of English, and the introduction is a masterly exposition. We augur well of a series which begins so satisfactorily.'—*Times.*

THE CHRISTIAN YEAR. By JOHN KEBLE. With Introduction and Notes by WALTER LOCK, D.D., Warden of Keble College, Ireland Professor at Oxford.

'The volume is very prettily bound and printed, and may fairly claim to be an advance on any previous editions.'—*Guardian.*

THE IMITATION OF CHRIST. A Revised Translation, with an Intro-

duction, by C. BIGG, D.D., late Student of Christ Church.

A practically new translation of this book, which the reader has, almost for the first time, exactly in the shape in which it left the hands of the author.

'A beautiful and scholarly production.'—*Speaker.*
'A nearer approach to the original than has yet existed in English.'—*Academy.*

A BOOK OF DEVOTIONS. By J. W. STANBRIDGE, M.A., Rector of Bainton, Canon of York, and sometime Fellow of St. John's College, Oxford.

It is probably the best book of its kind. It deserves high commendation.'—*Church Gazette.*

LYRA INNOCENTIUM. By JOHN KEBLE. Edited, with Introduction and Notes, by WALTER LOCK, D.D., Warden of Keble College, Oxford.

Leaders of Religion

Edited by H. C. BEECHING, M.A. *With Portraits, Crown 8vo.* 3s. 6d.

A series of short biographies of the most prominent leaders of religious life and thought of all ages and countries.

The following are ready—

CARDINAL NEWMAN. By R. H. HUTTON.
JOHN WESLEY. By J. H. OVERTON, M.A.

BISHOP WILBERFORCE. By G. W. DANIELL, M.A.
CARDINAL MANNING. By A. W. HUTTON, M.A.

CHARLES SIMEON. By H. C. G. MOULE, D.D.
JOHN KEBLE. By WALTER LOCK, D.D.
THOMAS CHALMERS. By Mrs. OLIPHANT.
LANCELOT ANDREWES. By R. L. OTTLEY, M.A.
AUGUSTINE OF CANTERBURY. By E. L. CUTTS, D.D.
WILLIAM LAUD. By W. H. HUTTON, B.D.

JOHN KNOX. By F. MacCUNN.
JOHN HOWE. By R. F. HORTON, D.D.
BISHOP KEN. By F. A. CLARKE, M.A.
GEORGE FOX, THE QUAKER. By T. HODGKIN, D.C.L.
JOHN DONNE. By AUGUSTUS JESSOPP, D.D.
THOMAS CRANMER. By. A. J. MASON.

Other volumes will be announced in due course.

Fiction

SIX SHILLING NOVELS

Marie Corelli's Novels
Large crown 8vo. 6s. each.

A ROMANCE OF TWO WORLDS. *Nineteenth Edition.*
VENDETTA. *Fifteenth Edition.*
THELMA. *Twenty-first Edition.*
ARDATH: THE STORY OF A DEAD SELF. *Eleventh Edition.*
THE SOUL OF LILITH, *Ninth Edition.*
WORMWOOD. *Ninth Edition.*
BARABBAS: A DREAM OF THE WORLD'S TRAGEDY. *Thirty-fourth Edition.*
'The tender reverence of the treatment and the imaginative beauty of the writing have reconciled us to the daring of the conception, and the conviction is forced on us that even so exalted a subject cannot be made too familiar to us, provided it be presented in the true spirit of Christian faith. The amplifications

of the Scripture narrative are often conceived with high poetic insight, and this "Dream of the World's Tragedy" is a lofty and not inadequate paraphrase of the supreme climax of the inspired narrative.'—*Dublin Review.*

THE SORROWS OF SATAN. *Forty-first Edition.*

'A very powerful piece of work. . . . The conception is magnificent, and is likely to win an abiding place within the memory of man. . . . The author has immense command of language, and a limitless audacity. . . . This interesting and remarkable romance will live long after much of the ephemeral literature of the day is forgotten. . . . A literary phenomenon . . . novel, and even sublime.'—W. T. STEAD in the *Review of Reviews.*

Anthony Hope's Novels
Crown 8vo. 6s. each.

THE GOD IN THE CAR. *Eighth Edition.*
'A very remarkable book, deserving of critical analysis impossible within our limit; brilliant, but not superficial; well considered, but not elaborated; constructed with the proverbial art that conceals, but yet allows itself to be enjoyed by readers to whom fine literary method is a keen pleasure.'—*The World.*

A CHANGE OF AIR. *Fifth Edition.*
'A graceful, vivacious comedy, true to human nature. The characters are traced with a masterly hand.'—*Times.*

A MAN OF MARK. *Fifth Edition.*
'Of all Mr. Hope's books, "A Man of Mark" is the one which best compares

with "The Prisoner of Zenda."'—*National Observer.*

THE CHRONICLES OF COUNT ANTONIO. *Fourth Edition.*
'It is a perfectly enchanting story of love and chivalry, and pure romance. The Count is the most constant, desperate, and modest and tender of lovers, a peerless gentleman, an intrepid fighter, a faithful friend, and a magnanimous foe.'—*Guardian.*

PHROSO. Illustrated by H. R. MILLAR. *Fourth Edition.*
'The tale is thoroughly fresh, quick with vitality, stirring the blood.'—*St. James's Gazette.*

28   MESSRS. METHUEN'S CATALOGUE

'A story of adventure, every page of which is palpitating with action.'—*Speaker.*

'From cover to cover "Phroso" not only engages the attention, but carries the reader in little whirls of delight from adventure to adventure.'—*Academy.*

SIMON DALE. Illustrated. *Third Edition.*

'"Simon Dale" is one of the best historical

romances that have been written for a long while.'—*St. James's Gazette.*

'A brilliant novel. The story is rapid and most excellently told. As for the hero, he is a perfect hero of romance'—*Athenæum.*

'There is searching analysis of human nature, with a most ingeniously constructed plot. Mr. Hope has drawn the contrasts of his women with marvellous subtlety and delicacy.'—*Times.*

Gilbert Parker's Novels
Crown 8vo. 6s. each.

PIERRE AND HIS PEOPLE. *Fifth Edition.*

'Stories happily conceived and finely executed. There is strength and genius in Mr. Parker's style.'—*Daily Telegraph.*

MRS. FALCHION. *Fourth Edition.*

'A splendid study of character.'—*Athenæum.*

'A very striking and admirable novel.'—*St. James's Gazette.*

THE TRANSLATION OF A SAVAGE.

'The plot is original and one difficult to work out; but Mr. Parker has done it with great skill and delicacy. The reader who is not interested in this original, fresh, and well-told tale must be a dull person indeed.'—*Daily Chronicle.*

THE TRAIL OF THE SWORD. Illustrated. *Sixth Edition.*

'A rousing and dramatic tale. A book like this, in which swords flash, great surprises are undertaken, and daring deeds done, in which men and women live and love in the old passionate way, is a joy inexpressible.'—*Daily Chronicle.*

WHEN VALMOND CAME TO PONTIAC: The Story of a Lost Napoleon. *Fourth Edition.*

'Here we find romance—real, breathing, living romance. The character of Valmond is drawn unerringly. The book must be read, we may say re-read, for any one thoroughly to appreciate Mr. Parker's delicate touch and innate sympathy with humanity.' — *Pall Mall Gazette.*

AN ADVENTURER OF THE NORTH: The Last Adventures of 'Pretty Pierre.' *Second Edition.*

'The present book is full of fine and moving stories of the great North, and it

will add to Mr. Parker's already high reputation.'—*Glasgow Herald.*

THE SEATS OF THE MIGHTY. Illustrated. *Tenth Edition.*

'The best thing he has done; one of the best things that any one has done lately.'—*St. James's Gazette.*

'Mr. Parker seems to become stronger and easier with every serious novel that he attempts. He shows the matured power which his former novels have led us to expect, and has produced a really fine historical novel.'—*Athenæum.*

'A great book.'—*Black and White.*

THE POMP OF THE LAVILETTES. *Second Edition.* 3s. 6d.

'Living, breathing romance, genuine and unforced pathos, and a deeper and more subtle knowledge of human nature than Mr. Parker has ever displayed before. It is, in a word, the work of a true artist.'—*Pall Mall Gazette.*

THE BATTLE OF THE STRONG: a Romance of Two Kingdoms. Illustrated. *Fourth Edition.*

'Such a splendid story, so splendidly told, will be read with avidity, and will add new honour even to Mr. Parker's reputation.'—*St. James's Gazette.*

'No one who takes a pleasure in literature but will read Mr. Gilbert Parker's latest romance with keen enjoyment. The mere writing is so good as to be a delight in itself, apart altogether from the interest of the tale.'—*Pall Mall Gazette.*

'Nothing more vigorous or more human has come from Mr. Gilbert Parker than this novel. It has all the graphic power of his last book, with truer feeling for the romance, both of human life and wild nature. There is no character without its unique and picturesque interest. Mr. Parker's style, especially his descriptive style, has in this book, perhaps even more than elsewhere, aptness and vitality.'—*Literature.*

S. Baring Gould's Novels

Crown 8vo. 6s. each.

'To say that a book is by the author of "Mehalah" is to imply that it contains a story cast on strong lines, containing dramatic possibilities, vivid and sympathetic descriptions of Nature, and a wealth of ingenious imagery.'—*Speaker.*

'That whatever Mr. Baring Gould writes is well worth reading, is a conclusion that may be very generally accepted. His views of life are fresh and vigorous, his language pointed and characteristic, the incidents of which he makes use are striking and original, his characters are life-like, and though somewhat exceptional people, are drawn and coloured with artistic force. Add to this that his descriptions of scenes and scenery are painted with the loving eyes and skilled hands of a master of his art, that he is always fresh and never dull, and it is no wonder that readers have gained confidence in his power of amusing and satisfying them, and that year by year his popularity widens.'—*Court Circular.*

ARMINELL. *Fourth Edition.*

URITH. *Fifth Edition.*

IN THE ROAR OF THE SEA. *Sixth Edition.*

MRS. CURGENVEN OF CURGENVEN. *Fourth Edition.*

CHEAP JACK ZITA. *Fourth Edition.*

THE QUEEN OF LOVE. *Fourth Edition.*

MARGERY OF QUETHER. *Third Edition.*

JACQUETTA. *Third Edition.*

KITTY ALONE. *Fifth Edition.*

NOÉMI. Illustrated. *Fourth Edition.*

THE BROOM-SQUIRE. Illustrated. *Fourth Edition.*

THE PENNYCOMEQUICKS. *Third Edition.*

DARTMOOR IDYLLS.

GUAVAS THE TINNER. Illustrated. *Second Edition.*

BLADYS. Illustrated. *Second Edition.*

DOMITIA. Illustrated. *Second Edition.*

Conan Doyle. ROUND THE RED LAMP. By A. CONAN DOYLE. *Sixth Edition. Crown 8vo. 6s.*

'The book is far and away the best view that has been vouchsafed us behind the scenes of the consulting-room.'—*Illustrated London News.*

Stanley Weyman. UNDER THE RED ROBE. By STANLEY WEYMAN, Author of 'A Gentleman of France.' With Illustrations by R. C. WOODVILLE. *Fifteenth Edition. Crown 8vo. 6s.*

'Every one who reads books at all must read this thrilling romance, from the first page of which to the last the breathless reader is haled along. An inspiration of manliness and courage.'—*Daily Chronicle.*

Lucas Malet. THE WAGES OF SIN. By LUCAS MALET. *Thirteenth Edition. Crown 8vo. 6s.*

Lucas Malet. THE CARISSIMA. By LUCAS MALET, Author of 'The Wages of Sin,' etc. *Third Edition. Crown 8vo. 6s.*

George Gissing. THE TOWN TRAVELLER. By GEORGE GISSING, Author of 'Demos,' 'In the Year of Jubilee,' etc. *Second Edition. Cr. 8vo. 6s.*

'It is a bright and witty book above all things. Polly Sparkes is a splendid bit of work.'—*Pall Mall Gazette.*

'The spirit of Dickens is in it.'—*Bookman.*

S. R. Crockett. LOCHINVAR. By S. R. CROCKETT, Author of 'The Raiders,' etc. Illustrated. *Second Edition. Crown 8vo. 6s.*

'Full of gallantry and pathos, of the clash of arms, and brightened by episodes of humour and love. . . .'—*Westminster Gazette.*

S. R. Crockett. THE STANDARD BEARER. By S. R. CROCKETT. *Crown 8vo. 6s.*

'A delightful tale in his best style.'—*Speaker.*

'Mr. Crockett at his best.'—*Literature.*

Arthur Morrison. TALES OF MEAN STREETS. By ARTHUR MORRISON. *Fifth Edition. Cr. 8vo. 6s.*

'Told with consummate art and extra-ordinary detail. In the true humanity of the book lies its justification, the permanence of its interest, and its indubitable triumph.'—*Athenæum.*
'A great book. The author's method is amazingly effective, and produces a thrilling sense of reality. The writer lays upon us a master hand. The book is simply appalling and irresistible in its interest. It is humorous also; without humour it would not make the mark it is certain to make.'—*World.*

Arthur Morrison. A CHILD OF THE JAGO. By ARTHUR MORRISON. *Third Edition. Cr. 8vo. 6s.*
'The book is a masterpiece.'—*Pall Mall Gazette.*
'Told with great vigour and powerful simplicity.'—*Athenæum.*

Mrs. Clifford. A FLASH OF SUMMER. By Mrs. W. K. CLIFFORD, Author of 'Aunt Anne,' etc. *Second Edition. Crown 8vo. 6s.*
'The story is a very beautiful one, exquisitely told.'—*Speaker.*

Emily Lawless. HURRISH. By the Honble. EMILY LAWLESS, Author of 'Maelcho,' etc. *Fifth Edition. Cr. 8vo. 6s.*

Emily Lawless. MAELCHO : a Sixteenth Century Romance. By the Honble. EMILY LAWLESS. *Second Edition. Crown 8vo. 6s.*
'A really great book.'—*Spectator.*
'There is no keener pleasure in life than the recognition of genius. A piece of work of the first order, which we do not hesitate to describe as one of the most remarkable literary achievements of this generation.'—*Manchester Guardian.*

Emily Lawless. TRAITS AND CONFIDENCES. By the Honble. EMILY LAWLESS. *Crown 8vo. 6s.*

E. W. Hornung. THE AMATEUR CRACKSMAN. By E. W. HORNUNG. *Crown 8vo. 6s.*
'An audaciously entertaining volume.'—*Spectator.*
'Fascinating and entertaining in a supreme degree.'—*Daily Mail.*
'We are fascinated by the individuality, the daring, and the wonderful coolness of Raffles the resourceful, and follow him breathlessly in his career.'—*World.*

Jane Barlow. A CREEL OF IRISH STORIES. By JANE BARLOW,

Author of 'Irish Idylls.' *Second Edition. Crown 8vo. 6s.*
'Vivid and singularly real.'—*Scotsman.*

Jane Barlow. FROM THE EAST UNTO THE WEST. By JANE BARLOW. *Crown 8vo. 6s.*
'The genial humour and never-failing sympathy recommend the book to those who like healthy fiction.'—*Scotsman.*

Mrs. Caffyn. ANNE MAULEVERER. By Mrs. CAFFYN (Iota), Author of 'The Yellow Aster.' *Second Edition. Crown 8vo. 6s.*
'The author leaves with us a most delectable addition to the heroines in modern fiction, and she has established herself as one of the leading women novelists of the day.'—*Daily Chronicle.*
'A fine conception and absorbingly interesting.'—*Athenæum.*

Dorothea Gerard. THINGS THAT HAVE HAPPENED. By DOROTHEA GERARD, Author of 'Lady Baby.' *Crown 8vo. 6s.*
'All the stories are delightful.'—*Scotsman.*

J. H. Findlater. THE GREEN GRAVES OF BALGOWRIE. By JANE H. FINDLATER. *Fourth Edition. Crown 8vo. 6s.*
'A powerful and vivid story.'—*Standard.*
'A beautiful story, sad and strange as truth itself.'—*Vanity Fair.*
'A very charming and pathetic tale.'—*Pall Mall Gazette.*
'A singularly original, clever, and beautiful story.'—*Guardian.*
'Reveals to us a new writer of undoubted faculty and reserve force.'—*Spectator.*
'An exquisite idyll, delicate, affecting, and beautiful.'—*Black and White.*

J. H. Findlater. A DAUGHTER OF STRIFE. By JANE HELEN FINDLATER. *Crown 8vo. 6s.*
'A story of strong human interest.'—*Scotsman.*

J. H. Findlater. RACHEL. By JANE H. FINDLATER. *Second Edition. Crown 8vo. 6s.*
'Powerful and sympathetic.'—*Glasgow Herald.*
'A not unworthy successor to "The Green Graves of Balgowrie."'—*Critic.*

Mary Findlater. OVER THE HILLS. By MARY FINDLATER. *Second Edition. Cr. 8vo. 6s.*
'A strong and fascinating piece of work.'—*Scotsman.*

'A charming romance, and full of incident. The book is fresh and strong.'—*Speaker.*

'A strong and wise book of deep insight and unflinching truth.'—*Birmingham Post.*

Mary Findlater. BETTY MUS-GRAVE. By MARY FINDLATER. *Second Edition. Crown 8vo. 6s.*

'Handled with dignity and delicacy. . . . A most touching story.'—*Spectator.*

'Told with great skill, and the pathos of it rings true and unforced throughout.'—*Glasgow Herald.*

Alfred Ollivant. OWD BOB, THE GREY DOG OF KENMUIR. By ALFRED OLLIVANT. *Second Edition. Cr. 8vo. 6s.*

'Weird, thrilling, strikingly graphic.'—*Punch.*

'We admire this book. . . . It is one to read with admiration and to praise with enthusiasm.'—*Bookman.*

'It is a fine, open-air, blood-stirring book, to be enjoyed by every man and woman to whom a dog is dear.'—*Literature.*

B. M. Croker. PEGGY OF THE BARTONS. By B. M. CROKER, Author of 'Diana Barrington.' *Fourth Edition. Crown 8vo. 6s.*

Mrs. Croker excels in the admirably simple, easy, and direct flow of her narrative, the briskness of her dialogue, and the geniality of her portraiture.'—*Spectator.*

'All the characters, indeed, are drawn with clearness and certainty; and it would be hard to name any quality essential to first-class work which is lacking from this book.'—*Saturday Review.*

H. G. Wells. THE STOLEN BACILLUS, and other Stories. By H. G. WELLS. *Second Edition. Crown 8vo. 6s.*

'They are the impressions of a very striking imagination, which, it would seem, has a great deal within its reach.'—*Saturday Review.*

H. G. Wells. THE PLATTNER STORY AND OTHERS. By H. G. WELLS. *Second Edition. Cr. 8vo. 6s.*

'Weird and mysterious, they seem to hold the reader as by a magic spell.'—*Scotsman.*

Sara Jeanette Duncan. A VOYAGE OF CONSOLATION. By SARA JEANETTE DUNCAN, Author of 'An American Girl in London.' Illustrated. *Third Edition. Cr. 8vo. 6s.*

'A most delightfully bright book.'—*Daily Telegraph.*

'The dialogue is full of wit.'—*Globe.*

'Laughter lurks in every page.'—*Daily News.*

C. F. Keary. THE JOURNALIST. By C. F. KEARY. *Cr. 8vo. 6s.*

'It is rare indeed to find such poetical sympathy with Nature joined to close study of character and singularly truthful dialogue: but then "The Journalist" is altogether a rare book.'—*Athenæum.*

E. F. Benson. DODO: A DETAIL OF THE DAY. By E. F. BENSON. *Sixteenth Edition. Cr. 8vo. 6s.*

'A perpetual feast of epigram and paradox.'—*Speaker.*

E. F. Benson. THE VINTAGE. By E. F. BENSON. Author of 'Dodo.' Illustrated by G. P. JACOMB-HOOD. *Third Edition. Crown 8vo. 6s.*

'Full of fire, earnestness, and beauty.'—*The World.*

E. F. Benson. THE CAPSINA. By E. F. BENSON, Author of 'Dodo.' With Illustrations by G. P. JACOMB-HOOD. *Second Edition. Cr. 8vo. 6s.*

'The story moves through an atmosphere of heroism and adventure.'—*Manchester Guardian.*

Mrs. Oliphant. SIR ROBERT'S FORTUNE. By. Mrs. OLIPHANT. *Crown 8vo. 6s.*

Mrs. Oliphant. THE TWO MARYS. By Mrs. OLIPHANT. *Second Edition. Crown 8vo. 6s.*

Mrs. Oliphant. THE LADY'S WALK. By Mrs. OLIPHANT. *Second Edition. Crown 8vo. 6s.*

W. E. Norris. MATTHEW AUSTIN. By W. E. NORRIS, Author of 'Mademoiselle de Mersac,' etc. *Fourth Edition. Crown 8vo. 6s.*

'An intellectually satisfactory and morally bracing novel.'—*Daily Telegraph.*

W. E. Norris. HIS GRACE. By W. E. NORRIS. *Third Edition. Crown 8vo. 6s.*

'Mr. Norris has drawn a really fine character in the Duke.'—*Athenæum.*

W. E. Norris. THE DESPOTIC LADY AND OTHERS. By W. E. NORRIS. *Crown 8vo. 6s.*

'A budget of good fiction of which no one will tire.'—*Scotsman.*

W. E. Norris. CLARISSA FURIOSA. By W. E. NORRIS. *Cr. 8vo. 6s.*
' As a story it is admirable, as a *jeu d'esprit* it is capital, as a lay sermon studded with gems of wit and wisdom it is a model.'—*The World.*

W. Clark Russell. MY DANISH SWEETHEART. By W. CLARK RUSSELL. *Illustrated. Fourth Edition. Crown 8vo. 6s.*

Robert Barr. IN THE MIDST OF ALARMS. By ROBERT BARR. *Third Edition. Cr. 8vo. 6s.*
' A book which has abundantly satisfied us by its capital humour.'—*Daily Chronicle.*
Mr. Barr has achieved a triumph.'—*Pall Mall Gazette.*

Robert Barr. THE MUTABLE MANY. By ROBERT BARR. *Second Edition. Crown 8vo. 6s.*
' Very much the best novel that Mr. Barr has yet given us. There is much insight in it, and much excellent humour.'—*Daily Chronicle.*

Robert Barr. THE COUNTESS TEKLA. By ROBERT BARR. *Second Edition. Crown 8vo. 6s.*
' Thrilling and brilliant.'—*Critic.*
' Such a tale as Mr. Barr's would ever receive a hearty welcome. Of these mediæval romances, which are now gaining ground, "The Countess Tekla" is the very best we have seen. The story is written in clear English, and a picturesque, moving style.'—*Pall Mall Gazette.*

Andrew Balfour. BY STROKE OF SWORD. By ANDREW BALFOUR. Illustrated. *Fourth Edition. Cr. 8vo. 6s.*
A banquet of good things.'—*Academy.*
' A recital of thrilling interest, told with unflagging vigour.'—*Globe.*
An unusually excellent example of a semi-historic romance.'—*World.*

Andrew Balfour. TO ARMS! By ANDREW BALFOUR. Illustrated. *Second Edition. Crown 8vo. 6s.*
' The marvellous perils through which Allan passes are told in powerful and lively fashion.'—*Pall Mall Gazette.*

R. B. Townshend. LONE PINE: A Romance of Mexican Life. By R. B. TOWNSHEND. *Crown 8vo. 6s.*
' It is full of incident and adventure. The great fight is as thrilling a bit of fighting as we have read for many a day.'—*Speaker.*

' The volume is evidently the work of a clever writer and of an educated and experienced traveller.'—*Athenæum.*

J. Maclaren Cobban. THE KING OF ANDAMAN: A Saviour of Society. By J. MACLAREN COBBAN. *Crown 8vo. 6s.*
' An unquestionably interesting book. It contains one character, at least, who has in him the root of immortality.'—*Pall Mall Gazette.*

J. Maclaren Cobban. WILT THOU HAVE THIS WOMAN? By J. MACLAREN COBBAN. *Cr. 8vo. 6s.*

J. Maclaren Cobban. THE ANGEL OF THE COVENANT. By J. MACLAREN COBBAN. *Cr. 8vo. 6s.*
' Mr. Cobban has achieved a work of such rare distinction that there is nothing comparable with it in recent Scottish romance. It is a great historical picture, in which fact and fancy are welded together in a fine realisation of the spirit of the times.'—*Pall Mall Gazette.*

Marshall Saunders. ROSE À CHAR-LITTE: A Romantic Story of Acadie. By MARSHALL SAUNDERS. *Crown 8vo. 6s.*
' Graceful and well written.'—*Saturday Review.*
'Charmingly told.'—*Manchester Guardian.*

R. N. Stephens. AN ENEMY TO THE KING. By R. N. STEPHENS. *Second Edition. Cr. 8vo. 6s.*
' It is full of movement, and the movement is always buoyant.'—*Scotsman.*
' A stirring story with plenty of movement.'—*Black and White.*

Robert Hichens. BYEWAYS. By ROBERT HITCHINS. Author of 'Flames, etc.' *Second Edition. Cr. 8vo. 6s.*
' The work is undeniably that of a man of striking imagination.'—*Daily News.*

Percy White. A PASSIONATE PIL-GRIM. By PERCY WHITE, Author of ' Mr. Bailey-Martin.' *Cr. 8vo. 6s.*

W. Pett Ridge. SECRETARY TO BAYNE, M.P. By W. PETT RIDGE. *Crown 8vo. 6s.*

E. Dawson and A. Moore. ADRIAN ROME. By E. DAWSON and A. MOORE, Authors of 'A Comedy of Masks.' *Crown 8vo. 6s.*
' A clever novel dealing with youth and genius.'—*Academy.*

J. S. Fletcher. THE BUILDERS. By J. S. FLETCHER. Author of 'When Charles 1. was King.' *Second Edition. Cr. 8vo. 6s.*

J. S. Fletcher. THE PATHS OF THE PRUDENT. By J. S. FLETCHER. *Crown 8vo. 6s.* 'The story has a curious fascination for the reader, and the theme and character are handled with rare ability.'—*Scotsman.* 'Dorinthia is charming. The story is told with great humour.'—*Pall Mall Gazette.*

J. B. Burton. IN THE DAY OF ADVERSITY. By J. BLOUNDELLE-BURTON. *Second Edition. Cr. 8vo. 6s.* 'Unusually interesting and full of highly dramatic situations. —*Guardian.*

J. B. Burton. DENOUNCED. By J. BLOUNDELLE-BURTON. *Second Edition. Crown 8vo. 6s.* 'A fine, manly, spirited piece of work.'— *World.*

J. B. Burton. THE CLASH OF ARMS. By J. BLOUNDELLE-BURTON. *Second Edition. Cr. 8vo. 6s.* 'A brave story—brave in deed, brave in word, brave in thought.'—*St. James's Gazette.*

J. B. Burton. ACROSS THE SALT SEAS. By J. BLOUNDELLE-BURTON. *Second Edition. Crown 8vo. 6s.* 'The very essence of the true romantic spirit.'—*Truth.*

R. Murray Gilchrist. WILLOW-BRAKE. By R. MURRAY GILCHRIST. *Crown 8vo. 6s.* 'It is a singularly pleasing and eminently wholesome volume, with a decidedly charming note of pathos at various points.'—*Athenæum.*

W. C. Scully. THE WHITE HECATOMB. By W. C. SCULLY, Author of 'Kafir Stories.' *Cr. 8vo. 6s.* 'Reveals a marvellously intimate understanding of the Kaffir mind.'—*African Critic.*

W. C. Scully. BETWEEN SUN AND SAND. By W. C. SCULLY, Author of 'The White Hecatomb.' *Cr. 8vo. 6s.* 'The reader passes at once into the very atmosphere of the African desert : the inexpressible space and stillness swallow him up, and there is no world for him but that immeasurable waste.'—*Athenæum.*

M. M. Dowie. GALLIA. By MÉNIE MURIEL DOWIE, Author of A Girl in the Karpathians.' *Third Edition. Cr. 8vo. 6s.*

M. M. Dowie. THE CROOK OF THE BOUGH. By MÉNIE MURIEL DOWIE. *Cr. 8vo. 6s.*

Julian Corbett. A BUSINESS IN GREAT WATERS. By JULIAN CORBETT. *Second Edition. Cr. 8vo. 6s.*

OTHER SIX-SHILLING NOVELS

Crown 8vo.

MISS ERIN. By M. E. FRANCIS.

ANANIAS. By the Hon. Mrs. ALAN BRODRICK.

CORRAGEEN IN '98. By Mrs. ORPEN.

THE PLUNDER PIT. By J. KEIGHLEY SNOWDEN.

CROSS TRAILS. By VICTOR WAITE.

SUCCESSORS TO THE TITLE. By Mrs. WALFORD.

KIRKHAM'S FIND. By MARY GAUNT.

DEADMAN'S. By MARY GAUNT.

CAPTAIN JACOBUS : A ROMANCE OF THE ROAD. By L. COPE CORNFORD.

SONS OF ADVERSITY. By L. COPE CORNFORD.

THE KING OF ALBERIA. By LAURA DAINTREY.

THE DAUGHTER OF ALOUETTE. By MARY A. OWEN.

CHILDREN OF THIS WORLD. By ELLEN F. PINSENT.

AN ELECTRIC SPARK. By G. MANVILLE FENN.

UNDER SHADOW OF THE MISSION. By L. S. McCHESNEY.

THE SPECULATORS. By J. F. BREWER.

THE SPIRIT OF STORM. By RONALD ROSS.

THE QUEENSBERRY CUP. By CLIVE P. WOLLEY.

A HOME IN INVERESK. By T. L. PATON.

MISS ARMSTRONG'S AND OTHER CIRCUMSTANCES. By JOHN DAVIDSON.

DR. CONGALTON'S LEGACY. By HENRY JOHNSTON.

TIME AND THE WOMAN. By RICHARD PRYCE.

THIS MAN'S DOMINION. By the Author of 'A High Little World.'

DIOGENES OF LONDON. By H. B. MARRIOTT WATSON.

THE STONE DRAGON. By MURRAY GILCHRIST.

A VICAR'S WIFE. By EVELYN DICKINSON.

ELSA. By E. M'QUEEN GRAY.

THE SINGER OF MARLY. By I. HOOPER.

THE FALL OF THE SPARROW. By M. C. BALFOUR.

A SERIOUS COMEDY. By HERBERT MORRAH.

THE FAITHFUL CITY. By HERBERT MORRAH.

IN THE GREAT DEEP. By J. A. BARRY.

BIJLI, THE DANCER. By JAMES BLYTHE PATTON.

JOSIAH'S WIFE. By NORMA LORIMER.

THE PHILANTHROPIST. By LUCY MAYNARD.

VAUSSORE. By FRANCIS BRUNE.

THREE-AND-SIXPENNY NOVELS
Crown 8vo.

DERRICK VAUGHAN, NOVELIST. 42nd thousand. By EDNA LYALL.

THE KLOOF BRIDE. By ERNEST GLANVILLE.

A VENDETTA OF THE DESERT. By W. C. SCULLY.

SUBJECT TO VANITY. By MARGARET BENSON.

THE SIGN OF THE SPIDER. By BERTRAM MITFORD.

THE MOVING FINGER. By MARY GAUNT.

JACO TRELOAR. By J. H. PEARCE.

THE DANCE OF THE HOURS. By 'VERA.'

A WOMAN OF FORTY. By ESMÉ STUART.

A CUMBERER OF THE GROUND. By CONSTANCE SMITH.

THE SIN OF ANGELS. By EVELYN DICKINSON.

AUT DIABOLUS AUT NIHIL. By X. L.

THE COMING OF CUCULAIN. By STANDISH O'GRADY.

THE GODS GIVE MY DONKEY WINGS. By ANGUS EVAN ABBOTT.

THE STAR GAZERS. By G. MANVILLE FENN.

THE POISON OF ASPS. By R. ORTON PROWSE.

THE QUIET MRS. FLEMING. By R. PRYCE.

DISENCHANTMENT. By F. MABEL ROBINSON.

THE SQUIRE OF WANDALES. By A. SHIELD.

A REVEREND GENTLEMAN. By J. M. COBBAN.

A DEPLORABLE AFFAIR. By W. E. NORRIS.

A CAVALIER'S LADYE. By Mrs. DICKER.

THE PRODIGALS. By Mrs. OLIPHANT.

THE SUPPLANTER. By P. NEUMANN.

A MAN WITH BLACK EYELASHES. By H. A. KENNEDY.

A HANDFUL OF EXOTICS. By S. GORDON.

AN ODD EXPERIMENT. By HANNAH LYNCH.

TALES OF NORTHUMBRIA. By HOWARD PEASE.

HALF-CROWN NOVELS
Crown 8vo.

HOVENDEN, V.C. By F. MABEL ROBINSON.

THE PLAN OF CAMPAIGN. By F. MABEL ROBINSON.

MR. BUTLER'S WARD. By F. MABEL ROBINSON.

ELI'S CHILDREN. By G. MANVILLE FENN.

A DOUBLE KNOT. By G. MANVILLE FENN.

DISARMED. By M. BETHAM EDWARDS.

A MARRIAGE AT SEA. By W. CLARK RUSSELL.

IN TENT AND BUNGALOW. By the Author of 'Indian Idylls.'

MY STEWARDSHIP. By E. M'QUEEN GRAY.

JACK'S FATHER. By W. E. NORRIS.

A LOST ILLUSION. By LESLIE KEITH.

THE TRUE HISTORY OF JOSHUA DAVIDSON, Christian and Communist. By E. LYNN LYNTON. *Eleventh Edition. Post 8vo. 1s.*

Books for Boys and Girls

A Series of Books by well-known Authors, well illustrated.

THREE-AND-SIXPENCE EACH

THE ICELANDER'S SWORD. By S. BARING GOULD.

TWO LITTLE CHILDREN AND CHING. By EDITH E. CUTHELL.

TODDLEBEN'S HERO. By M. M. BLAKE.

ONLY A GUARD-ROOM DOG. By EDITH E. CUTHELL.

THE DOCTOR OF THE JULIET. By HARRY COLLINGWOOD.

MASTER ROCKAFELLAR'S VOYAGE. By W. CLARK RUSSELL.

SYD BELTON: Or, The Boy who would not go to Sea. By G. MANVILLE FENN.

THE WALLYPUG IN LONDON. By G. E. FARROW.

ADVENTURES IN WALLYPUG LAND. By G. E. FARROW. 5s.

The Peacock Library

A Series of Books for Girls by well-known Authors, handsomely bound, and well illustrated.

THREE-AND-SIXPENCE EACH

A PINCH OF EXPERIENCE. By L. B. WALFORD.

THE RED GRANGE. By Mrs. MOLESWORTH.

THE SECRET OF MADAME DE MONLUC. By the Author of 'Mdle. Mori.'

OUT OF THE FASHION. B L. T. MEADE.

DUMPS. By Mrs. PARR.

A GIRL OF THE PEOPLE. By L. T. MEADE.

HEPSY GIPSY. By L. T. MEADE. 2s. 6d.

THE HONOURABLE MISS. By L. T. MEADE.

MY LAND OF BEULAH. By Mrs. LEITH ADAMS.

University Extension Series

A series of books on historical, literary, and scientific subjects, suitable for extension students and home-reading circles. Each volume is complete in itself, and the subjects are treated by competent writers in a broad and philosophic spirit.

Edited by J. E. SYMES, M.A.,
Principal of University College, Nottingham.
Crown 8vo. Price (with some exceptions) 2s. 6d.

The following volumes are ready:—

THE INDUSTRIAL HISTORY OF ENGLAND. By H. DE B. GIBBINS, Litt.D., M.A., late Scholar of Wadham College, Oxon., Cobden Prizeman. *Sixth Edition, Revised. With Maps and Plans. 3s.*

A HISTORY OF ENGLISH POLITICAL ECONOMY. By L. L. PRICE, M.A., Fellow of Oriel College, Oxon. *Second Edition.*

PROBLEMS OF POVERTY : An Inquiry into the Industrial Conditions of the Poor. By J. A. HOBSON, M.A. *Fourth Edition.*

VICTORIAN POETS. By A. SHARP.

THE FRENCH REVOLUTION. By J. E. SYMES, M.A.

PSYCHOLOGY. By F. S. GRANGER, M.A. *Second Edition.*

THE EVOLUTION OF PLANT LIFE : Lower Forms. By G. MASSEE. *With Illustrations.*

AIR AND WATER. By V. B. LEWES, M.A. *Illustrated.*

THE CHEMISTRY OF LIFE AND HEALTH. By C. W. KIMMINS, M.A. *Illustrated.*

THE MECHANICS OF DAILY LIFE. By V. P. SELLS, M.A. *Illustrated.*

ENGLISH SOCIAL REFORMERS. By H. DE B. GIBBINS, D.Litt., M.A.

ENGLISH TRADE AND FINANCE IN THE SEVENTEENTH CENTURY. By W. A. S. HEWINS, B.A.

THE CHEMISTRY OF FIRE. The Elementary Principles of Chemistry. By M. M. PATTISON MUIR, M.A. *Illustrated.*

A TEXT-BOOK OF AGRICULTURAL BOTANY. By M. C. POTTER, M.A., F.L.S. *Illustrated.* 3s. 6d.

THE VAULT OF HEAVEN. A Popular Introduction to Astronomy. By R. A. GREGORY. *With numerous Illustrations.*

METEOROLOGY. The Elements of Weather and Climate. By H. N. DICKSON, F.R.S.E., F.R. Met. Soc. *Illustrated.*

A MANUAL OF ELECTRICAL SCIENCE. By GEORGE J. BURCH, M.A. *With numerous Illustrations.* 3s.

THE EARTH. An Introduction to Physiography. By EVAN SMALL, M.A. *Illustrated.*

INSECT LIFE. By F. W. THEOBALD, M.A. *Illustrated.*

ENGLISH POETRY FROM BLAKE TO BROWNING. By W. M. DIXON, M.A.

ENGLISH LOCAL GOVERNMENT. By E. JENKS, M.A., Professor of Law at University College, Liverpool.

THE GREEK VIEW OF LIFE. By G. L. DICKINSON, Fellow of King's College, Cambridge. *Second Edition.*

Social Questions of To-day

Edited by H. DE B. GIBBINS, Litt.D., M.A.

Crown 8vo.   2s. 6d.

A series of volumes upon those topics of social, economic, and industrial interest that are at the present moment foremost in the public mind. Each volume of the series is written by an author who is an acknowledged authority upon the subject with which he deals.

The following Volumes of the Series are ready :—

TRADE UNIONISM—NEW AND OLD. By G. HOWELL. *Second Edition.*

THE CO-OPERATIVE MOVEMENT TO-DAY. By G. J. HOLYOAKE. *Second Edition.*

MUTUAL THRIFT. By Rev. J. FROME WILKINSON, M.A.

PROBLEMS OF POVERTY. By J. A. HOBSON, M.A. *Fourth Edition.*

THE COMMERCE OF NATIONS. By C. F. BASTABLE, M.A., Professor of Economics at Trinity College, Dublin. *Second Edition.*

THE ALIEN INVASION. By W. H. WILKINS, B.A.

THE RURAL EXODUS. By P. ANDERSON GRAHAM.

LAND NATIONALIZATION. By HAROLD COX, B.A.

A SHORTER WORKING DAY. By H. DE B. GIBBINS, D.Litt., M.A., and R. A. HADFIELD, of the Hecla Works, Sheffield.

BACK TO THE LAND: An Inquiry into the Cure for Rural Depopulation. By H. E. MOORE.

TRUSTS, POOLS AND CORNERS. By J. STEPHEN JEANS.

THE FACTORY SYSTEM. By R. W. COOKE-TAYLOR.

THE STATE AND ITS CHILDREN. By GERTRUDE TUCKWELL.

WOMEN'S WORK. By LADY DILKE, Miss BULLEY, and Miss WHITLEY.

MUNICIPALITIES AT WORK. The Municipal Policy of Six Great Towns, and its Influence on their Social Welfare. By FREDERICK DOLMAN.

SOCIALISM AND MODERN THOUGHT. By M. KAUFMANN.

THE HOUSING OF THE WORKING CLASSES. By E. BOWMAKER.

MODERN CIVILIZATION IN SOME OF ITS ECONOMIC ASPECTS. By W. CUNNINGHAM, D.D., Fellow of Trinity College, Cambridge.

THE PROBLEM OF THE UNEMPLOYED. By J. A. HOBSON, B.A.

LIFE IN WEST LONDON. By ARTHUR SHERWELL, M.A. *Second Edition.*

RAILWAY NATIONALIZATION. By CLEMENT EDWARDS.

WORKHOUSES AND PAUPERISM. By LOUISA TWINING.

UNIVERSITY AND SOCIAL SETTLEMENTS. By W. REASON, M.A.

Classical Translations

Edited by H. F. FOX, M.A., Fellow and Tutor of Brasenose College, Oxford.

ÆSCHYLUS — Agamemnon, Chöephoroe, Eumenides. Translated by LEWIS CAMPBELL, LL.D., late Professor of Greek at St. Andrews. *5s.*

CICERO—De Oratore I. Translated by E. N. P. MOOR, M.A. *3s. 6d.*

CICERO—Select Orations (Pro Milone, Pro Murena, Philippic II., In Catilinam). Translated by H. E. D.

BLAKISTON, M.A., Fellow and Tutor of Trinity College, Oxford. *5s.*

CICERO—De Natura Deorum. Translated by F. BROOKS, M.A., late Scholar of Balliol College, Oxford. *3s. 6d.*

HORACE: THE ODES AND EPODES. Translated by A.

GODLEY, M.A., Fellow of Magdalen College, Oxford. 2s.

LUCIAN—Six Dialogues (Nigrinus, Icaro - Menippus, The Cock, The Ship, The Parasite, The Lover of Falsehood). Translated by S. T. IRWIN, M.A., Assistant Master at Clifton; late Scholar of Exeter College, Oxford. 3s. 6d.

SOPHOCLES — Electra and Ajax. Translated by E. D. A. MORSHEAD, M.A., Assistant Master at Winchester. 2s. 6d.

TACITUS—Agricola and Germania. Translated by R. B. TOWNSHEND, late Scholar of Trinity College, Cambridge. 2s. 6d.

Educational Books

CLASSICAL

PLAUTI BACCHIDES. Edited with Introduction, Commentary, and Critical Notes by J. M'COSH, M.A. Fcap. 4to. 12s. 6d.

PASSAGES FOR UNSEEN TRANSLATION. By E. C. MARCHANT, M.A., Fellow of Peterhouse, Cambridge; and A. M. COOK, M.A., late Scholar of Wadham College, Oxford; Assistant Masters at St. Paul's School. Crown 8vo. 3s. 6d.

'We know no book of this class better fitted for use in the higher forms of schools.'— Guardian.

TACITI AGRICOLA. With Introduction, Notes, Map, etc. By R. F. DAVIS, M.A., Assistant Master at Weymouth College. Crown 8vo. 2s.

TACITI GERMANIA. By the same Editor. Crown 8vo. 2s.

HERODOTUS: EASY SELECTIONS. With Vocabulary. By A. C. LIDDELL, M.A. Fcap. 8vo. 1s. 6d.

SELECTIONS FROM THE ODYSSEY. By E. D. STONE, M.A., late Assistant Master at Eton. Fcap. 8vo. 1s. 6d.

PLAUTUS: THE CAPTIVI. Adapted for Lower Forms by J. H. FREESE, M.A., late Fellow of St. John's, Cambridge. 1s. 6d.

DEMOSTHENES AGAINST CONON AND CALLICLES. Edited with Notes and Vocabulary, by F. DARWIN SWIFT, M.A. Fcap. 8vo. 2s.

EXERCISES IN LATIN ACCIDENCE. By S. E. WINBOLT, Assistant Master in Christ's Hospital. Crown 8vo. 1s. 6d.

An elementary book adapted for Lower Forms to accompany the shorter Latin primer.

NOTES ON GREEK AND LATIN SYNTAX. By G. BUCKLAND GREEN, M.A., Assistant Master at Edinburgh Academy, late Fellow of St. John's College, Oxon. Crown 8vo. 3s. 6d.

Notes and explanations on the chief difficulties of Greek and Latin Syntax, with numerous passages for exercise.

GERMAN

A COMPANION GERMAN GRAMMAR. By H. DE B. GIBBINS, D.Litt., M.A., Assistant Master at Nottingham High School. Crown 8vo. 1s. 6d.

GERMAN PASSAGES FOR UNSEEN TRANSLATION. By E. M'QUEEN GRAY. Crown 8vo. 2s. 6d.

SCIENCE

THE WORLD OF SCIENCE. Including Chemistry, Heat, Light, Sound, Magnetism, Electricity, Botany, Zoology, Physiology, Astronomy, and Geology. By R. ELLIOTT STEEL, M.A., F.C.S. 147 Illustrations. Second Edition. Cr. 8vo. 2s. 6d.

ELEMENTARY LIGHT. By R. E. STEEL. With numerous Illustrations. Crown 8vo. 4s. 6d.

VOLUMETRIC ANALYSIS. By J. B. RUSSELL, B.Sc., Science Master at Burnley Grammar School. Cr. 8vo. 1s. 6d.

'A collection of useful, well-arranged notes.' —School Guardian.

ENGLISH

ENGLISH RECORDS. A Companion to the History of England. By H. E. MALDEN, M A. *Crown 8vo.* 3*s.* 6*d.* A book which aims at concentrating information upon dates, genealogy officials, constitutional documents, etc., which is usually found scattered in different volumes.

THE ENGLISH CITIZEN: HIS RIGHTS AND DUTIES. By H. E. MALDEN, M.A. 1*s.* 6*d.*

A DIGEST OF DEDUCTIVE

LOGIC. By JOHNSON BARKER, B.A. *Crown 8vo.* 2*s.* 6*d.*

A CLASS-BOOK OF DICTATION PASSAGES. By W. WILLIAMSON, M.A. *Second Edition, Crown 8vo.* 1*s.* 6*d.*

TEST CARDS IN EUCLID AND ALGEBRA. By D. S. CALDERWOOD, Headmaster of the Normal School, Edinburgh. In three packets of 40, with Answers. 1*s.*

METHUEN'S COMMERCIAL SERIES

Edited by H. DE B. GIBBINS, Litt.D., M.A.

BRITISH COMMERCE AND COLONIES FROM ELIZABETH TO VICTORIA. By H. DE B. GIBBINS, Litt.D., M.A. *Third Edition.* 2*s.*

COMMERCIAL EXAMINATION PAPERS. By H. DE B. GIBBINS, Litt. D., M.A. 1*s.* 6*d.*

THE ECONOMICS OF COMMERCE. By H. DE B. GIBBINS, Litt.D., M.A. 1*s.* 6*d.*

FRENCH COMMERCIAL CORRESPONDENCE. By S. E. BALLY, Master at the Manchester Grammar School. *Second Edition.* 2*s.*

GERMAN COMMERCIAL CORRESPONDENCE. By S. E. BALLY. 2*s.* 6*d.*

A FRENCH COMMERCIAL READER. By S. E. BALLY. 2*s.*

COMMERCIAL GEOGRAPHY, with special reference to the British Empire. By L. W. LYDE, M.A. *Second Edition.* 2*s.*

A PRIMER OF BUSINESS. By S. JACKSON, M.A. *Second Edition.* 1*s.* 6*d.*

COMMERCIAL ARITHMETIC. By F. G. TAYLOR, M.A. *Second Edition.* 1*s.* 6*d.*

PRÉCIS WRITING AND OFFICE CORRESPONDENCE. By E. E. WHITFIELD, M.A. 2*s.*

A GUIDE TO PROFESSIONS AND BUSINESS. By HENRY JONES. 1*s.* 6*d.*

WORKS BY A. M. M. STEDMAN, M.A.

INITIA LATINA: Easy Lessons on Elementary Accidence. *Third Edition. Fcap. 8vo.* 1*s.*

FIRST LATIN LESSONS. *Fifth Edition. Crown 8vo.* 2*s.*

FIRST LATIN READER. With Notes adapted to the Shorter Latin Primer and Vocabulary. *Fourth Edition revised.* 18*mo.* 1*s.* 6*d.*

EASY SELECTIONS FROM CÆSAR. Part I. The Helvetian War. *Second Edition.* 18*mo.* 1*s.*

EASY SELECTIONS FROM LIVY. Part I. The Kings of Rome. 18*mo.* 1*s.* 6*d.*

EASY LATIN PASSAGES FOR UNSEEN TRANSLATION. *Sixth Edition. Fcap. 8vo.* 1*s.* 6*d.*

EXEMPLA LATINA. First Lessons in Latin Accidence. With Vocabulary. *Crown 8vo.* 1*s.*

EASY LATIN EXERCISES ON THE SYNTAX OF THE SHORTER AND REVISED LATIN PRIMER. With Vocabulary. *Seventh and cheaper Edition, re-written. Crown 8vo.* 1*s.* 6*d.* Issued with the consent of Dr. Kennedy.

THE LATIN COMPOUND SENTENCE: Rules and Exercises.

Crown 8vo. 1s. 6d. With Vocabulary. 2s.

NOTANDA QUAEDAM : Miscellaneous Latin Exercises on Common Rules and Idioms. *Third Edition.* *Fcap. 8vo.* 1s. 6d. With Vocabulary. 2s.

LATIN VOCABULARIES FOR REPETITION : Arranged according to Subjects. *Eighth Edition. Fcap.* 8vo. 1s. 6d.

A VOCABULARY OF LATIN IDIOMS. 18mo. *Second Edition.* 1s.

STEPS TO GREEK. 18mo. 1s.

A SHORTER GREEK PRIMER. *Crown 8vo.* 1s. 6d.

EASY GREEK PASSAGES FOR UNSEEN TRANSLATION. *Third Edition Revised. Fcap. 8vo.* 1s. 6d.

GREEK VOCABULARIES FOR REPETITION. Arranged according to Subjects. *Second Edition Fcap. 8vo.* 1s. 6d.

GREEK TESTAMENT SELECTIONS. For the use of Schools *Third Edition.* With Introduction Notes, and Vocabulary. *Fcap. 8vo* 2s. 6d.

STEPS TO FRENCH. *Fourth Edition.* 18mo. 8d.

FIRST FRENCH LESSONS. *Fourth Edition Revised.* Crown 8vo. 1s.

EASY FRENCH PASSAGES FOR UNSEEN TRANSLATION. *Third Edition revised. Fcap. 8vo.* 1s. 6d.

EASY FRENCH EXERCISES ON ELEMENTARY SYNTAX. With Vocabulary. *Second Edition. Crown* 8vo. 2s. 6d. KEY 3s. net.

FRENCH VOCABULARIES FOR REPETITION : Arranged according to Subjects. *Seventh Edition. Fcap* 8vo. 1s.

SCHOOL EXAMINATION SERIES

EDITED BY A. M. M. STEDMAN, M.A. *Crown 8vo.* 2s. 6d.

FRENCH EXAMINATION PAPERS IN MISCELLANEOUS GRAMMAR AND IDIOMS. · By A. M. M. STEDMAN, M.A. *Tenth Edition.*

A KEY, issued to Tutors and Private Students only, to be had on application to the Publishers. *Fourth Edition. Crown 8vo.* 6s. net.

LATIN EXAMINATION PAPERS IN MISCELLANEOUS GRAMMAR AND IDIOMS. By A. M. M. STEDMAN, M.A. *Ninth Edition.*

KEY (*Fourth Edition*) issued as above. 6s. net.

GREEK EXAMINATION PAPERS IN MISCELLANEOUS GRAMMAR AND IDIOMS. By A. M. M. STEDMAN, M.A. *Fifth Edition.*

KEY (*Second Edition*) issued as above. 6s. net.

GERMAN EXAMINATION PAPERS IN MISCELLANEOUS GRAMMAR AND IDIOMS. By R. J. MORICH, Manchester. *Fifth Edition.*

KEY (*Second Edition*) issued as above. 6s. net.

HISTORY AND GEOGRAPHY EXAMINATION PAPERS. By C. H. SPENCE, M.A., Clifton College. *Second Edition.*

SCIENCE EXAMINATION PAPERS. By R. E. STEEL, M.A. F.C.S. *In two vols.*
Part I. Chemistry ; Part II. Physics.

GENERAL KNOWLEDGE EXAMINATION PAPERS. By A. M. M. STEDMAN, M.A. *Third Edition.*

KEY (*Second Edition*) issued as above. 7s. net.